The Countess and
The Miner

The Countess and The Miner

Olga Sinclair

ROBERT HALE · LONDON

Typeset in 11/14pt Sabon
by Derek Doyle & Associates in Shaw Heath.
Printed in Great Britain by
St Edmundsbury Press Ltd, Bury St Edmunds, Suffolk.
Bound by Woolnough Bookbinding Ltd.

For my wonderful husband,
Stan Sinclair (Stanislovas Jasinskas)

Prologue

THE procession of carriages was drawn by perfectly matched teams of horses, the reins held by gold-braided, white-gloved postilions, carrying the richest and most aristocratic ladies and gentlemen of Tsarist Russia to the great Cathedral of Vilnius. It was the wedding of the year. The bride was Anastasia, beautiful daughter of Count Suslenko; the bridegroom, Lord Eveson, heir to the Earl of Milton, whose estates included the richest coal mines in Scotland.

The poor country folk stared with wonder and stoical resignation at the lavish pageantry. Young Irena Militaite held tightly to her grandfather's callused hand, fearful of getting lost in the crowded city. They had walked ten miles to be there.

This was her first visit to Vilnius, where that day the streets were decorated with flags and flowers. The count's guards passed by, resplendent in gold encrusted uniforms, mounted on magnificent horses. A mild cheer rippled from the crowd when the carriage of the bridegroom appeared. Irena stood on tiptoe to see.

'He doesn't look at all pleased or excited,' she complained aloud.

'And you think he ought to be?' Grandpa sounded amused. 'Marriages are arranged for all sorts of reasons, you know that.'

'I thought the rich would marry for love,' she said. She accepted that when the time came for her to marry, the choice of husband would be negotiated by her parents, through the services of a match-maker. She hoped the man would be more handsome and happier looking than Lady Anastasia's new husband!

A murmur of excitement swept along the crowded street, as Count Suslenko's processional landau came into sight. The bride's head was veiled in a froth of white with a circlet of flowers, and among them was the compulsory sprig of rue, the *ruta*, the country's national emblem, said to signify virginity. Suslenko waved to his people and they bowed and curtseyed as expected.

Irena jumped up to get a better view. The movement caught Anastasia's attention and she stared at the fine embroidery on the child's national costume. A breath of wind lifted her veil. For the briefest of moments the eyes of the two met. The one haughty, aristocratic, well educated, the other an illiterate peasant girl. Irena was awe-struck, marvelling at such riches. She could not help a stab of jealousy. Neither would have believed their lives could ever be linked.

Chapter 1

1912, Scotland

IRENA Militaite stepped off the train at Ringbrae. A label tied to her shawl flicked over in the sharp breeze, hiding the writing on it.

She pulled the hand-crocheted garment closely around her thin shoulders with one hand. The other clasped the linen-wrapped bundle, which held her pitifully few possessions, the most important being the clothes specially made for her wedding. Five days ago she'd left her home in Lithuania. She looked conspicuously foreign and her homesickness was a physical choking pain. She was tired, hungry and scared. She gazed around wide-eyed, whilst the other passengers rushed past. She envied them – they knew where they were going. The train hissed and chuffed on again. For the hundredth time she felt the pocket of her skirt in which was pinned a letter from the matchmaker.

Duncan MacRaith had been watching her for some minutes. She was young and pretty, but what caught and held his attention was the lost, forlorn look about her, a feeling he knew well. Hadn't he felt just like that when he left the remote, wild and beautiful island in the Hebrides, his home for nearly twenty-six years? The bastard son of a local girl, he'd had to endure the taunts and slights from children and adults alike. He'd been left with his grandmother when but a few weeks old. She was the only person who'd loved him, cared for him, God rest her soul. His mother had disappeared into the mainland. He didn't know where she was, though he'd been told she'd married and no doubt had produced legitimate children. He'd fought his way through school days. Tough and agile, he'd beaten most opponents and earned grudging respect among the fishermen with whom he'd worked, until that tragedy when the boat was lost at sea. He'd been the sole survivor, and after that he couldn't bear to stay on the island. He'd moved south and found work as a coal miner. He would have scorned any suggestion that the lone figure of the girl awoke tenderness, yet he walked towards her and stopped.

'Are ye all right, lassie?' he asked. She took a step back and shook her head. He guessed that she had little or no knowledge of English. He reached out, turned the label over and read it aloud. 'Ona Green, 21 Half Mile Row, Ringbrae.'

'Ona,' the girl repeated, nodding vigorously. 'Sister.'

Duncan reached out to take her bundle from her, but she held on tight.

'I'll no hurt ye,' he said. 'I'll tak' ye there.'

Irena didn't understand, but his voice was soft, his face had a kindly expression and the hand he put on her arm was gentle. She allowed him to guide her out through the booking-hall. Her wood-soled shoes clattered on the boards. A policeman stood at the foot of the steps. Irena hesitated; to her men in uniform were all in the service of the Tsar. They kept the Lithuanian peasants in fear and poverty. Instinct told her to run but there was nowhere she could go. The stranger gripped her arm tightly as they walked down the steps and past the policeman.

It took all her self-control to appear calm. She held her head high, her woollen skirt swirled around her ankles, and she was unaware that she moved gracefully in spite of her ugly shoes.

Only four weeks ago her father had returned to the small family farm, after visiting the town-reeve, who read the letter from the match-maker for him.

'Well?' her mother had asked sharply. She'd rapped the wooden spoon on the rim of the iron pot hanging over the stove of whitened clay. 'What did the letter say?'

'It is as Ona said. A man has offered for Irena.' Her father had looked round the four of his daughters who were present. Irena could see he wasn't happy.

'What is he asking as a dowry?' her mother asked.

'Nothing.'

'Who is he, papa?' Irena asked softly.

'He is from our country, a Lithuanian, but he has lived in Scotland for over a year. He has work there, in the coal fields, and he has the means to provide for a wife. His name is Tamosinskas.'

It was as had been planned, but Irena was unable to avoid the fear that gripped her. She was to marry a stranger, a man of whom she knew nothing. If he were to walk into the room at that very minute she would not recognize him. But he wasn't there, he was hundreds of miles away, in this faraway place they called Scotland. The thought of leaving her home, saying farewell to all she knew and loved, was heart-rending.

She was eighteen, the middle one of five girls and, with no boys in the family, from early childhood she had been expected to do her share of work on the farm. She had never minded that, especially in the spring and summer. She loved the sun on her face, though her mother would chide her to pull her headscarf forward to protect her skin. She went to church on Sundays and Feast Days and said her prayers every night. Her days should have continued in that natural order, which would have made her a peasant farmer's wife, mother to bonny country children, there in the land she loved – but for the tyrannical domination of the Tsarist regime.

Irena felt no deprivation in being unable to read or write. She liked the seasonal routine on the farm, the care of the animals and hens, the sowing, the flax pulling, weaving, cooking, hand crafts. These were things she did well and did gladly. She would never have asked for more – except that somehow she had to find a husband.

Many of the young men left the country – they emigrated, or were conscripted into the army, sent away for seven years or more. Some girls married old widowers, but she didn't fancy settling down with any of them, even if one had asked her!

Her eldest sister, Magde had married when she was eighteen and brought her husband, to live at the farm. Ona was only sixteen when she married and soon afterwards she and her husband left for Scotland – it was they who had arranged the match for her.

'You may never get another offer, Irena,' warned Magde. She was irritable in the last weeks of her third pregnancy.

Irena knew the small farm couldn't support them all. If she didn't accept this opportunity she would grow old and become a laughing stock, poor old Irena, an ageing spinster. Almost anything would be better than that.

'I will marry this man, Tamosinskas,' she whispered.

Now here she was in Ringbrae. The stranger led her through the grimy streets, into the meaner part of the town where little low houses lined the long road. He was looking at the doors of the houses.

Half way along the street he stopped and knocked on a door. Irena waited anxiously. There was a clatter of footsteps, then it was flung open – her sister Ona was there! She rushed out with a shriek of joy. 'Reenie! Reenie! You're here! God be thanked. Oh, I can't believe it!'

Irena threw herself into her sister's outstretched arms. What a relief it was to see her sister and hear her own language!

Duncan MacRaith smiled at such ebullience.

'Is my sister,' Ona beamed at him. She spoke in broken English. 'Come in, come in.'

He would have turned away, but she caught hold of his sleeve and hustled both him and Irena into the house. A man standing with his back to the glowing coal fire nodded in their direction, but made no move. Irena spoke to him and he replied. Duncan noticed there was no welcome in his voice. Clearly he did not welcome this pretty young newcomer. Duncan guessed he was questioning her about him. He felt uncomfortable. He turned towards the door, but Ona wouldn't allow him to leave. 'You kind to my sister. You eat with us,' she said. Duncan looked at the man.

He nodded. It was not the warmest of welcomes, but Duncan was hungry and the soup smelt good. Ona caught hold of his arms and almost pushed him into a chair. He glanced towards Irena; although she still looked strained she smiled at him shyly.

A sturdy little boy of about two and a half sidled across the room to grasp his mother's skirts. Ona lifted him. Irena spoke to him softly. He wriggled closer to his mother. Her hair straggled lifelessly about her face and he noticed she had a bruise on her cheek. Petras growled in his foreign language and at once Ona stood Gavin down and fetched soup-plates and a loaf of bread. A pot steamed on the stove. Ona ladled out the soup and Irena carried the well-filled plates to the table. Petras drew up his chair, sat down and crumbled bread into the soup. 'Eat – eat,' he ordered Duncan.

Scampering footsteps brought a boy of about six hurtling through the door. His black tackety boots, clattered noisily.

'Stop that row, boy,' Petras shouted.

The eagerness died on the child's face. He edged along to his place at the table with downcast eyes.

'This is Dougie,' Ona said. Duncan winked at him, liking the round flushed face, the stubble of fair hair, close shaven above his pink out-standing ears. The boy ate his soup and bread as if he didn't have a moment to spare.

'It's long way from school,' Ona explained in her careful broken English.

Petras made a snarling remark, which Duncan couldn't understand. As soon as he finished his meal, he stood up and stretched, took a silver-cased hunter from his waistcoat pocket. 'Time I was away,' he said in English.

Ona placed Petras's boots beside his chair. She had already packed his 'piece' and filled a bottle with cold tea. Petras shook hands with Duncan, unhooked his cloth cap from behind the door, slammed it shut as he left. Ona relaxed. Dougie ran off back to school. Duncan found himself reluctant to leave. He hoped he might see Irena again somehow, but couldn't be so bold as to ask.

There were Lithuanians in almost every pit in the area and he'd noticed women out shopping, always wearing little white head scarves, but he'd never before been inside one of their houses. It was clean and bright with polished brasses, and hangings of crochet work. Now that Ona's husband had gone the two women were chattering freely. Irena carried the plates to a small table at the back of the room. There was no sink: the washing-up was done in a bowl on a small table. Irena glanced over her shoulder and smiled at him. Her hands grew pink from the hot water, a dash of soda added, her arms, bare to the elbow, were lightly tanned from working in the fields. She felt shy, then she darted a sidelong glance at him, smiling, and he seized Gavin, swung the toddler up high.

'His hands are sticky – don't let him touch your good clothes,' Ona warned.

Duncan held the child at arm's length, in mock horror. Gavin giggled and stabbed out with jam-stained fingers. Duncan growled, pretending to bite, and Gavin shrieked in fear and excitement. Then holding the tiny hand as if it was truly repulsive, he swung round towards Irena. She smiled, and blushed but kept her eyes on the laughing child, but Duncan flapped the sticky hand towards her until she had no option but to turn her face and look fully at him. Merriment danced in the depths of her eyes and he saw they were a lovely clear blue. He was memorizing her features and almost forgot the child he was holding. Brusquely Irena took the cloth to clean the boy's hands. Gavin wriggled down and ran to his mother.

'Irena going to marry very soon,' Ona said.

He took it as a warning. He wasn't surprised. He gave up all thought of asking her to walk out with him. He managed to say, 'I hope you will be very happy.'

'Thank you Duncan,' she said.

She watched him go with a touch of sadness in her heart. Ona shut the door behind him, then lifted the baby. She sat down with a sigh of relief and unbuttoned her blouse. The rose-bud mouth closed tight on the nipple of Ona's pale, blue-veined breast.

'Ona – who is this man I'm to marry?' Irena asked.

'Never mind about him now. Sit down, dear – I'm dying to hear about everyone at home.' Ona was avoiding her question. Something was wrong, she was sure of it. She concentrated on Ona's questions, relating the happenings from Mossenos, the faraway village of their childhood. Time slipped by.

Then, quietly, but with determination, Irena said, 'Now, tell me about Tamosinskas.'

Ona shifted the baby from one breast to the other, 'Petras will be seeing him soon,' she said.

'What is he like? Does he live nearby? Will I be near you when I'm married?' Fear tightened its grip.

'I can't tell you anything,' Ona sounded weary.

'Why not?' Irena persisted. 'Don't you know him?' Still Ona avoided the question.

'Petras will tell you. Oh! Irena, dear – please don't spoil today. It's like a breath from the past, having you here. We had such happy times, didn't we? Remember those picnics and dancing in the woods? How we used to decorate the wagons with greenery and paper flowers, and Vincie played his fiddle. Do they still do that, Irena?'

'Yes, sometimes.'

'I'd wear my prettiest blouse and skirt, and we'd dance and sing all night long—'

Why wouldn't Ona tell her about Tamosinskas? Suppose he was like Petras? Irena had never liked him. Ona looked so tired. The baby, satisfied, released the nipple with a milky burp.

Ona sighed. 'I must get ready for Ladislas. Bring up her wind, will you, Irena?'

She handed the baby over, buttoned up her blouse then poked the glowing coals of the fire to bring two big kettles to the boil.

'Who is Ladislas?'

'He's the lodger.'

The baby burped. 'I think she needs changing,' Irena said.

'There are dry nappies on the pulley.' Ona lowered the line and lifted off a clean towelling square.

Ladislas came in, bringing a damp, dank smell. Only the whites

15

of his eyes and his pink lips showed clean in his coal-blackened face. Irena had never seen a man so dirty. Ona stood a tub by the hearth and filled it from kettles of hot water and buckets of cold.

'This is my sister, Irena,' Ona introduced him.

Ladislas glanced shyly at Irena.

'Go outside' Ona hissed. 'He has to get washed.'

'In here?'

'There's nowhere else. It's no good fussing,' Ona told her sharply. 'Life's different here.'

Outside, beyond the single-storey houses was the great black bulk of a slag heap. A sulphurous smell hung in the air. There was not a tree, a flower or a bird in sight. Men squatted beside a wall; toddlers splashed bare-foot in a puddle; two women lounged in a doorway, talking to an old black-clad crone who sat squarely on a high-backed chair; a girl was bouncing a ball, chanting softly.

'Where are the coal fields?' Irena asked.

'There are no coal *fields*.' Ona emphasised the last word and gave a grim laugh. 'Only the pits. Underground – that's where the men work.'

Irena's bewilderment grew. 'Is the whole of Scotland like this?' she asked.

Ona shrugged. 'There are some lovely places, but not here.' Dougie came back from school, hungry. Bonnie had to be looked after. Later the boys were washed and tucked into the truckle-bed, pulled out from under the lodger's bed where it was kept in the daytime.

'If you'd like a good wash, this is the best time,' Ona said. 'Petras won't be in for over an hour.'

As she undressed and washed by the fire, a sad weariness pressed on Irena's eyelids.

'You can sleep there,' Ona drew back a curtain revealing a bed in the wall. 'I must get the water ready for Petras now.'

Tired though she was, Irena couldn't sleep. When she heard Petras crash into the room, she buried her head in the feather-filled covers, shutting out the sounds of his splashing and grumbling. Would her life be like this? Would she have to live here for the rest of her days? Who was this Tamosinskas she was soon to marry?

Chapter 2

THE house in Half Mile Row, where Duncan had left Irena, was typical of the two room dwellings, the miners' rows, provided by the coal bosses for their employees. He lodged in a similar dwelling, about two miles distant. He tried to put Irena out of his mind as he walked along the spit spattered pavement, thronging with black-faced miners wearily trudging homewards. The air was heavy with smoke, a blast furnace flamed in the distance, and the slag from the coal mines made mountains, called bings. He passed a small group of prostitutes, at a corner of the street, smoking, coughing. One of them called out to him, but he had no interest in them, with their painted faces. What a contrast they were to the sweet, shy girl he had escorted from the station. He recalled how difficult he'd found life in Ringbrae when he first arrived. He was accustomed to dangerous work: he'd made his living from the sea since he'd been twelve years old, but working in the pits was something different. He'd never forget that first day when he'd signed on. Geordie Walker had been his gaffer and Duncan had hesitated at the pit head, but Geordie pushed him inside the cage and slammed the grille shut. The cage dropped. He felt as if his feet had been knocked from under him leaving him suspended like the lamp he held by its hook in his hand. His nostrils filled with a sour, dank smell and the flickering lamps of the miners cast grotesque shadows. Down, down jerked the cage. It rattled then stopped suddenly in a cavity bright with electric lights. He choked, which added to his fear. He learned later this was due to a change in air pressure, it being so deep underground.

He followed Geordie and the other men through an opening where there was light for a short way. As the passage narrowed, they walked in single file. The roof got lower, there were only the lamps of the miners, each of about two candle power. Never in his life would Duncan have imagined such a place! He must be walking into the depths of hell! He made the sign of the cross on his breast as he followed the line of miners and kept close to Geordie, fearing to be left behind. The roof sagged down on boulders hung on pit props, bent and cracked with the weight of rock they were holding up. Fear made him think those rocks had been waiting just to fall and crush him. He scurried under and the men noticed and chuckled.

The passage narrowed yet more, the roof got lower. Then the men seemed to disappear. They were crawling up an opening. On his hands and knees he crawled after them. They all had a strap or a hook to hold their lamps. Duncan held the lamp in his teeth as he crawled along.

At last they came to where the coal was. The seam was about two hundred feet long and the men were spaced out along it. The coal cutting machine had already sliced under the coal, just above the rock, leaving loose stuff lying outside. 'Shovel it into the pans,' he was told.

There was just enough space for him to crawl into and he set to work. Hours passed. He was sweating and cramped, but determined to give his best. Seeing more loose stuff under the cut coal. He began to clear that.

Geordie yelled an instruction.

Duncan did not understand. How could he? He'd never heard the words before. He carried on clearing beneath the cut coal, anxious to show he was a hard and willing worker.

'Ni gumoak!' growled the old man again, more urgently.

Duncan paused. He withdrew his arm from under the coal. Then it happened! The coal fell. Duncan tried to jump back, but the place was too narrow. Pit props were knocked down. Falling lumps of coal hit him; his light went out.

Geordie picked up the broken shaft of a pick and went for

19

Duncan like a madman. Duncan crawled away as fast as he could down the tunnel. He scarcely knew what he had done wrong, loathed being down there, shut away from the sun; he was in pitch darkness, bruised and scared. He stopped, panting, ears strained to the strange noises of the pit.

Geordie called to him, more reasonably. 'It's all right. There'll be no more fall. You can come back.'

Duncan was still uneasy, but what else could he do? He would never find his way out of the pit without Geordie to lead him. Confidence in his own strength and agility reasserted itself. He crawled back to where a lamp glimmered.

'You could have had us buried alive. Geordie growled. 'Get on now, get those hutches filled.'

'I'll need my light.'

'You can't light it down here. You'll have to work beside that lad there and get what you can from his light.'

Duncan was appalled that men should labour under such conditions – boys too, for some of the lads were no more than thirteen, not yet fully grown, with pinched faces and scarcely enough strength to carry out the tasks they were set.

At last the shift was done. Duncan crawled back, following the others, through the tunnels and along the narrow passages. The roof cracked his head when he straightened too soon, he had only the dim light of the miner ahead of him as a guide. He would get used to it, but never forget the misery of that first day.

When he stepped out of the cage at the pit-head and drew in a draught of the sweet, fresh air it seemed as exhilarating as champagne. He blinked to accustom his eyes to the blessed daylight; glanced at the faces of his fellow workers and saw that fleetingly they all experienced relief and joy at being up on the good earth again.

Irena slept fitfully. It was only five-thirty when she awoke, and peeped out from behind the curtain. Ladislas was getting ready for the day shift. Ona had lit the fire, boiled a kettle and was packing his lunch-box. No wonder she looked worn. Irena dressed behind the curtains, then did what she could to help as the day's work began. The baby cried until she was fed, the boys ate doorsteps of bread and drank cups of milky tea. Dougie was tidied and sent off to school. Petras emerged from the other wall-bed, dressed in trousers and shirt, pulling braces over his broad shoulders.

'God be with you, Petras,' Irena said, politely.

He grunted, 'You might as well have stayed at home. That bloody Tamosinskas has hooked up to some other sly bitch.'

Stupefied, Irena turned to Ona. She couldn't believe what she heard.

'It doesn't matter, dear.' Ona hurried across and threw her arms around Irena. 'Don't be upset about it. There are better fish in the sea than Tamosinskas.'

'Huh!' snorted Petras. 'Meanwhile she makes another mouth to feed.'

Irena said, 'I don't understand. I have a letter from the match-maker. It is all arranged—'

'It was.' Petras growled. 'Some widow woman wheedled her way in. She's got a fully furnished house so he married her instead.'

'You're well rid of him.' Ona said. 'We'll find you another husband.'

Irena was shocked – and furious! She'd been cheated, made a fool of! Rejection twisted like a knife wound in her stomach. It touched her heart only to harden it, for she had never met Tamosinskas. Hurt pride added to her bitterness and desolate helplessness. She couldn't go back. She had no money for the fare. Anyway, what was there to go back for?

All she could do was make herself as inconspicuous as possible when Petras was at home, and more than pull her weight in house-work, cooking and mending. Then, on Friday Irena noticed an unusual nervous tension in Ona. It puzzled her; the week's work was finished, surely it should be a happy time? After his meal Petras left the house. Ona began packing a basket, with a can of water, a jug of milk, some little twisted doughnuts sprinkled with sugar.

'Making a picnic?' Irena asked, surprised and puzzled.

Ona avoided looking at her. 'Petras has gone for his pay, then he'll go to the bar. He gets mad when the drink's on him, so I take the children into the washhouse.'

'That's dreadful!'

'It's not his fault.' Ona snapped defensively. 'It's the drink – and the work. It's no life for a man like Petras, crawling about in those rat-holes all day. He's not the only one that goes wild on pay night.'

The washhouse held a dank smell of yellow soap trapped in the cracks of the scrubbed wooden table and the quarry tiles of the floor. Ona shared the little brick building with five other families. No one else wanted it at nine o'clock on a Friday evening.

Bonnie gurgled happily as she was carried out in her osier cradle. In the light of a single candle Ona spread a thick blanket on the table and put the boys to bed there, with pillows and a warm feather-filled quilt.

'I dare not light the fire,' she said. 'It could damage the copper unless I put water in it, and if I do that the place gets steamed up.'

It took three trips to carry out everything Ona thought they might need, including two wooden chairs, some cushions and blankets. The candle guttered, burning low. Ona fumbled in her basket. 'I meant to put in a new candle. Oh, don't say I've forgotten it!'

'I'll get another one.' Irena offered.

'You'll have to hurry – it's nearly closing time.'

Irena found the candle. She was returning across the yard when she heard drunken singing and a clatter of heavy boots. She ran. Ona stood at the open door of the washhouse.

'Quick! That's Petras—' Ona hustled her inside, slammed the door shut and locked it.

Irena stood by the window, watching as Petras staggered to the door of his house, flung it open and crashed inside, mouthing curses.

A few minutes later he burst out again.

'He's coming this way,' Irena said.

Ona was sitting on one of the chairs, very still and tense. 'Come away from the window and keep quiet. He can't get in here.'

'Woman – Ona – fucking hell woman. I know you're in there. You wait! I'll belt the lot of you.'

The wash-house door rattled as he fumbled with the latch. He bashed against it with his shoulder and Irena held her breath, terrified he would break in. There was a loud thud. He had slipped and fallen to the ground.

Cursing, he heaved himself to his feet again, pounded on the door and yelled obscenities with growling ferocity. Irena trembled. She put her hand on Ona's shoulder and her sister held it tightly, sharing her fear. Each gave courage to the other, until at last the shouting, banging and rattling on the door ceased. Petras's dragging footsteps shuffled away and he spat curses at them, at life, at everything.

Irena moved back to the window. Petras took a bottle from his pocket, swigged from it and threw it to the ground where it smashed into a hundred fragments. He went into the house.

'He'll sleep now,' Ona said. 'He'll be all right in the morning.'

The children had remained as quiet as mice, tucked up in their hard bed on the table. 'Has Dada gone, Mamyte?' Dougie whispered.

'Yes, my darling.'

'He can't come in here, can he?'

'Shh! Go to sleep. It's all right, now. I'm here with Auntie Irena.'

Dougie stuffed his thumb into his mouth and settled down beside his little brother. Irena and Ona ate some of the doughnuts. It was a long night on the bare wooden chairs covered only by a blanket.

Next day the routine of life was resumed as if nothing had happened. By afternoon Petras had recovered from his hangover sufficiently for Ona to trust the children to his care and she and Irena set off to do the week's shopping. Gangs of youths gathered at street corners, sitting on their hunkers, or with their legs stretched out over the pavement, whistling and catcalling. The local girls responded cheekily, but Irena was afraid of them.

'They don't like us,' Ona said. 'I don't know why. We've never done them any harm.' She pointed ahead. 'We're nearly there. That's Krepsys.'

It was a different world inside the shop, filled with appetizing smells. Smoked sausages hung from the ceiling, in clusters or singly. Varnished drawers held dried fruits, spices, sugars, or lentils. Sacks on the floor spilled out flour, oatmeal and potatoes. There were cucumbers, cabbages, beetroot; an open barrel of salt herring, seed-sprinkled loaves of rye bread, baps and rolls. On a marble slab behind the counter stood a round lump of butter and several big cheeses. Goods were weighed into thick blue bags or twisted 'pokes' of rolled newspaper. Over all hung a strong sweet-sour smell, an odour that repelled many, but to Irena it was mouth watering, as was the pungent smell of a freshly opened barrel of sauerkraut.

The chatter of Lithuanian voices flowed all around. Several women looked at Irena curiously, and she felt sure that they had heard that Tamosinskas had jilted her. She flushed, hating to be the object of their pity, then turned and moved towards the door.

'Don't go, Irena,' Ona caught hold of her arm.

'I'll wait outside.'

She stopped on the threshold, staring at a smart barouche that was approaching down the street, drawn by a matching pair of horses; two servants in green livery with gold braiding were mounted on the coachman's seat in front. The maroon bodywork gleamed whilst the hood over the rear seat was down, giving a clear view of the occupants.

'You know who that is?' Ona said. 'See the crest? It's Lord and Lady Eveson. She's the daughter of Count Suslenko.'

The years slipped away as Irena recognized them. 'Grandpa took me to their wedding,' she said. It was a day she'd never forgotten. They'd walked ten miles to join the crowds in Vilnius, to watch the grand procession of carriages, with bands and military outriders, as the aristocracy of Lithuania was conveyed to the cathedral.

Lord Eveson in grey top hat and morning coat glanced around the crowd with a supercilious air. His face wore the same bored expression it had on his wedding-day, pulling down the corners of his mouth beneath the waxed moustache. Something about him repelled her, still, whilst the cool loveliness of Lady Eveson excited her admiration. Her face, a perfect oval, was framed by red-gold hair, shielded by a wondrous be-feathered hat, held in position by a diaphanous veil of palest pink, Seven years after her wedding, she was if anything more beautiful. Impressive wealth, and aristocratic pride was emphasized by the way she held her head, and the slenderness of her shapely neck, rising from the softly draped neckline of her exquisite gown.

The horses were drawn to a halt outside the shop and Mr Brysinauskas, the owner of Krepsys, hurried out. He bowed, moved a few steps nearer, bowed again and waited until he was spoken to.

'That smoked sausage you sent – ' Lady Eveson began at once, speaking in Lithuanian.

'I trust it met with your approval, your Ladyship?'

'It most certainly did not. It was quite tasteless. I am sure it had no rye spirit in it–'

'Surely it had, your Ladyship. I—'

'It had not, I tell you. It is bad enough to be supplied with badly prepared food – it is intolerable to have my judgement criticized by a tradesman. Moreover it had not been properly smoked over branches of juniper trees in the manner to which I am accustomed.'

'Junipers are so very difficult to obtain—'

'If you sell sausage as a special type, you should ensure that it is true to its name. I might, in the circumstances, accept that there is a difficulty in obtaining juniper branches, but there is certainly no excuse for omitting the marjoram. Indeed I would go so far as to say it was quite flavourless.'

'Your Ladyship – I will see to it personally that such an error does not occur again. If you would allow me to fetch a freshly made sausage—'

'Send it to the castle and I'll look at it,' Lady Eveson's voice rang out imperiously.

'Certainly, your Ladyship. You are most gracious—'

She waved a dismissive hand and instructed the coachman to drive on. The barouche moved forward. Brysinauskas bowed and remained fawningly bent until the carriage was several yards away up the street.

A small crowd had gathered to watch and listen. Brysinauskas's two assistants stood poised, ready to attend immediately to any bidding from her Ladyship.

'Her husband is heir to the Earl of Milton,' Ona said, with a note of bitterness and envy. 'They own the pits and everything for miles around. The gentry live on the backs of the workers here, just as they do at home.'

Irena stared after carriage. How could some have such wealth in the midst of so much dirt and squalor? She recalled her father's anger when her grandfather had stated his intention of walking to Vilnius to see the wedding procession. 'I wouldn't stir a step to watch those bloodsuckers!'

Resentment stirred in her mind at the unfairness of life – yet something in Lady Anastasia's expression made her pause and wonder. Was her life with Lord Eveson happy? She too was far from home.

Chapter 3

'THERE'S no work for women,' Ona told Irena. 'Especially not for Lithuanian women. If you could speak English, you could get a job cleaning the houses of rich people, but there's nothing that you could do.'

'I've seen women working at the pit head, picking stone from among the coal,' Irena said.

'That's a terrible job,' Ona objected. 'And you'd get filthy – it's bad enough having to get Petras and the lodger cleaned up after work. Some widows do it, but they've no option. You'd make Petras mad if you took a job on the belts. He's been asking around for a husband for you.'

Irena sighed. If someone like Duncan MacRaith would offer to marry her, she'd jump at the chance – but the idea of being pushed off on any man who happened to want a housekeeper and a woman in his bed was a very different matter. That was how it had been when the marriage to Tamosinskas had been arranged, but somehow she'd seen that differently. Now she knew how hard life was for women in the miners' rows, she found the prospect quite frightening.

She prayed no one would want to marry her, but only two weeks later when Petras came home he sat down with a broad smile on his usually grim face and said, 'I've found you a husband, Irena.'

She glanced at Ona and saw the anxious expression on her sister's face.

'A mate of mine is willing to take you. I've asked a match-maker to see to the arrangements. I'm having it all done properly.'

Irena swallowed. 'Who – who is it?' she asked.

'Antanas Lazaraitis.'

The name meant nothing to her.

'Is he a good man?'

'As good as any others. I drink with him every week.'

Irena flinched and glanced at Ona.

Petras said, 'He's all right, I tell you. You be a good wife to him and he'll treat you well enough.'

A drinking pal of Petras's! They wanted to marry her off to a man like that! What could she do! She thought of visiting the priest and begging him to refuse to marry her to this man, but that would sound ridiculous. She would probably get a lecture on humility, be told it was her Christian duty to accept her lot. She felt shrivelled within herself.

Tight-lipped, like an automaton, she carried on with her tasks through the days that followed. Ona cast anxious glances at her from time to time. 'I'm sure Antanas will make as good a husband as Tamosinskas. You were quite willing to marry him, weren't you?'

'It seemed different. I didn't know what I was coming to.'

'Antanas brings in good money, and one man's much the same as another. Feed him well and don't argue.'

'You sound just like mother.'

'And why shouldn't I? It's plain common sense. You're here, and you need a husband, so you may as well make the best of it. There's a good many women would jump at the chance of marrying Antanas Lazaraitis.'

'Then let them!'

'Irena, you're being unreasonable. If you cross Petras on this I don't know what he'll do.' Ona looked drawn and upset. 'Nobody consulted me when my marriage was arranged.'

'Dadda wouldn't have insisted that you married Petras if you hadn't been willing.'

'Do you really think I had a choice? Who else was there? You know marriages depended on what you could offer as a dowry. Petras was the only one possible, as far as I could see. But it's worked out all right. He's a good man – and don't ever let me hear you say otherwise.' How could Ona be so blind! 'We'll make sure you have a really good wedding.'

Irena swallowed. 'When?' she asked.

'The week after Juozas Budreckis gets married.'

'But that's less than three weeks away!' Irena gasped. Juozas had sent home for his childhood sweetheart and Irena had agreed to be a bridesmaid.

'I do love a good wedding,' Ona said. She threw her arms around Irena, and gave her a hug, but the prospect of marrying this drinking pal of Petras's remained a leaden weight on Irena's heart.

The only relief for her was to walk, to get away from the miners' rows. She followed a track beside a railway line, crossing a meadow where cattle grazed. She had no fear of them, they were more gentle than many humans. The grassland sloped down to a gate and beyond that a little stream gurgled through grassy slopes leading to distant beech woods. Among the trees below she could see the chimneys of a very large house. It was where Lord Eveson lived with his beautiful wife, Lady Anastasia. One day Irena told herself, she would walk on further and see if she could catch a glimpse of the house itself.

She sat on the trunk of a fallen oak. She had first walked there with Dougie over a month ago, and since then it had become her refuge, a place that reminded her of home, being in the country-side, cut off from the desolation of the pits and the rows of mean little houses.

She sat there a long time and in loneliness and desolation she wept. Then she prayed. 'Dear Lord, there is no way out of this marriage, I know that, but let this man Petras has found for me, this Antanas Lazaraitis – please let him be kind, so that I may become a gentle, respectful wife to him.' But still as she walked back to the row, she was afraid.

*

29

At the end of each week's work, Geordie, the pit contractor, paid his men at his house.

'Dadda's gone to the pub,' the child who opened the door told Duncan.

'I've come for my pay.'

'He hasn't left it here. He's probably at the Duke's Bar.'

Having fallen asleep by the fire, Duncan was later than usual. He walked to the bar. Gas made balloons of fizzing light in the smoke haze and sawdust lay thick on the floor. Geordie was leaning on the counter; in front of him was a pint of beer and a smaller glass containing a double whisky.

'Why, Duncan! I didn't think you haunted these dens of vice.' He spoke with his cigarette drooping from his mouth, stuck to his lip.

Duncan grinned amiably. Mostly he spent his evenings at his lodgings, joining in a card game, or just wandering the streets, absorbing his strange surroundings. Geordie spat his cigarette stub to the floor and flattened it with his foot. He lifted his glass, poured the remaining half down his throat, pushed the glasses forward and ordered drinks for them both.

They clinked the whisky glasses together. Geordie threw back his head and swallowed the golden spirit, shaking the last drops into his beer. Duncan couldn't return the round: the money he earned barely paid for his food and lodgings.

Another contractor came in. He was a Lithuanian, but in the pits he was known as Jimmy Walker. All the foreign miners were given British names. It was a safety measure. The tally man needed names he could relate to when accidents occurred underground. Jimmy had a deep racking cough and spat frequently. He ordered a double whisky, downed it in one gulp and pushed his glass forward to be recharged.

'I needed that,' he said. 'Couple of my men got crushed today. I've just seen their widows.'

Geordie nodded. 'Poor buggers. Rock fall?'

'Aye. We dug 'em out and brought 'em up, but there was damn all we could do.' He sighed and shook his head.

They drank in bitter silence. Duncan thought of those fellow miners; he hadn't known them, but felt sad for them. He shuddered, seeing vividly rocks that seemed to be lying in wait just for him. It could happen at any time. He knew it. They all knew it. Every time they went into the pit, each man died a little death. A man's racking cough rasped through the smoky fug. Jimmy Walker moved across to the old miner, took his glass and had it refilled. He chatted with him briefly. Geordie drained his glass and moved away. Suddenly Duncan realised the contractor was walking out of the door. He leapt after him. 'You haven't paid me.'

Geordie showed exaggerated surprise.

'You know it,' Duncan growled.

'All right. All right!' Geordie took some coins from his pocket. 'Here you are. See you on Monday.'

Duncan counted the money – he'd been short changed. It would be like getting blood out of a stone to make the cunning old devil hand over the missing amount.

Others came in. Duncan recognized Petras, with two other men, their arms around each other's necks, as much to steady their steps as to indicate comradeship.

'Three pints and halves, Andy. We've gotta shel-shelebration—'

The barman drew the beer and stood a whisky beside each glass. 'What's the celebration, then?' he asked.

'My old pal here – that work along with me – where you are, Antanas?'

Antanas Lazaraitis shuffled slowly, unsteadily forward, a heavy-shouldered, thick-set man with short bowed legs.

Duncan finished his beer and decided it was time he went home. Petras caught him by the lapels of his coat. 'Wait till I tell ye.' His voice was slurred. 'Antanas Lash – Lashar – my good friend here is goin' ter get wed.'

'Oh, aye. Good luck to them both.' Duncan said.

Petras swallowed his whisky. He swayed, spun round and fell.

'Take that bloody sot home,' ordered the barman.

Duncan placed his feet firmly apart, grasped Petras's arms and

31

heaved, pulling him into a semi-upright position. Lazaraitis, who was less drunk, pulled Petras's arm over his shoulder and together they marched him out of the bar into the cool of the night. He muttered, incoherently as he was forced forward by his two supporters.

Half an hour later they came upon a square where a crowd had gathered. Petras lifted his head and straightened, like an out of condition pointer getting a scent on the wind. 'It'sh a wedding—'

'You're not going there,' Duncan said. He tried to guide Petras to the other side of the road.

'Next wedding'll be mine,' boasted Lazaraitis.

That day they were celebrating the wedding of Juozas Budreckis and Isabella at which Irena was a bridesmaid. For her, every moment of the elaborate nuptial ceremony had been a dreadful harbinger of the travesty of a marriage she was being forced into.

A week earlier Petras had brought Antanas Lazaraitis home. Meeting him had been even worse than Irena had feared. Her cool reception had done nothing to dampen his ardour. The sight of her made Antanas all the more eager for the match. He was physically repulsive to her, but she had no money, little knowledge of the language, no friends outside the immediate circle of the family. She could see no escape.

Lithuanian wedding festivities lasted almost a week, a ritual of eating, drinking, singing, and dancing. In the midst of it Irena felt remote, miserably alone. The wedding had been solemnized in the Church of the Blessed Virgin, and now the gaiety was in full swing.

Isabella wore a white head-dress with the veil thrown back, a frilled choker lightened her sensible dark dress, and pinned to her bodice was a bow of white satin ribbon with a centrepiece of feathery grey-green rue. Juozas sported a similar but smaller bow attached to the breast pocket of his dark, high-buttoned suit. Shy but happy, sweethearts for many years, they glanced longingly at one another, but they wouldn't be alone for many hours yet.

The reception was held in the living room of a small dwelling.

The table was piled with food, which the women were continuously replenishing.

Irena was reaching across the table with a fresh plate of sugar-sprinkled cakes of the kind called 'little ears' when she heard Petras's loud, slurred voice. She set the plate on the table, and looked towards the doorway. Duncan MacRaith was with Petras. Momentarily she was aware of no one else.

She had seen him only once since the day she arrived, and that was a month ago, at church. He'd been in the congregation. And he hadn't looked in her direction, but she'd been unable to take her eyes off him, so handsome and vibrant. She'd been unable to concentrate on the service.

She was shocked now to see him in the company of Petras and Antanas! Was he just another of their drinking pals? She regarded the trio with distaste. Petras, swaying slightly, unhooked his arms from around the shoulders of his companions and shouted for someone to get him a drink. Antanas stumbled towards her. He reached out to catch hold of her, and she stepped aside quickly to avoid his groping hands.

'Don't be coy, Reenie, my lovely,' he wagged a drunken finger playfully in her face. 'Don't forget it's to be our wedding next week.'

As if she could forget! She made no attempt to hide the loathing she felt. She stared at him with a fury of hatred, but he continued to push his way towards her.

The fiddler struck up a merry tune. 'Time for another dance,' he called. 'Outside – make a big circle.'

The tears Irena had held back all through this wedding welled into her eyes. She dashed them away with the back of her hand, refusing to allow herself to give way. Everyone around her seemed to be so carefree.

With a prancing step and a hop and a skip, the fiddler moved around the table and out of the door, playing a merry tune. Men, women and children followed him, holding hands, making a chain.

Antanas grabbed at Irena's hand. She snatched it away. He

lurched towards her, both arms outstretched. She swung around, desperate to escape but there was no back door to the little house. Then Duncan was there, rock solid in front of her.

'Come, Irena.' His voice was firm, but gentle. 'Dance with me.'

She was still agitated. 'I'm busy—'

'Leave the work. This is a day for dancing – have fun.'

If only she could! There had been so little fun since she came here. Duncan held out his hands and clasped hers. She left them resting in his and felt the pressure, the warmth, the roughened texture of his dry skin and found it comforting.

Antanas tried to push himself between them. 'I'm goin' to dance with her. She's goin' to be my wife.'

'She's not your wife yet.' Duncan shouldered him aside. He leaned towards Irena, his breath was on her cheek, he smelt a little of drink.

'Come on, Irena. Have I got to carry you out?'

'You wouldn't!'

'Wouldn't I?' His exuberance was infectious.

Wild excitement burst like a tumultuous chord of music within her. She threw back her head laughing, her mood fired to match his. He made to catch her up into his arms. She twisted away, but caught hold of his hand, and it was she who led him out into the gas-lit street.

The dancers formed a big ring, singing, circling around the bride and groom. The fiddler played with spirit and feeling, an abandoned energy that mirrored Irena's reckless mood. An age-old ritual of fertility magic from the fields of Lithuania was acted out on the hard-trodden, dusty ground of the square, with the bing flaring, sulphurous and menacing in the background.

The fiddler changed the rhythm, zipped into a polka. Duncan turned Irena to face him, put his hands on her waist, she lifted hers to his shoulders. They stood, smiling at each other as he waited for the beat, then swept her vigorously into the dance. She had learned in childhood and, held by Duncan, her feet seemed scarcely to touch the ground. She was conscious of him with every lightly springing step, but kept her eyes turned aside.

Only when the music swirled to an end and Duncan swung her round, lifting her off her feet, clasping her close, did she look up into his eyes. Both were breathing fast, her face was flushed. He threw back his head, laughter burst from his wide mouth, in spontaneous joy. They had matched so well – a pity it was only a dance! The rhythm of their bodies had been as perfectly in tune as if they had practised. Antanas was stumbling towards her, followed by Petras, both men coarse-looking, glasses slopping in their hands.

'You can't marry that man,' said Duncan. 'He's not right for you.'

'What else can I do? Petras has arranged it.'

Duncan was silent. His eyes were on the ground, where he slid his boot about, scuffing the dust. It was all very well for him to give her advice. She knew Antanas was not right for her!

Then, with a falsely flippant note, she said, 'I suppose you don't want a wife?'

He looked up. She tried to read his face – was he shocked? No decent girl would have made such an improper suggestion – but she didn't care! She had spoken in desperation, on impulse. Hot colour flooded her face, it burned her with shame, spreading up from her neck, over her cheeks. Duncan still scuffed one foot back and forth, looking down. Why should he take pity on her – for that was all she could hope for?

Antanas and Petras were only a step away, belligerent, scowling and ugly. She lifted her skirts, brushed past them and ran for the house.

'Come back. I want to dance.' Antanas shouted.

Petras gave an ugly laugh. 'You'll have to tame her after you're wed.'

Chapter 4

'I will marry Irena.'

She stopped dead still, her heart pounding. It was Duncan's voice – normally soft spoken, he had shouted the words for all to hear.

Slowly she turned round. Duncan was facing Petras, with his back towards her. Did he mean it – really mean it?

Petras snorted. 'You don't earn enough to keep a wife. The settlement's been made—'

'Irena doesn't want to marry Antanas,' Duncan said.

'It's my duty to see my sister-in-law is well provided for and Antanas has a house ready for them to move into. It's nothing to do with you, MacRaith.'

'You're a blasted selfish bully—' Duncan shouted.

'Take that back.' Petras hunched his shoulders, clenched his fists and stared threateningly into Duncan's face.

'Never!' Duncan drew himself up defiantly.

Irena drew in a deep breath as Petras lunged. He was strong, his reputation as a fighter almost legendary. Duncan dodged the blow and swung his fist at Petras's jaw. It glanced off. He stood no chance. She shuddered at the sound of fists thumping viciously into flesh, heard the grunts and growls and heavy breathing as punches struck home. She couldn't bear to watch – but nor could she turn away – her fear for Duncan, and not to know how the fight was going was worse.

More wedding guests ran up, excited and delighted – some thought a fight was a normal part of a wedding. No one asked what started it, they gathered in a wide circle, shouting in English and Lithuanian. Most were backing Petras, because they knew him, but others took Duncan's side. His quality as a fighter was unknown, they didn't think he had the remotest hope, but they were enjoying the spectacle.

Irena watched in horror as, grappling with each other, the two men fell to the ground. Their bodies heaved, they rolled over and over, their hands searched brutally for a hold on each other. She winced as Petras lifted Duncan by the shoulders and crashed his head down on a stone. Surely he must be knocked unconscious! But he kicked out, grasped Petras's throat, and with a mighty effort forced him off – and over. Then Duncan was on top drawing back his fist to deliver a mighty punch – Antanas leapt forward and grabbed Duncan's arm, pulling him back.

Angry shouts bellowed from the spectators. 'Let them fight fair.' Someone pulled Antanas away and landed a punch. He struck back. Then they too were fighting. The mood of the crowd, fired by drink, turned ugly. Fists were swung, blows struck. Where, only a few minutes earlier, there had been lively music and dancing couples, now there was uproar in the square. Pushed to one side by the surging mob, Irena almost lost sight of Petras and Duncan.

'Watch it – police!' The crowd scattered. Duncan delivered a mighty blow, with his full weight behind it, an uppercut that found its mark. Petras's legs buckled, he fell to the ground. Duncan stood over him, his face blood-stained, one eye almost closed, covered in dust. Two policemen ran up, one grabbed Duncan by the shoulder.

'I thought this was supposed to be a wedding and you're knocking hell out of each other!'

'Get up.' The other policeman nudged Petras with his foot, and dazed and swaying he staggered to his feet. 'You're under arrest – along to the station, both of you.' Meekly they shuffled off.

Ona snapped at Irena. 'It's all your fault, I just hope Petras won't be deported,' she said, bitterly.

'Oh, no!' Irena threw her arms around her sister, but Ona pushed her away.

'It's happened to some men when they've got into trouble with the police.'

Irena was aware of curious eyes sweeping over her; they made her feel guilty. Several people were talking at once, voicing different versions of how and why the fight had started. Ona was not the only one to blame her. She moved back till she was standing some distance away. She felt ashamed. How could she have been so bold as to offer herself to Duncan like that? It was so outrageous that, although she remained hidden in a shadowy corner of the square, her sense of humour bubbled up. She covered her mouth with her hand to smother a chuckle. With it came an uplifting sense of pride.

Duncan had been magnificent. She would never forget that moment when he had said, so clearly and firmly, 'I will marry Irena.' The fact that it had been a useless gesture did nothing to diminish her admiration for his courage. She had no hope the fight would change the marriage arrangement. That was already set up, but she was glad he'd knocked Petras out! Duncan's victory thrilled her, she knew she would never forget it.

Ona went into the house, weeping, supported by women friends. Irena's mood sobered. It would be awful if Petras and Ona were deported! If they were handed over to the Tsar's officials they might be sent to Siberia. She closed her eyes and prayed. She stayed there a long, long time.

Suddenly she saw them. Duncan and Petras were walking back, side by side. She did not move from the shadows. A resounding cheer was raised – people ran towards them. Ona rushed out of the house and threw herself into Petras's arms. Such a show of emotion embarrassed him and he thrust her aside in favour of the frothing pint of beer Antanas held out for him.

Someone handed a glass to Duncan. His face was puffy, bruised. He took the beer glass with tender hands, and sipped through swollen lips. He left the talking to Petras.

'What did the police say?'

'Have you got to go to court?'

'Yes. On Monday morning.' Petras's voice was husky. He was in a worse state than Duncan.

'A family was deported last week,' someone said. The atmosphere was brittle with anxiety.

'The judge said he was sick of men being brought before him for fighting.'

'It's not only the Lithuanian men that fight,' put in one of the women.

'The Scots and Irish fight more than our men do.'

'Aye, but they can't be sent anywhere else. This is their country.'

'You shouldn't have been fighting, either of you,' Ona said, with unexpected courage.

'You shut your face,' growled Petras. 'It was that wild bitch of a sister of yours that caused the trouble.'

'I've already told her that.'

Antanas turned on Duncan. 'You shouldn't have attacked Petras. If you wanted a fight, it should have been with me.'

'If that's how you feel – ' Duncan began aggressively, the words slurred by the swelling of his mouth. Two men grabbed hold of his arms and held him back.

'Leave it be, Duncan,' someone advised.

'I won't leave it. I've offered for Irena.'

'And I've said no! She's promised to my pal,' Petras flung an arm around the shoulder of Antanas, and grinned crookedly into his face. 'And the sooner you take her out of my house, the better pleased I'll be.'

'The match has been made,' Antanas said, smugly. 'It can't be changed now.' He looked around. 'Where is she? Where's my little bride-to-be?'

Irena would have drawn further back into the shadows, but there was no escape. With a whoop of triumph a couple of young men pushed her forward. She wished the ground would open up and swallow her.

'Come and take your place beside me,' Antanas ordered.

'No – let her come to me,' shouted Duncan.

The argument was silenced as the clear young voice of Isabella rang out. 'Irena should choose.' Everyone looked at the bride whose wedding party had been so violently disrupted.

'Yes – yes,' Duncan agreed eagerly.

'No,' roared Petras. 'I'm her guardian. I've made the decision and I won't change it.'

The wedding guests took up the argument.

'It's not something a girl should be consulted about.'

'She's got to live with the man – let her decide.'

Isabella ran to Irena and grasped both of her hands. 'My dear bridesmaid – what do you think? Do you want to accept the man that Petras has chosen for you? Or do you want the other?'

'Let me tell her what I have to offer,' said Antanas.

'Yes, she should know that,' said an old crone. 'And think about it carefully, my girl.'

There was a hush as Antanas Lazaraitis, straightened his shoulders and said, 'I've rented a house and I've bought a table and chairs and a good feather bed. I've got cooking pots and dishes and money in my belt here.' He opened it and took out five sovereigns. 'These you can have, lass – to buy anything that's needful for the home, and for your trousseau. There'll be plenty more where those came from.'

Irena neither looked at nor listened to him. Her eyes were fixed on Duncan – and she saw him lower his head. He looked defeated.

'Now, Duncan – you've offered for the lass.' The old crone's voice was derisive. 'Let her know how you can provide for her.'

Duncan lifted his arms then dropped them to his sides in a gesture of helplessness. He shook his head. She longed to run to him, to take his hands but she stood motionless because she was not sure whether he still wanted her.

'I'm sorry, Irena. I have nothing,' he said. Then he lifted his handsome head and looked defiantly around the assembly. 'But I'll work double time until I have all those things that Antanas has offered – and more besides.' He paused. Irena felt a pulse of excitement and drew in a sharp breath. 'I just need time. Give me a little more time.'

'No.' thundered Petras. 'I want her off my hands by the end of the week. It's settled. She will marry Antanas.'

'No,' Irena called out quickly. 'You said the choice was mine. I will marry Duncan MacRaith.'

There was a stunned silence. Then Duncan's great laugh rang out.

Petras stormed away, his face contorted with rage, shoulders hunched, growling like an angry bear. Antanas stumbled after him.

Together with Ona and the children, and almost in silence, Irena and Duncan walked back to number 21 Half Mile Row.

The house was in darkness, Petras had not yet returned. Duncan carried Gavin and Irena led Dougie by the hand. Ona, with Bonnie in her arms had hustled the children indoors.

Irena turned to face Duncan on the doorstep. 'I promise to be a good wife to you, Duncan,' she said.

Ona came to the door. 'Come inside, Reenie,' she ordered sharply. She rushed out and stood between them, arms akimbo. 'Make arrangements for the wedding as quickly as you can, Duncan MacRaith.'

'I'll speak to the priest tomorrow.' He took Irena's hand, held it warmly between both of his, and gave it a squeeze. 'Goodnight.' With a brief bow to each and a jaunty wave of his hand he swung away down the street.

Ona hustled Irena into the house. They stripped the children to their shirts, and tucked them into bed. Then they heard a clatter of boots outside. Ona's face looked tense and white in the lamplight.

'We should have gone to the wash-house,' she said.

The door crashed open. Petras's bulk filled the doorway, his big-boned head thrust aggressively forward.

'What's that whore doing in my house?' He jabbed his finger in Irena's direction, though he looked at Ona.

Ona's mouth moved, but only a small choking sound came from it.

'She'll not spend another night under my roof.' He spat out the words.

'Please, Petras – let her bide here until she's wed.'

'No. Not one more night! Not another minute!

'I've nowhere to go,' Irena pleaded. 'I'll leave in the morning.'

'You'll leave now. You've chosen to go your own way – refused the man I picked for you. Go to that bloody Duncan MacRaith – and I wish him joy of you!'

'You can't turn Irena out at this time of night—' Ona clasped her hands together beseechingly.

'Can't I?' Petras turned threateningly to Irena and she backed away. His hand shot out. She thought he was going to strike her and ducked. He grabbed her arm with vicious fingers that dug painfully through the thin fabric of her blouse, bruising her flesh. He was dragging her towards the door.

'Petras – don't – ' Ona pleaded with him.

He swung his free hand and caught his wife a blow that sent her toppling over backwards. At that Irena's resistance ceased.

'All right. I'll go. Just let me get my shawl.'

Petras tore the large woollen square from the peg. He still held her arm in a merciless grip, pushing her towards the door. He had left it open when he came in. A small group of people had gathered there, looking and listening with avid curiosity and Irena felt shamed to be the centre of the violent scene. She tried to wrest her arm free, but Petras twisted it viciously and she cried out with pain.

'Whore!' he shouted. 'Out in the street where you belong.'

The shove with which he ejected her sent her reeling towards the onlookers and they stepped back, as if merely to touch her would be a contamination. Petras flung her shawl after her into the dirt of the gutter.

'Go your own way, you whore, and don't come back here – ever.'

Chapter 5

PETRAS slammed the door shut. Irena recovered her balance
and stooped to pick up her shawl. She was bruised and angry.
She glanced at the faces that stared at her in the light of the street
lamp – there was no one she knew. They drew back a little,
unwilling to become involved. One man said something to his
neighbour, who guffawed in response. She could not understand,
knowing so little English.

She guessed it was derogatory and felt threatened. She cowered
away from them, drew her shawl close around her shoulders and
ran down the street. She was desperate to get as far away as possible from Half Mile Row and from Petras. She ran and ran until
she was breathless, on and on until the pain in her side became
unbearable and forced her to slow her step. She walked on, afraid,
alone, at night, in an unfamiliar part of town. She turned a corner
and found herself in Main Street. It was dark between the yellow
pools of gaslight.

A late tram rattled past. Irena had no money to pay a fare, even
if there had been somewhere for her to go. She had no idea where
Duncan lived – and it would be shameful to go to him anyway.
She looked nervously this way and that, kept to the middle of the
wide pavement, away from the alleys that gaped darkly between
the high buildings. Any one might be lurking there. Her imagination was tight-strung – she fancied she heard footsteps running up
behind her, turned round quickly. There was no one, but she
quickened her pace.

She passed two prostitutes leaning against a lamp post, slightly drunk, bedraggled feathers adorned their shoulders, their gowns so low-cut that their breasts were visible. The younger one of the two eyed her with defensive aggression, and stepped out to bar her way.

'Where you goin', hen?'

Irena shook her head. 'I no understand,' she said. Her eyes widened with fear and she pulled the shawl tighter around herself.

The other woman glanced at her, ran her eyes up and down, and dismissed her with a curl of her lips, as of no consequence. 'She's one of them foreign women,' she said. Irena hurried past.

On the opposite side of the road three drunks were arguing outside a pub. Broken glass showed their drinking had not ended with closing time. Irena turned down the next side street, but that was darker, narrower, ill-lit, filled with menacing shadows. Two policemen on their beat were trying locked doors. To Irena they, too, were a threat. She turned round another corner and ran again. She ran until her breath rasped, an iron-tight pain shot through her chest and she stopped. A door rattled on its hinges, a piece of cardboard blew over the cobbles with a scraping sound, a rat scuttled along in the gutter. She could smell a midden somewhere close by and felt nauseated. The town was terrifying at night. She wished she had taken the other direction, towards that grassy slope by the little stream. There she could have crawled in beneath a sheltering bush and drawn comfort from the sound of rippling waters, watched the stars twinkling in the wide sky.

Perhaps she could find her way there, even now. She would retrace her steps, but which way had she come? Nothing was familiar – should she turn left here, or right? Anxiously she sought some house or shop she might recognize, but the narrow streets were all strange to her. She began to run again, until the echoing of her own feet unnerved her, then she made herself walk, quite quietly. She was tired, frightened and lonely, but kept moving on and on, until suddenly she was in Main Street again.

She had no idea of the time, but the last tram had passed long ago. Even the prostitutes and the drunks had gone. Half way along the street was a church. Irena walked towards it. She did not remember seeing it before, and it seemed like a miracle that it should be there now. She climbed the stone steps and tried the door. It was locked. There was no admission to its sanctuary. She sat down on the stone steps; it was pointless to move further.

She leaned against a pillar that supported the arch over the door and closed her eyes. She had to rest. Time passed. She heard the sound of a carriage coming along the street. She stayed very still, well back in the shadows, untroubled by the gentle clip-clop of the horse's hooves, the crunch of wheels. Its lights came nearer and, as it passed, she recognized the crest on its door as that of the Earl of Milton. The carriage rolled on only a few yards further, then she heard a call of 'Whoa!' The horse was drawn to a standstill just beyond the steps where she sat.

A gentleman got out. He wore a black cape and a top hat, as if he had been to some elaborate function. He spoke to the driver, the carriage moved on. The gentleman walked towards the church where Irena was sheltering. She stood up, would have run away, but he had seen her and called out. She did not know what he said but it was a voice of command, the kind that expected to be obeyed. She hesitated, frightened, uncertain how to respond. She had recognized the carriage and the man – it was Lord Eveson.

He staggered a little, drunkenly. He held out a hand to her, frightened she shrank away from him. Her back was against the church door. He moved swiftly, his hands were spread out, one on either side of her, trapping her. She screamed and he slapped her so hard across her face that the jolting pain stifled her cry.

'Shut up,' he growled.

He pressed the bulk of his body against her, pinioning her against the door. The front flap of his trousers was unfastened –

in horror and disgust she realised he was rubbing his swollen penis against her. She tried to twist away from him, but his grip was like an iron vice. He pressed his face into hers, she smelt whisky on his breath as his open mouth searched for contact. Sweat trickled down from his forehead. It dampened his dark hair and wetted her cheek. Nauseated, she jerked her head to one side, struggled desperately but his skull cracked against her cheek, knocked her against an iron bolt in the door. She was strong for a woman, yet against his determination was helpless. He did not yield an inch and his weight was so heavy against her she could scarcely breathe, jammed tight into the corner of the solid wooden door and the cold stone of its archway. A large iron knob dug painfully into her shoulder.

She cried out wildly, in Lithuanian, but his hand whipped across her mouth, stifling the sound. With his other hand he was lifting her skirt and petticoat. She wore no other garment beneath. He was feeling his way up the inside of her thigh, grop-ing. Desperately she tried to escape – then with a suddenness that totally startled her, he whipped one leg round behind her knees with a pressure that made them buckle and threw her to the ground. Her head hit the stone step with such force that she was momentarily stunned. In that moment he forced her legs apart. His hat had fallen off and she saw his face, contorted with lust. He fell on her and pain screamed through her body.

It was quickly over. He withdrew. She lay there, bruised and bleeding and barely conscious. He threw a coin down beside her, picked up his hat and strolled away. She lay where he had left her, shamed and sobbing and wishing for death. She heard the carriage return, pick up its passenger and clip-clop away up the street. She tried to stand, but the pain was unbearable. She crawled into the most distant corner of the church porch before she lost conscious-ness.

In the morning the young priest came to unlock the church. He picked up the golden guinea and turned it over in his hand, in surprise. Then he found her.

Duncan attended court on Monday morning, escorted with brisk efficiency by the nine-year-old daughter of Connie, his Lithuanian landlady. It had been arranged for her to interpret for Petras, and assist Duncan if need be. Young Agnes was dressed for the occasion in a hand-embroidered linen smock over her thick tweed skirt and shining black buttoned boots. Her long golden ringlets, having been tightly screwed up in papers the night before, bounced on either side of her head. Duncan envied her composure as she led him through the impressively huge doorway of the court building. She was confidently bilingual and had acted as interpreter in several court cases before.

Petras was already there, his cap set at a rakish angle which only partly covered his eye, multi-hued, purple and yellow with a tinge of green. Duncan was not sorry to see the puffy state of his face. He had heard nothing of Irena since he had left her on Saturday night. Now, having decided in advance that he must make an effort to get on with his future brother-in law, he strode towards Petras, who grunted, and pointedly ignored Duncan's outstretched hand.

'Keep away from me,' Petras growled. 'You've caused nothing but trouble.'

Agnes caught hold of both men by their sleeves. 'If you fight here, they'll certainly send you to prison,' her young piping voice warned. 'And you and your family could be deported,' she added, looking at Petras. She need not have been alarmed. Petras's manner, though unfriendly, was not belligerent and Duncan certainly had no intention of fighting. The two big men stood one on either side of the little girl, meekly waiting for her advice.

'If you behave yourselves you'll probably get away with a fine,' she said, sternly. 'Have you brought any money?'

Petras tapped a well-stuffed money belt. Duncan had borrowed a sovereign from Connie.

The usher opened a door. 'Duncan MacRaith. Charles Smith,' he called out.

'Take your cap off,' Agnes hissed at Petras. Her golden ringlets bobbed around her pretty face as she led them into the court-room.

The charges were stated. In a clear young voice she translated for Petras. The men each replied 'guilty' as she had instructed them.

The clerk read out the facts. 'Your worship. This case concerns a fight between these two men, on the evening of last Saturday.'

He paused. Agnes translated. She nodded to the clerk and he continued, pausing several times for her to explain to Petras.

The procurator-fiscal asked for information about both men. Agnes explained he was a married man with three children and he had never been in any trouble before, he was sorry and would make sure it never happened again. The procurator-fiscal looked grimly disbelieving. Then he barked some questions at Duncan. How long had he been in Ringbrae? Was he married or single?

'Please your worship, I'm to be married next week,' said Duncan.

'I understand this incident occurred at a wedding. I trust you won't repeat this disgraceful performance at your own wedding?'

'I promise you Sir – I shall not fight on my wedding day,' Duncan said, his hand on his heart.

A flicker of amusement crossed the procurator-fiscal's face. He announced the sentence, the clerk scribbled, and Agnes explained. 'You must each pay one pound or go to prison for ten days.'

As they left the courthouse Duncan and Petras each gave Agnes a shilling, and with her ringlets bobbing about her shoulders the child skipped away down the street to take the money to her mother.

Petras hunched his shoulders and without a word, hurried away to the tram stop. Duncan shrugged and walked briskly to the pit.

His spirits were high. His shoulders were broad, his back strong, he could earn more money. As he worked underground he thought of Irena with hot-blooded excitement. The longing to touch her and kiss her and share a bed with her awoke a physical yearning that was almost unbearable. For so long he had wanted a woman. More than one had seemed to him irresistibly fascinating, but the restrictions of life in his home village had prevented anything more than a few stolen kisses.

He asked Geordie Walker about finding a cheap house and was told of a single-end that was available in Mick's Buildings. It was reached by walking through a passage that smelled of urine and was graffiti-decorated. 'UP THE TING A LEERIES', 'BLOODY POLES', 'UP THE BILLY BOYS', 'KICK THE POPE' read the messages. Half a dozen ragged little boys were kicking a tin can about in the courtyard. A flight of stone steps led up to a line of four little 'houses' of which Duncan had been offered the first.

He unlocked the door and stepped inside. The room contained a coal-burning grate, dulled by a film of dust. Old linoleum lay on the floor, cracked and scuffed. Duncan lifted an edge and stamped on a black beetle. There were two recessed beds, consisting only of bare wooden boards. How in the world could this bare, dismal room be made decent and homely? However, he would have a wife to help him – and he was whistling as he locked up, ran down the stairs, and walked along the street with a jaunty air.

His face was still blackened from the pit and he was ravenously hungry when he reached his lodgings. He walked into the room and was surprised to find Ona sitting with Connie. The two women were talking in hushed voices. Agnes was sitting in her usual chair, listening pale-faced. Three pairs of eyes turned towards him. Foreboding turned to certainty of disaster as he looked from one to another. Connie stood up and reached out her hands to him, tears were rolling down her plump cheeks.

'Oh, Duncan – Duncan – I'm so sorry – so sorry!'

'What is it? What's wrong?'

Connie wiped her wet face with her apron, then said, 'It's Irena. She's in the hospital of the Little Sisters of Mercy.'

'What's happened?' Duncan's heart was hammering in his chest as if it might choke him. 'For God's sake, tell me.'

'Why couldn't you let things be, Duncan MacRaith?' Ona said.

'The disgrace you've brought on us!'

'For heaven's sake! What have I done?'

'It's not Duncan's fault,' Connie muttered, her voice thickened by tears.

'Petras had arranged a good match for her – ' Ona began. Duncan strode forward and gripped her by the shoulders. 'Tell me – what's happened to Irena.'

Fear leapt into Ona's eyes. He loosened his grip slightly but did not let go. 'Petras wouldn't have her in our house – not after what happened. He meant her to go to you, or to friends – but she just ran out into the night and wandered about the streets—'

'You turned her out? On her own? Late in the night?' He couldn't believe it!

'Petras was so angry, he didn't think. Oh, Duncan – she was attacked—'

He tightened his grip on her shoulders. 'How – attacked?'

She avoided his eyes. Without another word, he understood. Rape. The word exploded into his mind.

'My God! Oh, no! No!' He strode across the room and back, beating his fist on his head, needing physical pain to stop the pounding of his brain. He stamped back to Ona and stared down at her, his face contorted, his voice rasping harshly from his throat: 'Who did it?'

'She says it was—' she paused and lowered her voice to the merest whisper – 'Lord Eveson.'

'Eveson?' he repeated, stupefied.

Ona shrugged. 'They say he haunts Main Street late at night, knows the whores who hang around there—'

'Irena's not one of them!' he exploded.

'Of course not – but you know what these aristocrats are like, they think they own the rest of us body and soul.' Ona spat contemptuously.

Duncan turned on her furiously. 'How could you have turned her out with nowhere to go?'

'You shouldn't have upset Petras,' Ona snapped.

Duncan remembered the strange way Petras had acted that

51

morning. He had known then, and said nothing!

'I went to see her today,' Ona said. 'At the convent.'

'And?' he prompted.

'Petras is willing to have her back until the wedding, but she refuses to come home with me. There's no need for anyone to know anything about this.'

The wedding? Duncan was in no mood to talk about that. Could the wedding still go ahead – after this? He couldn't think straight.

'It's terrible – terrible!' Connie moaned. Agnes ran over to her and climbed on to her knee, a frightened little girl, scarcely understanding. Connie cuddled her close.

'The sensible thing to do is to get on with the arrangements for the wedding,' Ona said.

'But Irena wants to stay at the convent?' said Connie.

'It's because she's upset. You'll have to see her, Duncan, and persuade her.'

'I don't know. Perhaps – she really wants to stay there – ' Duncan had heard of girls who decided to become nuns after being raped. This terrible event might have changed her. He had no wish to take a reluctant wife. He was not sure he could feel the same desire for her.

Ona's eyes hardened. 'Duncan MacRaith, you agreed to marry my sister, and marry her you will! This would never have happened if you hadn't come along with your fancy offers. I knew no good would come of interfering with the old ways. Quarrelling and fighting in public and having to go to court – and now this! The disgrace of it all!'

'The least said about it, the better,' Connie said.

'You said she'd changed her mind – about marrying me?'

'She can't do that.' Ona was definite. 'Irena made her promise in public. If this wedding doesn't go ahead, and quickly – the tongues really will be wagging.'

'You should go and see her, Duncan,' Connie said, gently. 'Ona is right, you know, you've got to think about what people will say.'

'To hell with what people will say,' he shouted.

Ona jumped to her feet. 'I must get back home. I've given you my opinion. Just see that you do the honourable thing, Duncan MacRaith.' She hurried out of the house.

'I need to get cleaned up before I can do anything,' Duncan growled.

Connie rushed to fetch in the bine. He washed thoroughly, then went into the bedroom and dressed quickly. His mind was in turmoil as he tightened a broad leather belt round his lean waist.

'Your dinner's ready, Duncan,' Connie called.

'I don't want any.' The hunger that had gnawed his stomach had gone, leaving a desolate emptiness. He made for the outer door without looking at her.

'Where are you going?' Connie's voice was high-pitched and anxious.

He strode through the door, clattered down the stairs. He didn't know himself where he was going. He just had to get away. He walked fast – thinking – thinking – perhaps Petras and Ona had been wrong. Perhaps even he himself had been wrong – and Irena too – to ignore convention. But the real blame lay on the perpetrator of the crime. Lord Eveson.

Eveson. The name throbbed sledgehammer blows into Duncan's brain, destroying rational thought. The despised son of the hated pit owner, the Earl of Milton. Blood-suckers who took immense profits from the pits, and squeezed the miners who did the work and lived on a pittance. They cared nothing for the safety of their workers underground. They might throw a few shillings when husbands or sons were killed, but they resisted every attempt to improve conditions. Duncan's fury boiled as his mind turned over the catalogue of grievances that every miner in Scotland had about the pit-bosses.

And now this! This unspeakable horror! Why should Lord Eveson be allowed to rape a sweet young woman and go unpunished? Duncan strode out in his heavy boots along the grimy pavements of Ringbrae, agonizing for Irena – drowning in pity and sorrow, anger and despair.

Revenge – that was what he wanted. That urge took precedence over every other emotion – it blanketed any other thought. It pinpointed the direction in which he walked – towards the big house. He was consumed with the need for physical action, driven to do something, anything, no matter what as long as it hurt Lord Eveson.

Chapter 6

DUNCAN moved fast, sometimes breaking into a run, scarcely knowing what he intended to do. Gripped by a sense of outrage, his emotions led him surely to the huge wrought iron gates of the big house. They were firmly locked. A light shone in the tiny window of one of the pair of gatehouse cottages. He walked alongside the high wall; broken glass was cemented on its top.

If Eveson believed he was safe behind that, he was much mistaken! He found a tree with a branch that overhung the wall, took a running leap up and caught hold. Hand over hand he edged himself along until he was able to swing himself up. The barbarity of that glass-topped wall added to his fury. He kicked, shattering the vicious points, then leapt lightly down on to the soft grass beneath. He crossed a stretch of parkland, grazed short by sheep. He vaulted the iron railings that separated the meadowland from the shrubbery and lawns. A gravelled drive circled a rose garden in front of the mansion. Duncan marched up the majestic flight of steps that led to the front door, grasped the bell pull and jangled it hard and persistently.

The door was opened by a butler, who was formally attired, and stared at him with disdain and a *frisson* of apprehension. His glance darted anxiously towards the blackness of the night, as if he feared more angry young men might lurk there.

'I want to see Lord Eveson,' Duncan said.

'His Lordship departed for London some hours ago,' the butler replied. His voice was haughty, his over-refined English accent barely comprehensible.

Duncan stepped forward and the butler moved back. He would have shut the door, but Duncan thrust his strong leather boot between it and the jamb. 'Take me to Lord Eveson.' he repeated.

'His Lordship's away.'

'I'll wait.'

'He may be absent for several weeks,' said the butler. He waved his hand in a vaguely southern direction. 'Lord Eveson left for London this morning.'

London. That was hundreds of miles away! Frustrated, Duncan shifted his stance. The butler slammed shut the door and shot home the bolts. The sound fanned the flame of fury in Duncan. He raised his fists to batter on the door, but almost immediately realised the uselessness of such a protest. He was, however, not yet ready to admit defeat. He descended the steps, moved across the raked gravel of the drive and into the shadow of a giant fir tree.

Most of the house was in darkness. He saw the flicker of a lamp in the ground floor rooms, the butler was making his round, checking that all were secure – no chance of making an entry through the lower windows or doors. The first floor had more possibilities.

Creepers festooned the walls. He judged them capable of taking a man's weight. Had the butler told him the truth, or was it a ploy to persuade him to leave quietly? Had Lord Eveson really gone to London? Who was in those first floor rooms where the lamplight glowed through heavy lace curtains? The creeper had grown vigorously, its branches trained to fan out at regular intervals. It would be as easy as climbing a ladder to get up that. The sash window immediately above was open a couple of inches at the top and obviously unfastened. He tested the strength of the creeper. It held. Quietly and carefully he hauled himself up. The curtains had not been closely drawn. He reached the level of the window-sill and peered inside. The soft light of oil lamps and the flickering glow of a coal fire revealed a bedroom, a brass half-tester bed gleamed like gold, its hangings of peach satin had a

sheen of wondrous softness. His gaze darted around in amazement, yet he remained alert, ready to drop back to the ground if
there was danger. He could see no one in the room.

He drew himself up a little higher. There was no movement
within. He put one hand under the centre bar of the sash and
pushed it up. It went easily. He froze, and listened with bated
breath. There was no sound. Assured the room was unoccupied,
Duncan swung one leg over the sill and with natural agility
ducked through the open window.

He stood for a moment, debating whether to shut the window,
to conceal the fact that he was there or leave it open as a means
of quick exit. Then a door opened and a woman entered. She was
tall, her hair had been loosened and rippled over her shoulders in
a brilliant red-gold cascade, reaching to her waist. She wore a
loose-flowing, lace-edged garment of shot silk, its colour changing from blue through mauve to pink as she moved.

He guessed she was Lady Eveson. She had moved a couple of
steps into the room before she saw him and halted, obviously startled. He saw her recoil. Her eyes met his, and fear leapt into
them. They stared at each other in silence. Then she spoke and
her voice was cool, clear and precise.

'What are you doing here?' she demanded.

'I wish to see Lord Eveson,' he said.

She walked a few steps forward, nearer to the fireplace, beside
which hung a long narrow drapery. Was there significance in that?

'Why do you wish to see my husband?' she asked.

'What I have to say concerns only him.'

Lady Anastasia was in her late twenties, a woman in the full
flower of her beauty. Her scoop-necked, lace trimmed negligee
had slipped carelessly off one shoulder, revealing a voluptuous
roundness which she made no attempt to cover. She was prepared
for bed and obviously had nothing beneath the flimsy garment.
The delicate fragrance of her perfume increased the heady effect
she had upon him.

He drew himself up to his full height. He was well-built and
proud of his physique. He drew in a deep breath and his chest

expanded beneath his high-necked shirt. He tucked his thumbs into the front of his wide leather belt with a swaggering air and stood rock-solid, his feet slightly apart. He held his own, with an extraordinary belief, under the circumstances, and made out that he was in control of the situation.

'I have a score to settle with your husband.'

'Then why come to my room?'

'Your man would not let me in.'

'I'm not surprised. Eveson's gone to London.'

'So he said.'

'Didn't you believe him?'

'No.'

She gave a dismissive shrug.

'When will he be back?'

'When he feels like returning. Anyway you wouldn't find him here. This is my room.'

It was a very feminine room, peach colour predominating in curtains and the floral design of the thick-piled carpet. Heaped coals glowed red in the fireplace. She moved towards it and sat down on a couch. Gracefully, unhurried, she leaned back with one arm stretched along the back. He realized she was no longer afraid of him.

'Close the window,' she commanded.

'I prefer to leave it open, until I am ready to leave.'

'You'll leave when – and if – I say. Make any trouble and I shall summon the servants. I have only to pull the bell.'

So. That was why she had moved so close to the elaborately embroidered hanging. It remained easily within her reach.

'I'd be away before they left the servant's quarters,' he told her.

Anastasia was a powerful woman, her strength of character showed in her face, her calm control, her assurance, as she waited. 'The draught's making the room cold,' she said.

He had no wish to leave. The reckless mood, the desire for revenge, the bravado that had driven him to enter the house had not changed. He was careless of his safety, for what had he to lose? He moved to the window, it slipped down silently.

His eyes shot back to Anastasia. A mocking smile played upon her beautiful face. She seemed amused by the situation and that irritated him. He walked to the door, turned the key in the lock and felt more in control. A tingle of excitement swept over him.

'Come.' With a gracious sweep of her hand, as if he was an invited guest, Anastasia indicated the other end of the couch on which she was sitting.

Duncan watched her closely. She was no more scared of him than he was of her. A smile twitched the corners of her shapely mouth. It suggested she found his appearance pleasing.

'Fetch that bottle of vodka from the side table and bring it here.'

Her tone was friendly, but he moved sideways, keeping watch on her. There were other bottles and he removed them from the silver tray, leaving only the vodka. He placed two delicately cut glasses beside it, carried the tray to a small table close to where she sat and poured a good measure for each of them.

She raised her glass to him. 'Why don't you sit down.'

He lowered his strong sinewy body to the opposite end of the couch.

'What is your name?'

He replied cautiously. 'Duncan.'

'Duncan what?'

'Just Duncan.' It could be unwise to reveal his full name.

He raised his glass to her. It was very good vodka, appreciatively he allowed it to trickle down his throat.

'Talk to me, Duncan.'

'I didn't come here to talk.'

'I am in need of conversation, of entertainment. I was so bored when you arrived, I could have screamed.'

'If you had some work in your hands, you wouldn't have time to be bored,' he told her.

'What sort of work? Do you suggest I should scrub floors?'

She was making fun of him. He refused to answer.

She waited a minute, then said again, 'Talk to me, Duncan. Tell me about yourself. What do you do?'

'I work. I have to earn money. You wouldn't understand that.' He made no attempt to hide the bitterness in his tone.

She sighed. 'Money doesn't necessarily bring happiness.'

He thought of the poor little room where he had expected to make a home for himself and Irena. 'It must be wonderful to live in a house like this.'

'A house can be nothing but an empty shell. I hate this bleak and horrible country.'

'Where do you come from?'

She tossed her head. 'From Lithuania – and I long to be back there. I think of it every day, the forests, the wide plains, the hunting, the glorious summer days, sleigh rides over the snow in winter. Here it just rains at every season – it's so dismally boring, so lonely!'

'Why didn't you go to London with your husband?' he asked.

'He didn't even tell me he was going until he was about to leave for the train.' She turned dark, searching eyes on him. 'Why did he leave in such a hurry, Duncan?'

Her question startled him. He did not answer. What had happened to Irena was not this woman's fault.

'You know why, don't you?' she persisted. 'Isn't there some connection that brought you here?' Her eyes seemed to bore into him.

If he told her, she would reach for the bell and call the servants. If they caught him he would be handed over to the police.

'You must ask him.'

'But you know, don't you?'

'Yes. I know.'

'You won't tell me?'

He shook his head.

'As you wish. I'm not really interested in what he does. Pour me another drink.'

He refilled their glasses. She drank with uninhibited enjoyment, moist lips parted, head tilted back, revealing the length of her slender neck. The alcohol brought a glow to her face.

'Tell me about yourself. Have you always lived in this godforsaken place?'

'No, I come from the outer isles, far to the north of Ringbrae, where the weather is wilder. I do not know my real parents. My grandmother brought me up. I don't know how she managed it, though my mother sent money when she could. I had a little schooling, went to sea with the fishermen when I was twelve. My grandmother had a husband. Life was dominated by him.'

'You did not like him?'

'I hated him,' Duncan said cheerfully. 'He had a vile temper.' He paused dramatically. 'And a wooden leg – he lost the other in the South African war. But I had to admire him. He was stronger than any other man I've known. Once, for a bet, he harnessed himself to a wagon and pulled it along like a horse for a mile or more. He'd gamble on anything.'

Duncan enjoyed telling a good tale. His tongue was loosened by the vodka. He launched into another story, flattered by Anastasia's rapt attention. She encouraged him and he recounted other almost unbelievable exploits of his step-grandfather. He used light touches of hyperbole, exaggerating the humour, delighted to make this beautiful woman laugh, using colourful and evocative phrases.

Growing up in poverty, where there was no other entertain-ment, the tradition of story-telling had been as much a part of his life as eating and drinking. He had the gift of remembering with pictorial clarity, and had developed the skill of colourful speech. She had a sharp wit and added comments that sparked him to counter with a quick riposte. Sometimes she caught the point before he got to it. Extrovert by nature he found it a challenge to converse with and amuse her and unconsciously, a delicate rapport developed between them.

He poured more vodka. Their hands touched as she took the glass from him. When he sat down the distance between them had somehow lessened. His muscular thigh was in contact with the long graceful line of hers, her silken gown was insubstantial, her perfume filled his senses. She told him of the series of governesses she had suffered as a child. She mimicked their attempts to make her conform, to force her to concentrate on her lessons and how she had played mischievous tricks, and sometimes ran away to ride her pony or to play out in the woods on her own all day.

A gentle smile played around her face, softening her features. Her beauty, liveliness and the magic of her femininity had him entranced. His anger subsided, but his sexuality was more and more aroused. Anastasia filled his senses. He could not tear his eyes away from her. The vodka bottle was almost empty. An irrepressible force was forging an intimacy between them, linking them in its primeval mystery.

Inhibition was loosened by alcohol, but it was more than that. She glowed with the full physical warmth of womanhood. It was unbearable to sit beside her and not touch her. Her hand was lying loosely in her lap and impulsively he reached out and covered it with his. She made no attempt to remove it. They stared at each other, questioningly, and he read a desire in hers that matched the hot unholy feelings that he was finding it more and more difficult to control.

'You are a very handsome man, Duncan,' she said.

He tried to steady his racing blood, reminded himself that he had come to this house, seeking revenge against Lord Eveson, but that now seemed remote. This was reality. The alluring woman held him in the palm of her pale hand, entranced. He wanted to tell her how beautiful she was, but his lips were dry, a lump choked in his throat and he said nothing. He just gazed and gazed.

'I thought at first that you had come here to kill me,' she said.

'No – oh no!' The thought shocked him.

'But you had some retribution in mind, did you not? Perhaps my husband has wronged both of us.'

Her voice was smoothly beguiling, her tone inflamed his senses beyond his strength of resistance. She spoke as if she knew what he was thinking – understood the retribution that had been in his mind when he climbed so boldly through the window of her boudoir. Unable to contain himself a moment longer he leapt to his feet, reached down, caught hold of her hands and drew her up. His arms fastened around her, clasped her glorious body tightly against his own, felt the quickening of his blood, the throbbing of his loins, the swelling of his penis as he bent his head and with a moan covered her lips with his own.

His joy was intensified as she reached up, curled her arms around his shoulders, ran her hands through the thickness of his hair, deepening the kiss. Then she pulled his head down to where the négligé had slipped from her shoulder, encouraging him to explore the smoothness of her skin. She shrugged the garment looser, revealing the glory of her breasts, the delicious dusky dark nipples hardening as his tongue caressed first one then the other.

She gave a moan of pleasure, echoing sensations that throbbed all over his body. Years of frustration increased the wonder of this glorious happening. Her hands began to unfasten his belt, ran sensually beneath his tunic and over his muscular torso. Their delicate touch made his flesh quiver as her questing fingers traced ever increasing circles over his chest, then boldly moved down through the hair of his flat stomach. Tenderly she caressed his swollen penis, and as she did so, drew her face back from his, shamelessly gazing into his eyes. With a smile that was also an invitation, she stepped back.

She threw aside her negligee and stood naked before him. Like a starving man Duncan feasted his eyes on her, his excited gaze raking over her firm breasts, dark nipples, the curve of her neatly buttoned belly, the triangle of hair, a darker red-gold than on her head. He had never before seen a woman unclothed, and was spellbound. The reality of her palely gleaming, luscious flesh was more beautiful than anything he had conjured up even in his wildest excess of imagination. Her expression told him she delighted in the passion she had aroused in his eager body.

He tore off his clothes, until he too stood naked. Excitement and joy suffused her face at the power of his erection. She held her arms open.

'Take me,' she breathed.

He swept her up, held her close, easily carried her to the big, soft bed, turned down ready to receive them. Every inch of his body thrilled to contact with hers. His mouth covered hers, kissed her and devoured her. She was experienced – and where his eagerness might have made him precipitate, her guiding hands led him to touch wondrous secret places. Her thighs parted to receive him.

Although he had never made love before he seemed to find an instinctive sensitivity to the sensuousness of her needs, keeping the intensity of his own strong sexual appetite in check, until his climax could be held back not a moment longer. A cry like a rutting stag ripped from deep within him, burst out of his open mouth. It was loud enough to waken the whole household – had the servants' quarters not been two storeys higher and in a different wing of the great house.

Anastasia stirred sleepily when Duncan rolled gently away from her and slipped out of her bed. She knew he was dressing, and watched him with half-closed eyes, unwilling to waken fully to the tedious reality of her everyday life – not yet, not in the 'wee small hours'. He stood for a moment looking down on her, and when her eyes met his, she smiled. His face was serious. Vaguely she wondered what he was thinking, but was not really concerned. It was comfortable in the bed where they had made love, pleasant to lie relaxed and contemplative and feel his eyes on her.

When she had first seen him last night, standing in front of the open window in her bedroom, her immediate impulse had been to summon the servants. She had stepped towards the bell-rope – yet hesitated to pull it. She had been so intolerably bored. She had dined alone in the vast dining-room and retired early.

Effie, her maid, had helped her to disrobe, turned down the bed and been dismissed. Anastasia had picked up the latest copy of *The Tatler*, glanced at the 'society' column then thrown it aside. Toying with the idea of writing a letter, she wandered into her sitting room, sat at her bureau for twenty minutes without bothering to pick up her pen. Restlessly she had returned to her bedroom and there was Duncan. Handsome, wholesome and – interesting! Immediately her mind had connected him with Conroy's hasty departure. That had been intriguing – but so too was the man who stood before her.

She felt no guilt over taking him to her bed. She knew Conroy had not been faithful to her, yet she had never before taken a lover. Wickedness was wonderful, she decided. Duncan had been a gift from the gods. The height of sexual excitement to which he had aroused her was unbelievably exhilarating after so many years of disappointment.

'Revenge is sweet,' she murmured.

Duncan looked puzzled. She didn't trouble to explain. She was lost in a world of wonder. How had this stranger, a lowly working man, a miner – even though he was soft-spoken, humorous, with keen intelligent eyes – how had he awakened her body to such ecstatically, wondrous sensations? Conroy, rich, well-bred, expensively educated, had never troubled to court her. From the start of their loveless marriage, arranged by their respective fathers, he had expected her to lie compliantly between the sheets whilst he took his pleasure. On their wedding night the experience had been painful and unpleasant, in the ensuing years sex had dropped into a bearable routine. A pointless exercise, since she did not become pregnant. Her discontent had increased as the childless years passed by. He blamed her and thrust himself upon her, frequently demanding, never giving.

'I have to go,' Duncan said.

Fully dressed, he was buckling on his wide leather belt, backing away from the bed obviously reluctant to take his eyes from her. With a dramatic gesture she reached towards him, one delicate hand inviting him to clasp it. She saw desire flare in his eyes again.

'Come back this evening,' she said.

He stood very still, stretched his powerful body up to its full height, holding his head high. 'Will you instruct your man to let me in?'

She laughed. The suggestion was ridiculous.

'Of course not.' She smiled beguilingly. 'I shall leave the window unfastened, as it was last night.'

'I shall not enter that way again, like a thief.' He spoke proudly.

'Don't say that, Duncan. It pleases me to have you climb up to my bedchamber.' Her tone was equally proud. 'You will come again.'

'No.' Abruptly he swung around, in two strides he was at the window, slid up the lower half and climbed out into the darkness of the night. He left without another word, as silently, as abruptly, as he had entered.

Despite his words she was sure that he would return. She lay back in the big, crumpled bed and drifted into a contented sleep.

In the morning she was still glowing, her body tingling, her head in the clouds. She stretched and felt pleasure in the cat-like movement. The doorknob rattled. There was a pause, then gentle knuckles knocked timidly. Anastasia remembered that Duncan had turned the key.

'Your Ladyship? Are you all right? The door's locked.' It was Effie, her maid.

Anastasia floated to the door and threw it open. 'Good morning, Effie.' She smiled and stretched again.

Effie murmured 'Good morning, your Ladyship,' and gave a brief bob of her head in lieu of a curtsy, restricted by the weight of the tray she was carrying. Experience had shown that her mistress's moods were unpredictable.

The routine of Anastasia's day began just like any other.

Two days later a letter arrived from Conroy, very brief, more of a note in fact. He made no apology for his hasty departure. '*My dear Anastasia – Mrs Asquith is arranging a special dinner party next month to which we have been invited, and she has personally expressed her wish that she should have the pleasure of renewing your acquaintance. I know you have formed quite a friendship with the lady. I have accepted the invitation on behalf of us both. No doubt you will wish to have a new gown made to grace the occasion, therefore I shall expect you to join me in London very shortly.*'

Such an invitation would normally have lifted her into a whirl of excited activity, and of course, she had to go. She could have no possible excuse for not attending Mrs Asquith's grand dinner at her husband's side and, of course, that meant having a fashionable new gown made in London. She would have to leave soon, to allow the dressmaker time to produce an exquisite model. The woman always made difficulties, but no one else had her skill in design. She would just have to keep the seamstresses whirring away at their treadle machines an hour longer into the night – they were lucky they no longer had to sew every stitch by hand, as their mothers had done.

Yet, for the first time since her arrival in Scotland, Anastasia found herself reluctant to leave. London seemed less alluring than previously. Each night she left the sash-window unfastened and lay awake late – and alone.

Although Conroy was absent, his father, the Earl was at home and it was customary for them to dine together, he at the head of the long and highly polished table and she on his right.

'When will you be joining Conroy in London?' the earl asked.

'Soon. We are invited to dine at Mrs Asquith's next month.'

'Humph.' He was not impressed. 'Socializing – that's all you young people think about. Having a good time.' He paused. 'You know what I want, don't you?'

She nodded. He had mentioned the subject almost from the day she arrived, and harped upon it with increasing frequency.

'An heir,' he snapped. 'That's what's needed here. Children about the place to liven it up.'

The discussion angered her. She agreed with him. A child would give purpose to her life but after more than seven years of marriage she had never become pregnant. When Conroy was at home he was in her bed two or three times a week. He, too, grumbled because she did not produce a child – his father would be more generous with his allowance if there was a family.

'I'd die happy if I had a grandson to take over after Conroy,' the earl persisted. 'It was a great disappointment to me that my wife had only one child – I hoped for better things from you and Conroy.'

'It's not for want of trying,' she said, tartly. She had almost given up hope, but there was no point in admitting that to her father-in-law. She added, more gently, 'I've heard of women who've been married for ten years or more before they conceived.'

'It certainly won't happen whilst you're up here, and that son of mine takes himself off to London. Go down and join him, Anastasia.'

'I will. Next week.'

To her relief he allowed the subject to drop. As they parted for the night he said, 'Tomorrow, I'm going to a visit to an old friend in Glasgow. I'd be pleased to have your company.

'Of course, papa.'

Chapter 7

THE priest who found Irena on Sunday morning carried her to the convent. The nuns prepared a hot bath and made up a narrow iron-framed bed in their infirmary. They gave her a cotton night-gown and closed the prettily flowered curtains so she had a cubicle of privacy. A doctor, elderly and kind, examined her, patted her hand gave her two tablets and departed. Two nuns brought in a hot dinner but she couldn't eat it.

Sister Superior came and said a prayer in Latin and asked her some questions. Irena pretended she didn't understand. She did not want to talk about it. She wanted to die, to be buried and forgotten, never again to see anyone she knew.

Sister Superior sent a message to the Lithuanian priest, and on Sunday evening he called at the convent. He insisted Ona must be told, and Irena knew she could no longer hide from reality. They brought back her clothes, washed and ironed. Somehow life would go on.

Ona came to see her, tears streaming down her cheeks, moaning, condemning everyone she could think of – except for herself and Petras.

'Did you recognize the man?' she asked.

'It was Lord Eveson.'

Ona's mouth dropped open. 'Are you sure?'

'I saw his carriage with the crest on the door.'

'Have you told anyone else?'

'No. I don't wish to talk about it. I shall ask the sisters if I can stay at the convent.'

'But you're going to be married.'

'Not now.'

'Why not? No one need know – you needn't tell Duncan -'

Irena was shocked. 'I couldn't do that – especially to him.'

'Come home with me and we'll talk about it.'

'Petras turned me out.'

'He's calmed down now. You know what he's like when the drink's on him, Irena. I promise you, he won't say a word about – anything – come home.' Ona wept and pleaded.

'No.' Irena was adamant. She would never marry now. Work. That was what she needed, to act as a panacea. She sought out one of the nuns and managed to make her understand. The sisters were reluctant but eventually they brought torn sheets that had to be turned sides to middle. Irena stitched all that day and continued the following morning but her mind remained haunted by that terrible night. After lunch, whilst the nuns were at their prayers, she put the sheets aside and wandered outside.

The nunnery garden was surrounded by a high wall. Its lawns were shaded by mature trees and beyond was a shrubbery with a statue of the virgin and child. A path led to a vegetable garden. Someone had started digging, turning over a bed. That was the sort of work she needed, physically hard, out in the fresh air. A spade had been left, thrust into the earth, Irena seized it and set to. She could almost imagine she was at home on the farm again.

'Irena.'

The gentle voice of Sister Clare floated across to her. She carried on digging.

'You must go to Sister Superior's room at once.'

Irena pretended she didn't understand but Sister Clare wrested the spade from her hand. Reluctantly she followed the elderly nun to the washroom to clean and tidy herself and then to Sister Superior's room.

'You have a visitor. Mr MacRaith.'

Duncan. Part of her wanted to see him but there could be no marriage now. He would not want her, and she would not expect it.

Duncan was waiting in the parlour, a small room, sparsely furnished, smelling of Mansion Polish. A framed photograph of the Pope hung on one wall and a Madonna, painted in heavenly blues and gold, stood on a corner bracket; a candle in a red glass glowed at her feet. Sister Superior was seated on one of the upright chairs, acting as chaperone.

Duncan had his back to the window, his face was in shadow. 'Irena.' He said. 'I am very sorry – about – what happened – ' He stumbled over the words.

'It is all right,' she said tonelessly. 'Please do not concern yourself about me.'

'But I am – I came to say we will be married – just as we planned—'

'I shall not marry you, Duncan,' she said gently.

'I don't care what has happened—'

'But I do!' Her interruption was so fierce that he flinched.

'I didn't mean it like that. I should have said it doesn't alter—'

'It alters everything for me.' She couldn't shrug off the awfulness, the ugly feeling of being soiled. 'I shall stay here, if the sisters will have me.'

'You can't want to become nun!' he exploded.

'I never want to see any man, ever again. I hate this country, hate Scotland, hate Ringbrae. I wish I'd never come here.'

Tears glistened in his eyes. 'I'll take you back to Lithuania one day, Irena. I'll work and save.'

'No.'

She moved towards the door and he stepped quickly forward to intercept her, his hand held out to her.

'Don't touch me.'

'You offered to be my wife,' he said. His words jolted her. 'Didn't I fight for you? Go to court for you?'

She felt a tinge of shame. She had been thinking only of herself.

'I told the judge I'm to be married. It was a promise – on oath.'

'You can find someone else.'

'No. We promised each other. It's you I want, Irena.'

She began to waver. 'I – I don't know—'

'I've seen the priest. I've found a little house. We'll have the wedding party at Connie's house. Nobody need know.'

'Suppose I have a baby?' She saw him swallow a lump in his throat. 'You see? You doubt if you would be able to accept such a child.'

'I would accept it.'

'You're a kind man, Duncan.'

'I shall try to be kind always, but I'm no angel. I have more faults than you know of.' He paused. He looked very serious, very different from the laughing, carefree young man who had swept her away into the polka, and fought for her. 'I wish to marry you, Irena.'

'I couldn't wear the *ruta* at my wedding.'

'Wear it, Irena. I'll deal with anyone who dares say you should-n't!'

Despite everything it made her smile. He took that as assent.

'You will marry me, Irena. It will go ahead as arranged.'

The sky was overcast, as grey and dull as the streets of Ringbrae when Irena walked to the church on her wedding day. She wore the hand-embroidered blouse and the new skirt she had brought from home for her wedding to Tamosinskas. Ona had pinned a sprig of grey-green *ruta* in her veil. She strode along her head held high; in spite of everything she had a feeling of elation. They waited briefly in the cold, lofty porch of the church. Petras crooked his arm for Irena's hand and marched forward without giving her a glance. The organist played the wedding march. She looked straight ahead avoiding the eyes she knew were watching her.

Duncan was waiting. He had borrowed a dark suit. It was too small and looked uncomfortable. She felt detached, as if she was watching someone else's wedding. She heard a voice making vows, but scarcely realized it was her own.

Then it was over. Rain bucketed down. Duncan would have walked straight out into it but someone clicked open an umbrella and he held it over her. She tucked her hand into the crook of his arm and followed by the whole congregation they walked towards the house where Duncan had been lodging.

It was Saturday afternoon, the pavements thronged with shoppers, some stared at the wedding party. Delivery boys whistled at the girls. Trams rattled along the centre of the cobbled street, horse-drawn carts moved at walking pace. The gutter was awash. Her boots let in water and she clung to Duncan's arm, sheltering under the umbrella.

A carriage came up alongside and terror struck her as she recognized the heraldic device on its door. The coachman reined in the horses, drawing it up beside the wedding party. The window was lowered and she recognized Lady Anastasia but not the man beside her.

'It's the earl!'

Men doffed their caps and bowed, women bobbed curtsies and ordered their children to do the same. Irena would also have curtsied, as became a humble peasant, but Duncan stood straight and still and held her arm so tightly that she could not. An ostrich feather in Lady Anastasia's hat trembled, otherwise she sat motionless, very upright, with her hands folded in her lap. Her eyes were fixed upon Duncan and he stared boldly back. It was as if they knew each other! Irena dismissed the foolish thought. Duncan always acted as if he owned the world.

'Pennies for the wedding,' shouted one of the boys.

The usual bunch of ragged children jumped and clamoured around the carriage. It was customary to throw money to children at weddings. The earl threw out handfuls of coins, they scattered on the road, the pavement, plopped into the overflowing gutter, rolled among the feet of the wedding party. Children whooped after them.

Anastasia turned her head and her eyes met Irena's, as they had done all those years before. This time Irena was the bride but in no other way had their circumstances changed. Anastasia regarded her with condescending disdain, an expression that stirred a fury of resentment in Irena. What had that woman to be proud of, married to the callous brute who had raped her! Did she know? Would she care if she did? Irena's fingers tightened on

Duncan's arm. The earl raised the window and the carriage rolled away. Duncan covered her hand with his and that was comforting. The wedding party walked on to Connie's house.

Connie had a reputation for organizing parties. The table, covered with an embroidered linen cloth, held boiled hams, salami, meat loaf, pickled herrings and yellow chanterelle mushrooms along with horse-radish, gherkins, bread (brown and white), sauerkraut, beetroot and a big bowl of cucumbers in sour cream dressing. There were bottles of whisky and wines in the centre of the table, bedecked with red ribbons, together with a barrel of beer ready-tapped in the corner.

Amid a babble of talk, glasses were raised, clinked together, the food and drink began to disappear down many receptive throats. Some men brought extra bottles and when the beer ran out Duncan's best man had a whip round and fetched another barrel in a wheelbarrow.

Duncan's great laugh rang out again and again and it pleased Irena to see him so happy. She still felt remote from it all, content to fade into the background. The room was crowded, yet more and more pushed their way in. They began to sing, the music of a fiddle filled the room with the haunting songs of their Lithuanian home, late into the night.

'The rain's stopped,' someone called out. 'Let's see the young couple home.'

'I'm afraid it's not much of a place,' Duncan muttered to Irena. 'I haven't had time to get things together.'

'We'll manage,' she said.

Some people went to their own homes, the rest of the revellers surged out into the street. They sang as they went, in harmony, surprisingly sweetly considering the drink they had consumed. Duncan walked beside Irena. They did not hold hands, but once or twice he brushed against her and the sensation that evoked was pleasant. The streets shone wetly where gas lamps made pools of yellow light. It was over a mile to Mick's Buildings. They traversed the graffiti scrawled passage, and made their way up the outside stair.

Duncan and Irena were pushed through the doorway. An oil lamp had been lit and placed on the table, two chairs, newly painted, stood on either side of it, some foodstuffs were set out. It was better than she had expected. Duncan was looking around in bewilderment.

'I don't understand,' he said.

'We all found something for you. Couldn't let you start with nothing.'

A rag-rug covered the old linoleum. Curtains were drawn over the window, another pair, crimson chenille and fringed, were hooked back by one of the wall-beds. The bed was covered by a crocheted bedspread in white cotton with a design of reindeer and flowers worked in scarlet. Duncan swung around, face beaming, arms held wide. She remembered how Antanas Lazaraitis had offered many worldly goods and she had rejected him in favour of Duncan. Not for one moment did she regret that decision.

'Thank you – thank you so much,' Duncan exclaimed, over and over again. 'Fill your glasses, drink up.'

More than an hour passed before the guests started to leave, promising to return and carry on the party the following day. Then they were alone. Irena began to clear the table, picking up the glasses and bottles. Duncan took them from her. He placed gentle hands on her waist and turned her to face him. She trembled beneath his touch and at the desire she read in his eyes.

'Irena.' His voice was soft.

She bowed her head, unable to meet that look.

He put his arms around her, and his lips found hers. They had been married twelve hours and it was the first time he had kissed her. The sensation surprised her with its sweetness.

'Well, little wife,' he said.

She nodded. He had been so kind. It was time to become fully his wife. He lifted the veil with the ruta from her head and placed it on the table. She tried to relax as his arms closed around her. The urge she read in his eyes was powerful, but he wasn't hurrying her. Gently but persistently he kissed her. She felt his arousal as he pressed her body against his, and her own sexuality – her primitive feminine instincts responded. She had known, from the first moment she saw him, there was something special about this man.

'Husband,' she murmured.

He swung her up off her feet and carried her easily across to the bed in the wall. He took off her skirt and the exquisitely embroidered blouse. Submissively she lay back and he made love to her with tenderness and care. He had not put out the lamp and by looking fixedly at Duncan's face she managed – almost – to blot out the image of Lord Eveson. Afterwards she lay awake for some time, listening to Duncan's contented breathing and was happier than she had expected. She had begun to fall deeply in love with her husband.

Chapter 8

'KEEP awa' from the pit, Duncan.' The warning was hissed out of the darkness of five-thirty on a wet morning in February. Rain bucketed out of a leaden sky. It penetrated the old sack he had flung around his shoulders. He had been walking with his head bent, struggling against the blast. At the sound of the voice he stopped and looked around. The road behind him was ominously quiet. Where was the usual tramp, tramp, tramp of heavy boots? Where were the voices, the coughing and spitting?

The miners were on strike.

A swirl of brittle gaiety enveloped London society after King George V was crowned in the summer of 1911. The new reign brought many changes, but the brilliance of life for the rich and privileged continued as uninhibited as before. Anastasia danced, dined, rode in Hyde Park, dressed magnificently for the opera, visited and gave parties.

She brushed aside the first bout of morning sickness and yet it was unusual. She prided herself on having the constitution of a horse – or more accurately and bitterly – of a barren mare. She was never ill. Surely – it couldn't be?

Doubt and wonder turned to certainty. She had no doubt who had fathered the baby she cherished in her womb, yet felt not a shadow of guilt over its conception. It was purely for her own pleasure that she delayed announcing her condition to her husband, even though she knew both Conroy and the earl would be overjoyed – as long as they never learned the truth.

*

'I see he's put you in the family way, then.'

Irena straightened herself. She winced as she recognized the cackling voice which came from the open door of the wash-house. How could that old busybody know? Mrs Miller, a fat old witch of a woman had spoken with absolute certainty, confirming Irena's fears.

She had just stepped back from the tub, leaving the heavy wooden dolly bobbing in the sudsy water. The smell of boiling linen caught at her throat. She lifted her head trying not to let the old woman know how she had startled her.

'Don't tell me you didn't know,' Mrs Miller's voice held a note of triumph. 'Written all over you, it is!'

'Of course I know,' Irena snapped. 'And I'm pleased.'

'Huh! You won't be when you're expecting your sixth. How many months have you missed?'

'That, Mrs Miller, is my business.'

The old woman sniffed. Irena had never liked her. Dewlaps of fat hung from her sallow cheeks, and her sharp little eyes were so deep sunken they almost disappeared – but they missed nothing. Was it possible that she had heard about – about what had happened that dreadful night? 'I've been married for two months.' Irena snapped.

'Barely seven weeks, by my reckoning,' Mrs Miller sniffed, then shuffled away from the doorway, her voice raised to shout at her son.

The dread Irena had struggled to smother welled up again. The interfering old woman was right. She was pregnant. But she could feel no joy. If only she could have had one period since that night of terror: but she had seen nothing. She was carrying a child, and could not be sure who had fathered it.

She seized the dolly and thumped it up and down – if she induced a miscarriage, so much the better. She did not want this baby – when it might be Eveson's! She felt trapped by it. Did Duncan suspect? They had not spoken of the possibility of pregnancy since that day at the convent. Suppose it looked like Eveson – would she herself be able to love it? She thrust the bleached wooden copper stick into the boiling soapy water and lifted out a sheet, hot and heavy, the steam almost scalding her face. She dropped it into a galvanized bath of cold water. Two rinses, then it had to be fed through the wringer, into a large basket, and carried from the wash-house to the drying ground.

She had been taking in washing for two weeks now. A neighbour had told her about Mrs MacEwan, who was looking for someone to wash for her and Irena had immediately offered to take on the work. She had not told Duncan, sensing that his pride might be hurt. He had shown her only kindness and generosity, but she suspected he might hold the same view as Petras when it came to his woman working outside the house.

The drying ground was on a scrubby bit of green, part of the big square yard that held the facilities for Mick's Buildings. A block of four closets adjoined the wash-house and a tap, housed in a small timber stand.

By late morning some garments were ready to take in. Irena stood two flat irons against the black-leaded bars of the glowing fire, covered the table with a folded blanket and spread a sheet over it. She took special care over the finishing of Mr and Mrs MacEwan's assortment of shirts, blouses, underwear and bed-linen. Mr MacEwan was head-gardener to the earl at Achil House. They lived in the Lodge Cottage, beside a tall pair of wrought-iron gates, at the top of the drive which led to the big house. Irena had been worried about that, but so far she had seen no sign of any of the grand folk – and she hoped she never would – especially Lord Eveson.

It was a two mile walk, and the bundle of laundry was bulky and heavy, but Irena was strong. She was accustomed to walking and she found pleasure in escaping briefly from the mean streets of Ringbrae.

Mrs MacEwan was a kindly woman, tall, large-boned, elderly, and unable to do her own washing. She smiled in greeting. 'Come in, my dear. I've got your money ready,' she said. It was even more useful now Duncan was on strike.

Mrs MacEwan had taken quite a fancy to this young foreigner

who returned her laundry immaculately clean and neatly folded. Irena had joined a class to learn English and was becoming quite fluent. 'Will you dig up a couple of turnips for me,' Mrs MacEwan asked? 'Tak' some for yourself.'

Carrying the garden fork Irena followed Mrs MacEwan to the vegetable patch at the side of the cottage, close to the road. 'We've a fine crop this year.'

The old lady gave her a small sack to put them in, and told Irena to fill it up with cooking apples, fallen from the tree. She was about to leave when she heard a carriage approaching. Instinctively she stepped back, hiding behind the hedge. Mrs MacEwan hurried out as quickly as her stiff legs would carry her to swing open the high black-painted wrought-iron gates. Peeping through a small opening in the hedge Irena saw the single occupant was the old gentleman who had accompanied Lady Anastasia when they had stopped to throw money for the children on her wedding day. Mrs MacEwan bobbed a curtsy as the carriage passed.

'You've no need to be afraid of the old earl,' she said to Irena. 'He's a real gentleman.' She paused then added, 'Can't say the same for his son, though – and as for that foreign woman he married, I don't think she even knows ordinary folk exist. It's no' that often the old earl gaes oot. An' the two young 'uns are awa' doon to London. Shan't see them till the spring, I reckon.'

Irena doubted whether Lord Eveson would recognize her – yet she was with child, and it might be his. She fretted about that terrible night as she walked back to Ringbrae. She believed Duncan had agreed to go through with the marriage only because he was sorry for her, and had been pressurized by Ona. Who had fathered the child that was growing in her body, uninvited, unwelcome, and immovable? She would keep her condition secret for as long as she could. If Duncan did not know till later, and they did not talk about dates, then perhaps he might accept the child as his.

Anastasia hugged her secret to herself, even on the journey to Lithuania three days before Christmas to spend the festive season

with her family. She sat opposite Conroy in the private compart-
ment as the express train steamed along its thousand mile journey
from Berlin to St Petersburg, via Vilnius. The line crossed the
wide plains of East Prussia, passing comfortable farmhouses and
red-roofed villages, prosperous towns, high spired churches and
castles with fairy tale turrets. Day merged into night, the express
cut through the darkness, warm, brilliantly lit, until ten and a half
hours after its departure from Berlin, when it halted at the
German border. Passports were checked, and soon the train
moved on again, only to grind to a halt a few minutes later at
Wirballen, the frontier of the great Russian Empire.

Russian bureaucracy caused a stop of at least an hour. Porters
in fur caps, baggy trousers and high boots hurried to assist passengers to get their luggage through customs. Conroy left all that to
his valet. Anastasia took her husband's arm as they walked along
the snow-packed platform to the first-class waiting room, their
breath steaming in the frosty air. The solidly furnished room
smelt of leather and sheep-skin coats and sunflower oil. To her it
was a warm, familiar smell.

An hour later the train was ready to steam onwards and those
going to St Petersburg settled into their berths for the night.
Anastasia was thankful that for them only three hours' travelling
remained. Preoccupied by her own thoughts, she took little notice
as they crossed the flat snowbound land of *Suwalki* – land fought
over for centuries, inhabited by Lithuanians, Poles, Russians,
Germans and Jews. She glanced at Conroy. He was twiddling that
waxed moustache of which he was so proud, absorbed in a book.

She smiled to herself. She was almost three months pregnant.
Probably Effie knew, but the maid was far too well trained to
mention it. The thought that her condition might be common
knowledge in the servant's hall, long before her husband knew,
did not trouble Anastasia in the slightest. Servants were non-
people, of no importance, so long as they attended to their work
efficiently, punctually and with due deference. She was accustomed to talking freely whilst they served her, just as if they did
not exist. She had already decided to make her momentous

announcement when the family was all gathered together at Christmas.

The train chuffed on, skirting the Niemen, into the valley of the Vilayá and entered a long tunnel through the Ponári Hills to reach Vilnius. It was at this stage of the journey that Anastasia found stirrings of nostalgia for half-forgotten things. Youthful memories, emotions and happenings from those impressionable years had rubbed deep into her, more so than she would have believed. Not all were happy. When the train emerged from the darkness into the glow of the station at Vilnius, a tingling excitement took her by surprise. She had returned only twice before in the four and a half years since her wedding.

The bustle of leaving the train began. Effie hurried to assist her mistress, ensuring that her toilette was impeccable, whilst Conroy's personal valet attended to the same services for his master. A retinue of servants, smartly turned out in Count Suslenko's green and gold livery were lined up on the platform. The carriage in which Anastasia and Conroy had travelled was privately hired, at the front of the train, easily recognized by its newly painted shining cleanliness, compared with the grime which covered the rest.

Juozas, the coachman, immaculate in a bottle-green coat, stepped forward. He swept off his top hat, decorated with a golden cockade, and bowed so low the feathers swept the platform. 'His excellency asked me to convey his greetings to you. He is unable to come and meet you himself, but awaits your arrival with impatience.'

'Thank you, Juozas.' Anastasia translated the information into English for Conroy as they walked through the high, marble-pillared portico.

Outside the station the count's winter vehicles were drawn up in line, headed by a green and gold sleigh piled high with fur rugs for Anastasia and Conroy. Four perfectly matched white horses champed their feet on the snow-crusted road. Harness leather gleamed and brass-work twinkled in the glow of gas-lamps. There were larger sleighs for the servants and behind those two long sledges for their baggage. Conroy handed Anastasia into the sleigh and she sank back into the luxurious comfort of the fur-covered seat whilst Effie hurried forward to wrap her around with more soft fur, making an impregnable cocoon of warmth from the sharp frosty air. Conroy took his place beside her.

They sped swiftly, almost silently, through the streets of Vilnius. The hour was late, yet the city had a busy air. Every street was familiar to Anastasia. Soon they were rushing along the route over which she had been driven as a bride to her wedding in the cathedral. Over the bridge then away into the moonlit snow-bright countryside, mantled in a glitter of crushed diamonds, where the blue-shadowed frost of winter held everything in its death hard grip. Sound was stilled, apart from the merrily jingling sleigh bells. They flashed by woods of fir and silver birch. Juozas whipped the horses into a canter and they swept through the tall double gates of the Suslenko Palace. The mile-long drive passed through an avenue of ornamental trees, their branches drooping to the ground beneath the weight of snow. As a child Anastasia had imagined they were bowing to her, just as the serfs and the servants did.

The sleigh drew up below the elegantly broad steps, which led to the beautiful blue, white and gold palace. The wide doors of the house were swung open and Count Suslenko stepped out to stand silhouetted against the yellow light. Behind him were the butler, the housekeeper and other servants, all standing to attention in hierarchical order. Outdoor servants held up lanterns, making the place almost as light as day. Anastasia waved to her father and saw him as older, more stolidly Russian-looking, for although he had Polish and German blood in him, the genes of Russian ancestry predominated. He was shorter than she remembered, his heavy jowl broadened by a thick beard, dark hair unexpectedly turned grey. She had been afraid of him as a child, had sheltered behind the skirts of countless housekeepers and governesses, unable to give love, when she seemed to receive so little of it from him.

He belonged to a male-dominated generation that took families for granted. His marriage had been arranged when he was in his late twenties and although he had respected his wife, and had even come to like and admire her, that emotion had been inspired more by her quality of efficiency than by love of her as a person. Countess Suslenko had been a true Lithuanian, tall, slender and shapely, a woman of great beauty and charm. She was intelligent and cultured but what Anastasia remembered most about her was her quiet, gentle manner. When she died the count had been surprised at the extent of the distress he had experienced, but he had had no idea of the devastating effect that trauma had on his daughter. Only twelve years of age she had been deeply affected and there had been no shared sorrow, no special affection, or even understanding from her father, from which she might have drawn comfort.

'Anastasia.'

She mounted the steps, kissed his cool cheek, looked deep into his eyes and saw welcome there. Was it possible that age had mellowed him sufficiently to care? For her part she realized that her approaching motherhood had already wrought subtle changes in her. She felt a stirring of affection for him. Soon she would tell him that next year he would have a new grandchild. Her baby would not be heir to the Suslenko estates, her brother's brood of three sons would take care of that. Nevertheless, the infant she carried was his flesh and blood, no matter who had fathered it, and somehow that seemed to present a bond between them. She knew she could never tell him the truth, even though it was said that he had fathered several children among the serfs. Were they perhaps two of a kind in some ways? She chuckled at the thought.

There was the usual large gathering at the Suslenko Palace which increased daily as Christmas approached. There was Anastasia's brother, Stanislovas, her sister-in-law, Katya, and their three sons whose ages ranged from twelve to seven, plus a multitude of aunts, uncles and cousins, relatives from both the Russian and Lithuanian sides of the family, who always turned up at Christmas. They also congregated at one or other of their several palaces for weddings, funerals or christenings. Had anyone read out their names it would have sounded like the trumpeting of an Eastern European version of Debrett, listing the most ancient lines of Russian and Lithuanian aristocracy, with some German and Polish names thrown in. Naturally, they almost all took up residence in St. Petersburg for the 'season' immediately after Christmas. It had already been arranged that Conroy and Anastasia should also stay there as guests of her aunt and uncle.

It might have been expected that such close personal contact would cause them to tolerate the policies of each other's governments, but not so. Friendly they might be in personal contact, but that would all be put aside if the interests of their respective countries – and therefore of their own wealth and well-being – were threatened. An undercurrent of unrest regarding the situation in Serbia rippled through the conversation of the Suslenko household that Christmas, though no one had the remotest idea of the magnitude of the calamity their countries were racing towards. As far as unrest among the peasants was concerned they easily brushed that aside, convinced that the army of the Tsar would be able to deal with that as effectively as in 1905 and on other occasions since.

Christmas Eve was the traditional and most important part of their ritual celebrations. In the grand dining-room of the Suslenko Palace a tall pine tree was decorated, and so many candles were lit that a footman was ordered to stand with a large can of water. There were presents on and all around it for the children, and when they were ushered into the room they ran and skipped and shrieked, bubbling with excitement, despite the efforts of their nannies and governesses to maintain some sort of order. They were all arrayed in fancy dress, as pirates, Cossacks, fairies, elves and snowmen. There were old costumes brought out of the storerooms and new ones made from paper and cardboard. It took some time to quieten them and line them up and set them to walk around the room in single file as tradition dictated, circling the long dining table. Then they were formed into a choir to sing a selection of the old songs and carols, traditional airs which they had been practising for weeks in advance and they performed very creditably for they had skilled music teachers. Anastasia knew all the words and sang joyfully with the children, as she remembered the excitement and awe she had felt on this occasion when she had been little.

The singing was applauded warmly and in the expectant silence that followed there came a loud knocking on the door. It heralded the arrival of *Kaledis*, or Old Man. Uncle Albertis was playing that part, just as he had done for several years, though she had never recognized him then, any more than the children did now. Wide-eyed, they stood rooted to the spot, even the boldest showing some apprehension, the youngest holding tightly to their nannies' hands.

Old Man was dressed in a ragged coat, a hood over his head was pulled forward to shield his face, his long grey beard swept almost down to his knees and he leaned heavily on a thick staff. Anastasia, in the role of go-between, stepped forward and held out her hand.

'God be with you, *Kaledis*. Have you come to see the children?'

Uncle Albertis mumbled in a deep growl. 'I've come to see if they have all been good during the past year.'

Anastasia turned to the anxious children. 'What shall I say? Can I tell *Kaledis* that you've been good?'

'Yes! Yes!' they chorused.

Old Man teased them by pretending to leave.

Cries of 'oooooh' from the children made him stop.

'Don't go, *Kaledis*,' Anastasia called out. 'The children have all been very good, and they promise to be even better next year.'

'That's all right, then,' growled Uncle Albertis. 'Because I've left presents about here somewhere. They'll have to hunt to find them – I'm so old I can't remember where I've left them—' A great sigh of dismay burst from the children. 'I think there may be some under the table, and some behind the curtains, and something out in the entrance hall.' The little ones could scarcely contain their excitement, but they were not allowed to move. Old Man held up a hand commanding silence, then when all were breathlessly still he relented and chuckled 'Now I must get on my way – there are other children waiting for me. Goodbye, everyone.'

He shuffled out of the room and the children sprang away, rushing this way and that. Some dived under the table and hauled out boxes tied up in pretty coloured paper, others rushed to the windows, pulled the curtains aside and found more things. Her brother's son rushed out of the room, then shouted, 'Look what I've got! A new sledge!'

Excitement was intense as papers were ripped off. Lifelike jointed dolls, magnificently attired in satin and lace were cuddled and crooned over. Boys had model railways and yachts, fully rigged for sailing on the lake. The room became a wonderland of expensive toys, delicious sweetmeats, amusing automatons and pretty trifles. The adults played with the children and enjoyed the fun until it was time for nannies and governesses to hustle them off to the nursery wing, and for the adults to dress for dinner.

'You played go-between very well, Anastasia,' Katya remarked as they left the room together, their long gowns rustling.

'I enjoyed it,' Anastasia replied honestly.

'I didn't know you were so fond of children.' Her tone was irritatingly patronizing. 'It must sadden you – eight years married, and nothing to show for it.'

Her words sparked a flash of anger in Anastasia, catching her off guard. 'I shall have – next year.'

Katya stopped, amazement lengthened the features of her narrow face. Her eyes darted inquisitively down to the region of Anastasia's stomach. 'You're going to have a baby – at last?' Her voice suggested she could scarcely believe it.

'That's what I said.'

'Of course I noticed you'd put on weight since last I saw you. When is it due?'

'Early summer.' Anastasia was deliberately non-committal.

In the huge entrance hall her soft-soled shoes made little sound as she moved over the inlaid teak and mahogany parquet floor, towards the wide sweep of the marble stairs with their magnificent balustrade. The house was warmed to near-tropical temperature by huge wood burning stoves.

Katya hurried to keep up with her. 'Conroy must be over the moon! Or haven't you told him yet?'

'He's as thrilled as I am!' Anastasia snapped.

She was confident that he would be pleased, if only because of the financial advantage her pregnancy would accrue. The earl had promised to increase their allowance liberally when they had a child.

She was almost at the foot of the stairs when loud voices, heavy footsteps and the noisy opening and shutting of doors heralded the return of the hunting party. Conroy and Stanislovas strode into the house. They had set out early in the morning, with about twenty guests and had been away all day. Faces were red, ice and snow clung to beards and moustaches and spread on riding clothes. Fur hats were flung aside, thick leather coats unbuttoned, and dropped for servants to pick up. Laughter boomed through the hall and it was not simply the icy air that gave a glow to their faces. They had lunched well and imbibed freely at one of the lodges on the vast estate.

Katya raised her voice to carry above the hubbub. 'Conroy, I've just heard your wonderful news! Congratulations!'

He swayed slightly. A vacant smile spread over his face, puckered around his eyes as he tried to focus his thoughts.

'What news?' he asked.

'Anastasia's just told me.' Katya glanced back and Anastasia caught a glimpse of spite in her eyes. It was as if her sister-in-law was aware that Conroy had not known until that moment.

'Why—' Katya began.

'Of our coming parenthood,' Anastasia interrupted swiftly, studiously maintaining her poise.

'Good God!' exclaimed Conroy.

'I know we intended to make the formal announcement this evening after dinner, darling,' Anastasia said. 'I told Katya in confidence. I hardly expected her to set herself up as a town-crier.'

Her tone was as barbed as the line of icicles that hung from the roof outside. The noise and chatter was stilled. A brittle silence hung almost tangibly over the tousled heads of the hunters, as they sensed a drama, listened for any hint of scandal, which they would immediately relay to their wives, most of whom were already upstairs. The servants hurried away almost buried beneath piles of outdoor clothes from which the snow was melting in puddles, which other servants were mopping up.

Giving her sister-in-law no time to utter another malicious word, Anastasia called to Conroy, 'Darling – come upstairs—'

Her honeyed voice held an invitation, readily pounced upon by the men with a guffaw of vulgar laughter and boorish comments.

Stanislovas thumped Conroy heartily on the back. 'You're a damned lucky fellow.'

Conroy laughed and sprang towards Anastasia, his reputation as a bit of a rake in no way diminished. She lifted her long skirts, pretending to run from him, whilst he followed, leaping up the stairs two at a time. He almost caught up with her at the top, but she sped along the corridor and flung open the door of her bedroom, with Conroy close on her heels. She was laughing as she turned to face him.

'Is it true?' he asked, breathlessly.

'Absolutely.'

'Why didn't you tell me?'

'I wanted to be sure. I've had disappointments before.' She paused. 'I'm sorry Katya blurted it out like that. I spoke to her in confidence.'

'Blasted busybody! She quizzed me yesterday about a family and I told her there was no sign yet.'

'Well, now she knows differently.' She paused then asked, softly. 'Are you pleased?'

'Of course.' Suddenly he chuckled. 'I knew I could do it! I knew there was nothing wrong with me. I knew it!'

'Your father will be pleased.'

'I'll send him a telegram. He'll make over at least another couple of thousand a year. More if you have a son.'

'That's not within my power to promise,' she warned.

'But if we can do it once, we can do it again. We can have more children.'

'Why not?' she agreed. The thought brought a smile to her face, reflecting her mood – making her look seductive, womanly, wanton and beautiful.

Conroy stepped towards her and took her into his arms, with rather more gentleness than he usually demonstrated. Then he lifted her off her feet and threw her on to the bed, and within minutes he had tossed aside his clothes and was on top of her. For the sake of her child and its inheritance, she welcomed him in a spirit of friendship.

Chapter 9

'I shall take a ride in the park,' announced Anastasia. 'Have a horse saddled for me, Anderson.'

She and Conroy had been back at Achil House for two weeks. They had broken the long train journey from St Petersburg by stopping off for a week at Vilnius, staying again at the Suslenko Palace. The count gave Conroy every facility to make arrangements for more men to be recruited from the villages and sent to Scotland, to help his pit managers break the strike.

When they finally reached Ringbrae the earl was at the station and greeted Anastasia with more warmth than usual. From then on he had cosseted her like a queen bee. He had the names of three experts in the field of gynaecology and had arranged that all three should attend upon her, in addition to two qualified midwives.

At first Anastasia found it quite agreeable to be so pampered. She was fatigued by the long journey and as the weather was drizzly and dull for the first two weeks, felt no desire to venture out of the house. Conroy was as good as his word and the fires were banked up, day and night, so that even she could not complain about feeling cold.

Then a day dawned when the sun rose brilliantly in a sky of Mediterranean blue and she could no longer bear the inactivity. To sit indoors was unthinkable.

'Begging your pardon, my lady – the earl would not—'

'Don't tell him. It's my order, Anderson. Have a horse saddled for me, immediately.'

'Yes, my lady.'

Anastasia rang for Effie and without waiting for her began to remove her morning gown.

'My riding habit,' she instructed. 'I'm going out.'

'But, my lady—'

'No buts. I've made up my mind. Help me to change.'

Effie did as she was told, but her face was puckered with disapproval, anxiety made her clumsy, and Anastasia's impatience turned to anger. It spilled over even more furiously when she realized that there was no way she could get into the riding habit.

'You really shouldn't, my lady—' Effie repeated.

An imperious knock on the door disturbed them. Anastasia looked round in dismay to see the earl standing there.

'What nonsense is this?' he thundered. 'You'll not ride again until after you have been delivered of my grandchild.'

'I can't bear being shut indoors—'

'Be sensible, my dear,' he said more gently. 'You'll do yourself a damage.'

'Nonsense. I know of several ladies who continued to ride, to hunt even, all through pregnancy, and it did them no harm.'

'That's as maybe. We've waited too long for this child, and I absolutely forbid you to take such a risk. You may go out in the carriage.'

She had to acquiesce and relinquish all thought of riding, the servants were given strict instructions to keep a close watch upon her. If she walked too long around the garden, the housekeeper would bustle out saying, 'My lady, it's time you came in for a rest.' If she instructed the coachman to whip the horses up faster, he would turn and say 'Beg your pardon, my lady, but my instructions are never to travel above a trot.'

Anastasia's restlessness did not lessen as the weeks passed, even as she came nearer her time. But the vigilance of the staff lapsed a little, perhaps because it seemed less likely that she would wish to venture far. Then, in the unexpected heat of a brilliant June day, she wandered dreamily to the far edge of the garden and turned, realizing there was no one hovering behind her. She stood at the edge of the lawn walk, where a little gate opened on a foot-path leading to the Bridie Burn. It wound through high banked rhododendrons; the temptation to continue her walk was too strong to resist. She felt perfectly well, and her spirits lifted, making her feel young, as if she was again escaping from her governess and the confines of the schoolroom.

The path meandered, skirting a lake, part of the gardens, laid out in the previous century. The melodious sound of rippling water caught her ears, and she turned towards it, through greenery which hid the stream from view. She picked her way carefully between overgrown shrubs and trees, pushing aside overhanging branches, drawn to the gurgling, swirling, water.

And there it was! A trickling burn, shallow, stone bedded, blue-black water, edged with a froth of white twisting around craggy rocks, riotously, boisterously running free. Translucent, it sprayed dew drops on the ferns that sprouted from niches in the rocks, dragged at lissom sprays of silver birch twigs. The Bridie Burn. She knew its name. She had been driven over it by the hump-backed bridge which, some said, had been there since Roman days. This was a sheltered, secret place. She drew in a breath of sheer pleasure as she walked forward then stood stock still. A man was there.

He was as motionless as she, stretched out face down on the bank, camouflaged in dark clothes against the shadowy under-growth. In momentary shock she thought he was dead – then he moved slightly. His long back and broad shoulders showed him to be a big man, bareheaded, his hair darkish, thick and curled up where it rested damply on his neck. The sleeves of his collarless striped shirt were rolled up and with one bronzed, muscular arm he was reaching into the water. Suddenly he made a quick scoop-ing movement. His hand flashed up clasped around the thrashing body of a fine silvery fish.

It was a trout, glistening, thickly spotted, symmetrical in shape from its gasping mouth to its broad fleshy tail. In the execution of that swift scooping movement with which he had caught the fish, the man had lifted his body from the ground. Duncan. His full attention was on his catch, her immediate thought was to step back. Yet she stayed. She made no movement, just gazed until he became conscious of her presence. His eyes, deeper-set than before, darker than she remembered, flashed a message that brought a constriction to her throat. The feeling engendered between them nine months previously was undiminished.

'Duncan.'

He scrambled to his feet. The fish lashed its tail in fury, but Duncan seemed unaware of it. His eyes held an intensity that made them seem almost black. She scanned his face. He was thinner. Beneath the light golden tan on his skin, his face had a drawn, hungry look. The silence stretched between them. She had to break it.

'I've never seen anyone fish like that before.' Ordinary, mundane words covered a depth of emotion.

'They call it guddling,' he said, at last.

'Hadn't you better put it out of its misery?'

He knelt and placed the trout on a flat stone almost reverently, held it firmly and cracked it sharply on the head with a short length of piping which had been lying beside his jacket. The fish jerked and lay still. He placed it beside two other fish which had been hidden from view, secreted under bushes, carefully wrapped in leaves. He moved back to the stream and rinsed his hands, shook the drops off and dragged the palms and fingers down against his shirt wiping them indifferently. Then he turned towards her again. His eyes slipped from her face to the roundness of her shape which proclaimed so much. He showed no surprise.

'How are you, Anastasia?' he asked.

His voice had the same pleasant resonance that she remembered so well. There was no humility in it, they were again man and woman, rank counted for nothing between them.

'I'm well enough,' she replied to his question. 'And you?'

He shrugged. 'I manage.'

Feeling a little unsteady she reached out and rested her hand on the trunk of a tree. Perhaps she had been foolish in walking so far.

An expression of concern crossed his face. 'Shouldn't you sit down? There's a fallen tree over there – I'll cover it with my jacket.'

He spread it lining up over the broad trunk and brushed the material with his hand, though no amount of attention could render it spotless. She moved towards the seat he had prepared but she had taken only a couple of steps when he was at her side, solicitously holding out his hand to assist her to settle comfortably. He dropped lithely down on the grass and sat cross-legged, tailor fashion, his hands resting on his knees, facing her.

'Are you on strike?' she asked.

'That's why I'm fishing.'

'To pass the time?'

'For food,' he replied drily.

'You've lost weight.'

'Aye – we all have. It hasn't been easy.'

'Why don't you go back to work?'

'We've held out this long, we can't give up now. They think they can starve us back, but we'll show 'em.'

'If the industry doesn't make a profit, they'll have to close the pits, and then there'll be no jobs.'

'Is that what they tell you?' His tone was dismissive. 'We're only asking for a decent living wage.'

'I don't know. I don't really understand it.'

'That's quite evident.'

'Conroy spoke of the strike when we were in Lithuania at Easter, on our way back from St Petersburg. It was a fabulous season. The Tsar was celebrating three hundred years since his family became rulers of Russia.'

'I heard he'd been over there. On a recruiting drive, wasn't it? Bringing in more blackleg labour.' His voice was bitter.

'The men were eager to come here.'

'Poor devils!' He heaved a sigh.

'Why do you say that?'

'They have police escort everywhere they go. Nothing will get me back now until it's all settled.'

95

'They say they'll never give in to you.'

'We shall see.'

Absent-mindedly he began to pluck blades of grass. She wanted to reach forward and run her fingers through the dark wavy hair that sprang with such vigour from his high forehead. She sensed his coiled up vitality. What was it about this man that exercised such power over her? Several seconds passed.

He looked up, a slow curving smile lightened his features. He didn't ask if the baby was his – perhaps he guessed.

A sharp pain stabbed into the lower part of her abdomen. She covered her rounded belly with her hand and felt the child within her kick violently. She gasped, it was half-moan, half scream. Surely – it couldn't be?

Concern leapt into Duncan's face. He leapt up in one strong and fluid movement.

She gathered her mind together. The discomfort passed. Perhaps it was indigestion. She didn't really believe it could be the baby coming, but she knew she must return to the house. She struggled to stand up and was grateful when Duncan stretched out a firm steady hand to help her. She gripped it tightly.

The pain came again.

'Can you walk?' Duncan asked.

'Of course.'

'Take my arm.'

She leaned heavily on him as together they began to retrace her steps through the woodland. When a pain came she had to stop and cling to him. Thankfully the contractions were not too frequent but she was in no doubt that she had started labour.

'Shall I carry you?' Duncan asked.

'You don't realize what a weight I am.' The light laugh died on her lips, as again a pain clamped her stomach into a vice.

'Let me lift you—'

'No. I prefer to walk. Let me lean on you.'

'As much as you like, my dearest.' His lips were close to her ear. Even in her present state that tender word gave her a glow.

'My lady. My lady.' Voices were calling from the gardens of the big house. 'My lady – where are you?'

'Answer them,' commanded Duncan.

'I'm here – by the little gate.'

Her hand clasped the gatepost, she felt Duncan transfer her weight from his shoulders, then he left her. She managed to turn, glimpsed his back disappearing, leaving only the swaying branches of a rhododendron to show where he had been.

'Oh, my lady!' Effie panted. 'We've been looking for you every-where.' Her voice rose in panic as the sight of Anastasia told her all.

Late that night her son was born. Conroy visited her when it was safely over. He had been drinking; she was glad he did not stay long.

The earl came to her room the next day. After the briefest of greetings he walked to the cradle. He bent over it, as if making an examination of the child tucked in so closely that the little face was barely visible between the woollen bonnet and the elabora-tion of frills on his gown. Lightly, gently, she pulled back the covers to look more closely at the screwed up little face with eyes tight closed. Anastasia held her breath. Was the shrewd old man looking for any special family characteristic? Something which could never be there? He stood in silence, leaned over and gazed at the child for a long time, then with long arthritic fingers, replaced the covers and moved towards the bed.

Anastasia watched warily as her father-in-law moved towards her. Surely he could have no doubts about the child – and yet he looked at her with such a serious expression that she felt uneasily he must have something immensely important to announce.

'I should like him to be called James Alexander Conroy,' he said. 'James after my father, Alexander after me and Conroy after his own father.'

Anastasia thought of that pedigree and a smile played about her lips. Her son could bear no resemblance to any of the three men after whom he was to be named. 'I am agreeable to that,' she said. Those names were like a blessing on her child.

Irena felt enormous and clumsy. She tried to get comfortable in the old chair with its sagging seat, shivered and pulled her shawl more closely around her. The grate was empty, and although it was June and the month had started off warm and sunny, the weather had changed abruptly. Indoors and out it felt damp and chilly. She dared not light the fire. Only two or three buckets of coal remained of the ton that had been delivered as part of Duncan's wages when he'd been at work. She was saving it for boiling kettles and to warm the room when the baby came. Surely it could not be long now!

Duncan had left the house late in the evening. 'I'm going with some of the men to get coal,' he had said.

His words had filled her with dread. They had no money, the strike had been on so long. There was nothing left to pawn.

'How?' Irena asked.

'There's a scheme on. It's secret.'

She knew it had to be illegal and dangerous. 'Oh, Duncan—'

'Don't worry, lass. Tomorrow our troubles will be over. We'll have a fire roaring up the chimney and sit and brew tea all day long.'

'You're going to steal it,' she accused.

'It's not stealing. The coal bosses are not going without coal, and I reckon we miners have more right to it than they have. We're the ones that sweat to hew it out of the ground.'

'But the police guard the pit-head,' Irena objected. 'The town was full of them today. I heard they'd brought extra men up from England.'

His face split with that infectiously wicked grin she knew so well. 'Don't tell a soul but the plan is to send decoys to Campbell's farm, just outside the town. They'll scatter the hens and let out the pigs and kick up a good old rumpus.' He laughed aloud.

The idea was so ridiculous that Irena smiled.

'Can't you just imagine it?' Duncan continued. 'They'll think we're after turnips or oats or an old hen to put in the pot. That'll send the police chasing over there, so they won't be watching the coal.'

There was no arguing with him, not in that arrogant optimistic mood. He was heading for the door. 'Don't wait up for me.'

That had been three hours ago, and midnight had passed long since. Being Duncan he was sure to be in the thick of any venture. He was always like that and now she sensed the desperation in him. He was thin and hungry, permanently restive, tight-wound, incapable of relaxing. He worried about her, she knew that, and the strike went on, week after weary week.

Every day they went to the communal soup kitchen for a mid-day meal. When it had first been set up she had helped there, scraping and peeling vegetables, stirring the pot, plucking a fowl if someone managed to get hold of one. Then, as her time drew near, the other women had told her to take more rest. They were right, but she missed their company. Despite the hardship of their lives they made light of things, cracked jokes and sometimes they were convulsed with laughter. She hadn't always understood what they were saying, but their merriment would always make her smile. Without the soup kitchen the miners would never have been able to hold out for so long.

Her sense of helplessness made her angry. She vowed that as soon as she was strong and on her feet again she would find some way of improving their circumstances. With help from a neighbour, called Eva, she had managed to keep up with the MacEwan's washing. Her friendship with the kindly Scots woman had deepened. She was now able to speak and understand English quite well. She wished Duncan could find some other work. It was a terrible job, and when the strike ended, would conditions be any better?

Irena had long since put down her crochet work. She was making another little bonnet for her baby. She hesitated to light the lamp as paraffin oil was costly. She was hungry. As the baby kicked in her womb she rose heavily to her feet, dipped a cup into the bucket beneath the table and took a cool refreshing draught of water. She found a dry crust and nibbled it as she moved back into the old chair.

What a celebration it had been when Duncan brought in those beautiful trout three days ago! He had burst into the room with a great clatter and she had thought at first that the strike must be over. His face was beaming, eyes shining, mouth open with a great smile as joyous as if he had been given the whole world. He had not looked so happily alive for a long time.

'Look Irena – look what I've got!'

He had opened his jacket, she had seen the bulge beneath his shirt, and teasingly, like a conjuror, he had paused, keeping her in suspense so that she wondered what on earth he was going to produce. The gleam in his eyes had told her it was something good, but she could not guess. Then he had unbuttoned his shirt and leaned over the table. A trout slithered out. Inadequately wrapped in leaves, it dropped on to the scrubbed pinewood. When it was followed by two more, she could scarcely believe her eyes.

'My apologies that I couldn't present them to you with more elegance,' he grinned. 'But there was no other way I could bring 'em home without being seen. I know it's greedy, but I've no intention of sharing them.'

He took off his jacket and shirt, walked over to the washing bowl on the table and, soaping a piece of flannel, washed the evidence of the fish from his chest and abdomen.

'Where did you get them?' she asked.

'A spot I know. It's on the earl's land.'

'You'd have been in serious trouble if you were caught.'

'But wasn't it worth it?'

She shook her head. She wouldn't encourage him. But she had to admit that his open fearless audacity was part of his attractiveness. His face was now as familiar to her as her own, every line and curve of it etched deeply into her heart.

Never had fish tasted better! She had grilled them over the fire with the utmost care and they had eaten every scrap, including the skin, then they sucked the bones and wiped bread around the plate till there was not a shred of flavour left. For the first time for weeks they left the table feeling fully satisfied.

She had thought back on that evening with pleasure more than once. After they had washed up she and Duncan had taken a stroll along the street, and she had felt secure and loved, with her hand on his arm. Proud too, because so many of the miners knew him, and were pleased to have a chat with him. Where was he now? Had they managed to lure the police out of the town? The stockpile at the Ringbrae Colliery was beside a railway siding, awaiting shipment. It was surrounded by a high chainlink fence, topped with barbed wire. Why had Duncan been such a long time?

A pain gripped the base of her stomach. The baby! Oh, no! Don't come now – not when I'm here on my own, she prayed. She sat frozen in the chair, then as the spasm passed, stood up carefully. She wanted to go to the toilet, and walked slowly to the door. Dawn was breaking, its pale light rose unwillingly into the dull grey sky, shadowed by the buildings that closed in on the yard. Still it rained.

She stood for a moment on the stone balcony and its iron handrail wobbled when she touched it. Duncan had warned her not to put too much weight on it. She began slowly to make her way down the stone steps when another pain stabbed into her. She had no doubt about it this time; even though it was her first, she knew without a doubt that the baby was coming. Her body was preparing for the birth. Still her immediate need was to get to the toilet block, and with caution and determination she continued on her way.

As she came back she heard the sound of men's voices. Thank God! Duncan was one of them. With him were Petras and another. Relief turned to horror as two policemen chased into the yard immediately behind them. She drew back into the shadow of the toilet block, and gripped its rough brick so hard it hurt her fingers. Another pain threatened to tear her apart inside.

Lazaraitis, Duncan and Petras didn't move. Lazaraitis had a whisky bottle in his hand. One of the policemen held up a lantern. Duncan was unsteady on his feet. Where had he got the money for drink? Lazaraitis passed the bottle to him – that explained it. He always had money. The old women had told her that, when he wanted to marry her. If she had accepted, she would not be living in this poor little single end, but she would not change Duncan for any other man in the world. If only she could be sure that this baby was his!

'What's going on here?' one of the policemen asked.

Duncan's words were blurred and he spoke too loudly. 'Good evening,' he grinned foolishly.

'We have reason to believe you've been stealing coal,' said the policeman.

Duncan stayed quiet, the other two men spoke to each other in their own language, as if they did not understand. One of the policemen brought out a notebook. 'What's your name?' he asked. He licked his pencil and pointed it at Petras. 'Name,' he said again, more loudly, as if that would make his request clearer.

'Petras Jousas Kalinauskas.'

'Christ! How do you spell that?'

'Spell? What spell?'

The policeman sighed and turned to the others. 'Let's have your names then?'

'Antanas Algierdas Lazaraitis.'

Duncan muttered something foreign sounding.

'How the hell do I write that down?'

The policeman looked at his companions helplessly. They were new to the area. He put his notebook back into his pocket. 'Shove off home,' he said.

'Have a drink.' Lazaraitis offered his bottle of whisky.

The policeman glanced over his shoulder, took a good swig and passed the bottle to his comrades, who did likewise and handed it back. They left the yard at a leisurely pace, chortling as they tried to mimic the funny accents of the foreigners.

Irena waited a moment then moved out of the shadows. 'Duncan,' she called.

His head jerked up. He looked towards the landing outside their room.

'Duncan,' she called again, more urgently.

He spun round and in a moment was at her side. 'What the hell are you doing out here?' He leaned towards her looking closely into her face. There was whisky on his breath, a smell that always reminded her of Petras. Lazaraitis was following him.

'The baby's coming.'

'Christ!' Anxiety made his voice crusty.

'Help me back to the house—' Her voice faded as a strong pain gripped her.

'I'll carry you—'

'No.' Her voice was sharp. 'You've been drinking—'

He grinned. 'Not a drop – well scarcely any. That was to fool the police. Come on, Irena, you must get into the house.'

Slowly she walked forward. He shouted, 'Fetch Ona.'

'Right away.' Petras ran off immediately.

His arm was wonderfully strong and steady. Leaning heavily on him she was able to climb the stone steps.

Within fifteen minutes Ona bustled into the room. She had become the self-appointed midwife for the Lithunaian women. At first she had worked with an older woman, and had learned the folk traditions associated with childbirth. Untrained, but knowledgeable, she was worth her considerable weight in gold.

'You're doin' fine,' she assured Irena after timing the contractions. 'No hurry. You'll be some time yet.'

'Duncan, for goodness sake, get that fire lit and put the kettle on.' This was one of the few times when a woman could order a man about and get away with it.

'I was just going to do it,' he protested, but mildly. He had already brought out some paper, kindling and a bucket of coal from under the bed. 'I told you we'd have the fire roaring up the chimney today, didn't I, Irena?'

'You got coal?' Irena could scarcely believe him.

'Three sacks of best quality. It's hidden under some gorse bushes.' He chuckled. 'I'll fetch it later.'

Irena smiled and relaxed. The pains came regularly, but they were easier to bear now she was sitting in her own room, being looked after. Ona had taken over with an authority that was comforting. She was in her element attending to women in child-birth, using her expertise and ordering people about.

'I'll prepare the bed. Where do you keep your spare linen, Irena? Don't get up. Just tell me.'

Irena pointed to the bottom drawer of a chest, and Ona lifted out sheets and towels and selected a few of the baby clothes that Irena had so carefully stitched and crocheted.

Duncan had lit the fire, blowing to encourage the flames. He knelt on the rag rug at Irena's feet. She ran loving fingers through his thick wavy hair, thankful that he had returned home safely. 'I've been so worried, Duncan.'

'No need.' He looked up at her, his face was flushed from blowing at the fire. 'The expedition went like clockwork. So easy, you wouldn't believe it! The decoy worked a treat. The police were lined up and marched away to Campbell's farm. Not one stayed behind to guard the coal. We managed a good hour's work before word went round that they were coming back at the double. Then we nipped off prettly quickly!'

'But those policemen – they followed you home?'

'They caught up with us just down the street. We pretended we didn't know what they wanted, and that we'd been drinking.'

'I thought you had too.'

Duncan piled coal on the fire and settled the kettle over the flames. He sat back on his heels. 'I pretended I was Lithuanian too – made up a name. You should have seen the mess that copper made of it when he tried to write it in his notebook.'

'Don't just sit there preening yourself,' Ona snapped. 'I'll need more water, fill the buckets up again, Duncan. Then you can fetch the doctor and keep out of the way until I call you.'

Duncan stood up. He leaned over and patted Irena's shoulder encouragingly. 'You'll be all right?'

She did not feel in the least bit right. Her body was out of her control and she was being bullied by this infant who was strug-gling cruelly with her. The contractions were coming quicker, she managed only a ghost of a smile for Duncan.

'Of course she'll be all right. You do what I've told you and then go off and get some more of that coal you've been boasting about.'

Ona waved her hands at him as if he was a goose she was trying to shoo out of the house and Duncan obeyed without a murmur. By the time he came back with the bucket of water, Ona had helped Irena to change into her nightgown and told her to climb up on to the freshly made bed. Duncan hesitated briefly in the doorway. She wished he could have stayed with her, but that was unthinkable. This was women's work.

'Get out.' Ona hustled him away.

As soon as the door had closed behind him she returned to Irena. 'You're doing fine, dear. Lie on your side, and catch hold of your knee. Push when you feel like it – good girl.'

The first sight of her new baby brought a stab of disappointment. Nothing in the furious little red face, topped by spiky dark hair, bore the least resemblance to Duncan. Irena sighed, and yet felt an infinite tenderness towards this scrap of humanity lying in her arms. His newness, his innocence, his need of her, brought an outpouring of love that transcended the pain and struggle of his birth.

'A fine boy!' the doctor declared.

He beamed as if he had actually done something to help the infant into the world. In fact when he arrived, the baby had been there, lying between Irena's sprawled out legs, protesting noisily, with Ona crowing over him in sing-song Lithuanaian baby-talk. The doctor had cut the cord, waited for the afterbirth, weighed the infant, made some notes and departed.

By the time Duncan was allowed into the room Ona had washed and tidied up both mother and baby. Irena was sitting up in bed cradling the infant in her arms. He was making funny little noises and movements but his face was barely visible in the wrappings of flannel and wool. Duncan put something down by the door and tiptoed into the room.

Irena smiled. 'You don't have to be so quiet, Duncan. You won't disturb him.'

His eyes scanned her face, his attention all for her – did that mean that he had dismissed the baby even before he saw him?

'How is it?' he asked.

'The baby—?'

'No. You. How are you?'

'I'm fine. Glad it's over.'

'It took a long time.'

'Yes. I suppose so.' She didn't want to be reminded of that now. 'The doctor said he's a fine baby.'

'Good.'

She wished Duncan would lean over, pull the wraps back from the baby's face, show some paternal interest in him, but she would not ask him to. That would have to come spontaneously.

Chapter 10

'IT'S a sell-out!'

The Union meeting was packed. Anger greeted the announcement of the small improvement that had been won in the miners' pay and working conditions. They could hold out no longer. Sheer miserable poverty defeated them. The hope that had sprung into Duncan's heart at the start of the dispute, the idea that ordinary working people might have some power over their own destiny, had died as the struggle for existence got worse every week.

Since the birth of Marty, three weeks earlier, he had been worried about Irena. She was so thin; she wasn't getting enough to eat for herself, let alone to feed a clamouring, hungry baby.

'Those in favour of accepting this offer?'

Duncan held up his hand, as did the majority.

It was a relief to be back at work, to use his abundant strength on physical activity, to have money and good food again. Within a few weeks that pinched, starved look disappeared from Irena's face, and the glow of health and contentment returned. Motherhood suited her and Marty thrived in her care. Duncan accepted his lot.

Every day began with the walk to the pit head through the morning-dark streets, shadowy black figures of colliers passing beneath the gas lamps, their boots making a steady tramp, tramp, tramp. The bing sprawled, its ugliness merging into the darkness, the clank of steam-driven machinery, the gush and throb of the ventilating pumps grated on the ears as the stark structure of the wheels of the pit head came into sight.

Duncan filed into the shed to collect his lamp. The checker stood by the cage. Each man handed over a token with his number, a tally of those below. Petras was there and they exchanged their customary curt nod. They worked in the same pit and on the same shift. Duncan avoided close companionship with him, but he had to admit that, as a worker, Petras was strong and skilled.

A gate of rusty metal clanged shut behind them. Mesh rolled down over the cage entrance. A grunt, a shout, a short wait and it plunged; the brick sides fled upwards as if they were dropping down a well. A draught of air came as they passed an old seam, worked out fifty years earlier. Down, down to the bottom of the five hundred yards deep shaft. They stepped out into a wide gallery. He looked into the stables. The smell of horses was strong, more pleasant to him than the dankness of the pit.

'Ho, Duncan – all right there?' The ostler was friendly. A lad was mucking out, wheeling a barrow load of manure to the second shaft. The ostler loved his ponies, bedded their stalls thickly, fed and watered them with care, groomed and rubbed them as if they were to draw the Lord Mayor's coach, instead of hutches of coal.

Duncan followed the other men down the road, through tightly fitting doors that directed the incoming air. A cool blast struck as he pushed his way through. Some ponies were working there, hauling filled tubs up from the face, a couple of miles distant. Further down where the roof dropped lower the ponies were smaller, strong, black Shetlands, gamely pulling the heavy loads. Duncan gave each an encouraging pat, greeted the lads who worked with them, took a crust from his pocket. He always brought a titbit for his favourite. Blackie stopped and reached forward with his head. Duncan held the bread in the flat of his hand, the soft wet lips swept his skin.

At the coal face Duncan dropped to his hands and knees and began to crawl along to his place. Other colliers squatted, shuffled aside, paused in their work to let him into the narrow, low road between the props, the trees, the crossbeams. He spat on his hands, crouched on his kneepads and began the long day's toil, chipping away the coal with his pick.

Above ground daylight dawned. There in the bowels of the earth there was only the dim glow from the lamp on his cloth cap. He had no means of telling the time, only his stomach told him when lunchtime was approaching. It was a welcome break to put aside his pick and crawl out to the road where he could sit upright and stretch his legs out in front of him. He took a long swig at the bottle of cold tea, tore hungrily at a hunk of cheese with strong teeth, ignoring the grit.

Frank Lee, a Lithuanian, sat beside him, tried to talk to him, but his stumbling words provoked an outburst of laughter from the other men who were Scots or Irish. It was friendly; there was camaraderie among the miners.

Duncan lifted the cap from his sweat-wetted hair and sat back to relax for the last few minutes before the contractor gave the word for them to crawl back to their places.

Then came the explosion! Deafening. It erupted, and was everywhere. It enveloped the whole road with a din that felt as if it was crushing his ear-drums. His head – his lungs – his heart – all seemed to be bursting. Something hit his temple. He reeled and lost consciousness.

He came to, choking, spluttering, gasping for breath; the air was filled with dust. Echoes of the explosion died away, the rumble of falling coal and rocks continued. Darkness was complete; he was locked in an impenetrable blackness. Was this the end? Would he ever see the blessed daylight again? He made the sign of the Cross over his chest, then struggled to pull his shocked body into a sitting position.

A cough rasped beside him. Then voices.

'Holy Mother of God, what was that?'

'Gas. Must have been!'

'Fuckin' hell!'

'I can't see a bloody thing. Hasn't anybody got a light?'

'Christ Almighty – you want tae set off another explosion?' It was Robbie, the contractor. 'Call your names,' he commanded.

'Peter Green.'

'Andy McNab.'

'Frank Lee.'

'Duncan MacRaith.'

Two Liths and two Scots. The voices guided the men towards each other. It was comforting to make contact with another human being, to jostle against a shoulder. A hand reached out and grasped Duncan's, a strong grip that exchanged the reassurance of life.

'Paddy Mahoney?' the contractor called. 'Where's Paddy Mahoney?'

Paddy, the tough little Irishman. He had been sitting quite close to Duncan.

'He was over here somewhere – Paddy – Paddy – ' He groped around, feeling the dry dust on the floor, calling the name. He put his hand on a bottle – broken. The jagged glass cut his palm. He swore in pain.

'Paddy.' Andy McNab was also searching. 'Is that you Paddy? He's here! Say something, Paddy. Oh, my God – there's blood all over his head.'

Duncan crawled towards the voice, reached out and felt the inert body. He helped Andy to lift the Irishman.

'That's everyone accounted for on this section, then,' Robbie said. 'We'll see if we can get oot. Ye'll ha' tae carry Paddy. Keep low and follow me.'

Paddy groaned as Duncan and Andy lifted him.

'He's alive!'

'Aye, but for how long?'

Stumbling, following the sound of the contractor's voice, carrying Paddy, progress was slow. The air was thick with dust. Duncan had never believed darkness could be so intense. Perhaps he had been blinded – perhaps they had all been blinded. Would they ever get out? How horrible to die, choked and trapped in filthy darkness. His mind flashed wildly, a kaleidoscope of jumbled memories, of home in the Isles, of his grandmother, Anastasia, Irena – did he have a son to carry on after him? He was not sure. Would he ever know? Had Anastasia borne his son? What difference did it make? Next he was guddling for trout; how would Irena manage without him? There was little talk, the tension was too great for that, except for the necessary words that kept them together, kept them moving on, taking turns at carrying Paddy.

'See that!'

'There's a light.'

It was true! There were lights in the distance, five or six hundred yards away, stars of hope in the blackness. Help was coming. The rescue party took over.

Paddy had wounds on his face that would leave him scarred for life. Duncan's forehead was gashed and his hand bleeding from the cut on the broken bottle. Funny how little it had hurt him after that initial stab of pain. Someone gave him a rag to wrap around it. The other men were in a similar state.

'You came off luckier than those poor sods at the other end of the face,' said one of the rescuers.

They had brought stretchers. Paddy was lifted on. The walk to the bottom of the shaft continued.

'They're digging 'em out there. Explosion brought the roof down at that end.'

Petras had been working there. 'Don't know who they've bloody got out yet. One poor bastard had his leg blown off. They've taken him up.'

Duncan was numbed. How close was life to death! Was there nothing in life but patient acceptance? He squatted on his hunkers close to the bottom of the shaft to await his turn in the cage.

The ostler came out of the stables carrying the humane killer and head-mask. Two of the ponies had been badly injured. Blackie might be one of them. He was small and could work down the lowest roads. The ostler went off to carry out his grim task.

They brought out another couple of men, one with his face and hand so badly injured as to be unrecognizable. Petras was not there – he was bulkier than either of those men.

'Have you seen Petras, the Lith?' Duncan asked a stretcher-bearer.

'If the poor bugger's doon there, they're diggin' him oot. There's nae mair alive.'

The injured men were taken away. Duncan went up in the cage. At the top he handed in his token, and stepped out into the blessed sweetness of the clear fresh air. The sky was overcast, threatening rain, what did it matter? He was alive, he could see, breathe, he had been lucky. But how long would it hold? He couldn't go home until he knew about Petras. He leaned with his back against the wall and waited.

The men who should by now be working the backshift stood about in the colliery yard. There would be no more coal-getting that day. They awaited the report from the mines inspector on safety. Colliery firemen had gone below, testing for gas, seeking other explosive pockets. The miners waited. They talked together in subdued voices. Another rescue party might be needed, or men to carry out urgent safety work. They waited, ready to go to the aid of any still trapped below.

Almost an hour passed before the bodies were brought out. There were three of them and Petras was the last. The police would notify Ona. It was not a major disaster. It made only a few lines in the local paper. Three men had been killed, another four seriously injured. Work would begin again tomorrow. A knot of women had gathered outside the colliery gates. They, too, moved away. Duncan started to walk home. Blood had congealed in a crimson trickle down his blackened face from the gash on his temple. His hand was sore. He tucked it inside his jacket to ease the throb. In the town men and women had gathered at the street corners. Duncan was stopped once or twice. He told them about Petras, and Paddy, and others whose names he knew, and they shook their heads and silently sorrowed.

Irena was sitting in the armchair, the glowing fire from the black-leaded grate reflected a pretty peach colour on her face and splashed auburn tints into her dark hair. She had been working on a cloth, but the crochet hook which had been deftly looping and twisting the fine white cotton stayed poised, as she swung round. At the sight of him, in the doorway, she jumped to her feet. He took her into his arms to calm her – and comfort himself.

He made light of the accident. 'I came out of it all right,' he ended.

'Yes – this time.'

'Accidents happen.'

'You should get out of the pit,' she said.

'What else can I do?' he snapped.

She was talking nonsense. He had been close to death more than once. Malicious demons lurked deep down, they played with the frailty of the men who chipped and picked and bore away the fossilized black treasure from the bowels of the earth. A man must not stop and think too much.

'Jeasu sunau Dievo gyvojo susimylk ant dušiu. Jesus, son of God, have mercy on his soul.'

The Lithuanians were singing the fifteen decades of the rosary at Petras's wake. An old man with a deep, mournful voice led the assembled company. Duncan joined in the oft-repeated phrase.

Petras's body, cleaned and decently robed for burial, lay on the brass-knobbed iron bed in the room where the lodgers usually slept. The blinds were drawn and two big candles had been lit. Their glow flickered over the faces of friends and neighbours. Petras's features were set with a serenity that had seldom been there when he was alive. His arms, crossed on his chest, gave him an air of resignation. His hands bore the scars and knots of the toil that had brought him death.

Jesus, son of God, have mercy on his soul.

Ona sat by her husband's head. She moaned and rocked herself inconsolably. Irena had come with Duncan earlier in the evening, but she had left some time ago, taking Ona's children with her, back to Mick's Buildings for the night. The lugubrious chanting went on. Duncan stayed for about an hour, then he and some other men moved out to the kitchen. Food and drinks were passed round. One end of the table had been cleared to make space and cards were being dealt out, glasses of beer close by.

'You want to join in?'

Duncan shook his head. They were playing for money and he had little to spare. The chanting rose and fell in the background. Duncan poured himself a glass of beer, took a slice of sausage and a hunk of bread and joined a group sitting by the fire.

'I went to a wake last year, where there wasn't a body,' one man said. He paused for effect, then continued. 'The house had only one room. I looked around for the body, but I couldn't see it anywhere. They were telling jokes and playing cards, just like this, the body was in the way, so they pushed it under the bed.'

Duncan's glass was empty. The bottles on the table were empty too. Lazaraitis took a half-sovereign from his money belt. 'We can't let Petras go without a proper send-off. Let's get some beer.'

They borrowed a handcart and pushed the barrel of beer back to the house. Petras had been respected for his strength, for his capacity to drink.

At the funeral Duncan acted as a bearer. He borrowed a navy suit from a friend and the undertaker handed to him a bowler hat. The rim sat hard on Duncan's forehead. He stood in front of the mirror, pleased with what he saw – a smart, dandy young man. The square lines of his chin, clean-cut above the stiff white collar, black tie knotted to perfection, the high-buttoned waistcoat lacked only the refinement of a gold watch-chain. He tilted the angle of the bowler slightly and his dark eyes twinkled. He restrained his mouth from opening in a wide grin of approval, remembering where he was. If he saved some money he could buy a suit to walk out on Sundays. He turned to see if Irena was impressed, but she was not looking at him. She was holding a glass to Ona's lips, persuading her to take a sip of something to strengthen her for the ordeal ahead.

The hearse was drawn by two black horses, their manes and tails braided with black ribbons. The bearers walked alongside. Duncan glanced back as they turned a corner. Irena was helping Ona, both women heavily veiled in black. Dougie walked alongside his mother, diminutive, pale-faced and solemn. Gavin and Bonnie had been left with neighbours, as had Marty.

The family mourners were followed by miners, four abreast, stretching back as far as the eye could see – Scots, Irish and Lithuanians. All dark-clad, each would lose a day's precious wages, an essential gesture to pay their last respects to a fellow-collier. After the Mass and the interment, Duncan walked from the graveside with Ona and Irena. A high wall squarely enclosed the bleak cemetery. Ona halted beside an elaborate stone, sculptured in the shape of a weeping angel. 'I'd like a monument like that for Petras,' she said.

Duncan and Irena had moved on a few steps. They both turned to look back.

'She can't mean that!' he said. 'An angel? For Petras?' He chuckled.

'Shh! Duncan!' Irena's voice was a sibilant whisper of reproof.

She placed a possessive hand on his arm, and when he looked down there were tears in her eyes. 'I can imagine how Ona feels. It's frightening, the danger you face, in those dreadful pits.'

Chapter 11

IRENA shifted the bundle of fresh laundry from one hip to the other, without pausing in her steady swinging walk. A fresh white headscarf covered her hair, her shawl hung loose around her shoulders, her long skirt floated around her ankles with the vigour of her easy strides.

Marty was almost a year old, standing on firm straight legs, walking if anyone held his hand, and otherwise crawling into mischief. She had left him with Ona and knew he would be taken good care of. Several people said how like Duncan he was and when Irena looked at his dark eyes and blond hair and funny little pug nose, she could almost believe it. She wanted to believe it, more than anything in the world. She loved both her son and her husband with an intensity that sometimes frightened her. Yet doubt remained.

One advantage of doing the weekly wash for Mrs MacEwan was that it brought her out into this glorious sweep of countryside, so different from Mick's Buildings. It would have been perfect if Duncan could be there with her, instead of down in those dark, dangerous pits! The horror of that accident had left its mark, not only on Duncan (though he made light of it) but on her too, perhaps even more on her! If anything happened to Duncan she might as well be dead herself. How could she live without him? Ona's suffering had become partly her own. Irena looked in on her almost every day, even if it was only for a few minutes. The Friendly Society of St Casimir had paid the funeral expenses and a whip round at the pit had provided some ready cash to see Ona over the immediate period of her mourning, but her grief was pitiful to see.

'Why?' she kept asking. 'Why did it have to be Petras?'

It was almost an accusation that Duncan should be alive when Petras was dead. Tears constantly filled her eyes and she would rock herself inconsolably. Kindly neighbours called in and kept her company, offered sympathy and practical help, made meals for the children, knitted extra woollies, rallied round. They all knew that any day the same thing might happen again, another explosion, another roof fall, a fault in the descending cage, a runaway hutch crashing, so many things that caused death and injury. Irena had been only dimly aware of the dangers before, now she saw with frightening clarity the things that could happen, that did happen. She also saw that they happened to anyone. It was unbearable. She pleaded with Duncan to leave the pit, but he would not hear of it.

'Don't talk like that,' he said brusquely. 'I came here to make money and I'm not leaving empty handed.'

'Money isn't everything.'

'There's not much you can do without it.' She knew what he said was true. 'But you will be careful—' she insisted.

'Of course. I've no intention of dying young, if I can help it.'

He was so cheerful, she wished she could feel the same, but her thoughts turned in only one direction. There must be some other job he could do, and if it meant less money, she would manage somehow. Even on this bright spring morning, that thought dominated her mind.

'Ah, there ye' are, hen. I've been looking oot fer ye,' Mrs MacEwan, beamed at Irena. 'The kettle's on the boil, how aboot a wee cup o' tae?'

'Thank you very much.' Irena's English was only slightly accented now.

The kitchen-living room was bright with sunlight. Cups and saucers, sugar bowl and milk jug had been placed on the table.

'I've been watchin' oot fer ye,' she said. 'Ye'll never guess whit's happened.'

Irena thought a moment. 'Your daughter is coming home?'

Mrs MacEwan longed to see her only child, who had emigrated to Canada. The old lady shook her head, taking her time over making the tea. 'Nae. I doot she'll manage it this year.'

Irena waited. She had been doing the washing for Mrs MacEwan for over a year and their liking for each other had developed into affection. The old lady sat down to allow the tea to brew. 'Ye mind ye telt me how you wanted your man tae get oot o' the pits?'

'I'm so afraid for him—'

'Mr MacEwan says there's a job goin', in the gardens here.' Irena's heart jumped. 'A job? In the gardens? You think my Duncan might be able— Oh, Mrs MacEwan! That would be wonderful.'

'I cannae say fer certain that he'd be suitable, ye ken.'

'But he would! I know he would. He's strong and clever and he knows about growing things. Please you tell your husband—'

'Nae, lass. It's no up to him. It's the steward up at the big hoose he maun see. Mr Anderson. He's in charge o' all the outdoor staff.'

'My Duncan's working late today. I see this man – I tell him Duncan's good worker.'

'Nae. Nae. It's your man Mr Anderson'll want tae see, hen.'

'But I should tell him, about Duncan, so he no take on someone else.'

'Aye, weel – maybe ye're right aboot that.'

'Where I find this Mr Anderson?'

'Up at the hoose. He has an office at the back.' Mrs MacEwan glanced at the clock. 'Two-thirty. He might be there noo.'

'I go. Right away—'

'Nay, lass, ye've time tae finish ye tea.'

Reluctantly, but remembering her manners, Irena sat back. 'I so much want my Duncan away from the pit,' she apologized.

'I cannae blame ye fer that. There's a wee hoose gaes wi' the job.'

'Oh!' Irena was speechless. 'Oh! Mrs MacEwan!' It sounded like heaven! Imagine getting away from Mick's Buildings!

'I could still wash for you, Mrs MacEwan.'

'That'd suit me fine. Off ye go, hen.' Mrs MacEwan walked with Irena to the door, still chatting. 'Ye might see her ladyship on the terrace wi' her wee laddie. But it's tae the back o' the hoose ye've tae go, mind. An' ye can tell Mr Anderson I sent ye.'

She gave the old lady a hug and hurried on her way, hope surging through her veins.

The front of the huge house faced south. Built in white freestone, it almost shone in the sunlight, the gables and multitude of chimneys sharply outlined against the Mediterranean blue sky. The portico was embellished with Corinthian columns supporting an elegant entablature, the earl's cypher carved in stone. Irena marvelled at the immense size of the place but she hurried on, through an archway in a high brick wall. Doors at the back of the house obviously led to kitchen, dairy, laundry, stores, and other domestic rooms, but one had the word 'office' worked into a panel of elaborately frosted glass. Irena knocked and waited.

No response. She knocked again. No sound from within. Her eager anticipation began to drain away. Mr Anderson was not there. What was she to do? Deflated, she contemplated sitting on the doorstep and waiting, but she might be there for hours, and she had to get back to Mick's Buildings, to her baby and to prepare for Duncan's return from work. She heard voices coming from one of the outbuildings. A lad came along pushing a wheelbarrow piled high with sawn logs. He stopped whistling when he saw her.

'Steward's oot,' he announced.

'When he be back, please?'

'No' the day. He's awa' tae toon. I seed him gae, a guid hour since.'

Irena felt almost physically drowned in the disappointment that flooded over her.

'Reckon he'll be here the morn,' said the boy helpfully.

'Thank you.' Slowly she turned away. The lightness had left her step. She told herself that she could come back tomorrow. Or Duncan could come then, if he would. Perhaps that would be better, but she knew his desire to find different work was not as powerful an urge as it was for her. She was afraid Duncan might allow himself to be brushed aside. Most of all, she feared that someone else, hearing of this wonderful opportunity, might snatch it from her grasp. A job and a house, that was too much to hope for – and yet it could be theirs.

Where the side path joined the main drive Irena paused. In no great hurry now, she stood and surveyed the huge honey-coloured mansion, then she noticed a lady just below the wide sweep of steps.

It must be Lady Anastasia, tall, wearing a lace gown, with a huge feathered hat pinned to her piled-up hair hiding her face. She wheeled a large perambulator and walked steadily in Irena's direction. Lady Anastasia, whose wedding procession she had watched in Vilnius, vividly remembered. Dare she speak to such a high-born lady? Irena hesitated, but need overrode her shyness. She rushed forward.

'Your Highness,' she called, in Lithuanian. 'Your Highness.' She threw herself to her knees on the gravel. 'Be so good as to hear me. I throw myself on your mercy, your kindness.'

Anastasia halted. She took a step back, drew herself up haughtily, unaccustomed to being so unceremoniously accosted. Yet she was intrigued at hearing her own mother tongue. A footman ran from the house to protect his mistress, calling on others to help him.

'I mean you no harm.' Irena pleaded.

The footman grabbed hold of Irena's arm. He was hurting her, but she would not stop her supplication.

'I ask only to have a few words with you, your Highness.'

'How dare you approach her ladyship! What are you doing here?' Roughly, he twisted Irena's arm, wrenching her up on to her feet.

The butler hurried up, overweight and panting. 'My lady, are you all right?'

'Perfectly, Ferguson.' Anastasia's voice was cool.

'We'll take this woman inside and send for the police.'

The footman gave another more vicious twist to Irena's arm, so that she gave a cry of pain.

'Please. Please, your Highness. I have no wish to cause trouble.' She gazed at Anastasia with eyes full of appeal. The two men were about to drag her away as if she was some dangerous criminal.

'Your Highness.' Irena pleaded, 'I mean no harm to you. I watched you drive to your wedding in Vilnius.'

'Wait,' Anastasia instructed the servants. 'You come from Lithuania?'

'Your Highness, I come to beg a favour.'

Anastasia spoke to the servants in English. 'You may leave us. I am perfectly safe.'

'Your ladyship?' The butler would have protested, but she stamped her foot. 'Leave us, I say.' He drew back a few paces, taking the footman with him. They remained within call, watching and listening.

'What is it that you want?'

'Your Highness, there is a vacancy for a man to work in the garden here. I hoped my husband might be able to do that.'

'That's nothing to do with me,' Anastasia shrugged. 'Speak to the steward.'

'He is not in his office.'

'Then come back tomorrow.'

A small baby sound came from the perambulator. Anastasia leaned over and pushed back the hood, which had been half up to shield her son from the sunlight. 'Hello, my sweet. Did you have a lovely sleep, then?'

'Tomorrow may be too late!' Irena cried. 'Please, your Highness, don't you see, by then someone else may have been granted the position. My Duncan is a fine man, clever, strong. He will keep your gardens beautiful.'

Lady Anastasia turned her attention back to Irena and regarded her steadily. 'What is his name?'

'Duncan MacRaith.'

'Did he tell you to come to me?' Her voice was suddenly sharper.

'No! He would be angry if he knew. He is a proud man, he would never beg for help.'

'Then why are you here?'

'Because I'm so scared that he will be killed if he stays in the pit. There are so many accidents. He makes light of it, laughs at me, but I know he would be happy if he could work here in the gardens for you.'

A strange little smile played around the corners of Lady Anastasia's mouth. Irena wondered what she could be thinking and felt uneasy. She waited patiently. This chance was too important to be missed.

Anastasia's son began to cry. Little Lord James was awake and demanding attention. He quietened as his mother leaned over, making soothing sounds as she lifted the child into a sitting position and plumped up the frilly pillows behind him. A bonny child, glowing with health, plump cheeks, little pug nose, fine hair towsled.

Irene stared at him and felt a deep sense of shock. A beautiful child, and so like Marty! Her worst fears were answered! Her own precious son was the double of Lord Eveson's son. She gazed in horror as Lady Anastasia fussed over her baby. Irena had little actual recollection of the features of Lord Eveson, but there was nowhere else such a resemblance could have sprung from. Duncan would see it, just as she had. She felt sick.

'I will leave. I should not have troubled you. Forgive me, your Highness.' She backed away.

Lady Anastasia looked up, her eyebrows raised, an unfathomable smile on her face. 'I will speak to the steward. If the position is still vacant, it shall be offered to Duncan MacRaith.'

'Th – thank you.' Irena stammered.

Lady Anastasia dismissed her with a sweep of her hand, then swung the perambulator around and strolled back towards her grand home. A middle-aged nanny, her plain brown dress covered by a huge white apron, hurried anxiously towards her mistress. She bobbed a curtsy and they exchanged a few words. Lady Anastasia moved on whilst the nanny took charge of little Lord James and wheeled him away. Irena turned and ran. The opportunity she had expected would bring her peace of mind, had left her in torment. The likeness between her darling Marty and little Lord James could mean only one thing. They must be half-brothers!

Set against that fear was her determination to get Duncan out of the pit, and there might never be another opportunity.

'I wouldn't have thought you'd want me to be employed by *them*. Not after what he did to you!' Duncan sounded quite angry. 'Let alone live in one of their cottages.'

Irena shrugged. 'I don't suppose Lord Eveson will even notice me now. After all, I'm a wife and mother.'

'You're still very pretty, Irena.'

She gave a wry smile. He didn't often say that. 'I'll keep out of his way. The cottage is on the edge of the estate, out of sight of the house and they say he spends most of his time away in London, anyway.'

'You seem to know quite a lot about them.'

'Only what I hear from Mrs MacEwan.' She eyed him thoughtfully. 'Why don't you want the job, Duncan?'

'I didn't say I didn't want it. I just didn't expect you to go begging for work for me behind my back.'

'But we have talked about you getting other work, I only asked Mrs MacEwan – no one else. I thought you'd be pleased.'

'But working there, up at the big house. I don't know.'

'It's a good job, Duncan. You'd be working under Mr MacEwan. He's very pleasant, the cottage is just lovely, it's got a kitchen, a parlour and two bedrooms.'

'A palace!'

'To me it would be,' she said wistfully. 'Please Duncan, just walk up there tomorrow morning and see the steward. You don't have to take the job if you don't want it.'

'Oh, all right, since it means so much to you.'

She said softly, 'There's another reason why I'd like us to move away from here, Duncan.'

'What's that?' His voice was quite sharp.

'I'm going to have another baby.'

'I had wondered. You're quite sure?'

'I've missed two months.'

Her eyes roved anxiously over his face. 'Do you mind?' she asked.

He shook his head, gave her a wry grin. 'Mind? Of course not! It just takes a bit of adjusting to.'

'I wouldn't want Marty to be an only,' she said.

'No, well, I never expected that he would be.' He sounded resigned rather than pleased.

'There's a bit of garden with the cottage,' she said, persuasively. 'It'd be lovely for the children to play in, and we could grow vegetables and save a bit of money.'

'You really want this, don't you?'

'Yes, but not if you don't,' she said hurriedly.

'I'll go and see Mr Anderson in the morning.'

They said nothing more about the matter. Irena. passed a restless night. Had she done the right thing? Surely the move, the change of job, would be good for all of them?

Duncan left the house early in the morning. It was near midday when he returned. She had his dinner ready, and set it on the table straight away.

'I'm starting in two weeks' time,' he said as he sat down. 'You can get ready to move house.'

Irena waited for him to say more, but that was all. She wondered if he'd seen the cottage, if he'd met Mr MacEwan, what he thought about the work. He offered no further information. He ate his meal and left for the pit.

'Ferguson tells me you were accosted by a young woman in the grounds today,' the earl remarked at dinner that evening.

Anastasia tensed. She was not surprised that he knew, the butler was totally loyal to his master, and the incident had been unusual, witnessed also by the nanny, and a footman. No doubt by now it had been blown up into a great drama in the servants' hall. To Anastasia it was an annoying reminder of how virtually impossible it was for any encounter to pass unobserved.

'It was no problem at all,' she replied coolly.

They were not entertaining and there were only the three of them at table. The roast Aberdeen Angus had just been carved by the earl and served by two footmen under the watchful eyes of Ferguson. She was seated on her father-in-law's right hand. Conroy, opposite her, lifted his wineglass and sipped from it.

'Who was it?' he asked, as if with mere idle curiosity. Was he afraid that one of his escapades was catching up with him? It amused Anastasia that he might think so.

'A young woman from Lithuania,' she answered. 'Apparently she was in Vilnius on the day of our wedding. Remarkable, don't you think?'

'There were thousands of peasants in Vilnius that day. Your father put on a good show for them. Surely she didn't come here just to tell you that? What was she after?'

'She'd heard there was a vacancy for an under-gardener, and asked that her husband should be considered for the position.'

'What impertinence!' The earl's voice was exasperated. 'She ought to have known better than to trouble you over such a matter, my dear.'

'It was no trouble, father. I found it amusing to speak Lithuanian again and she was perfectly respectful. Actually I felt sorry for her. She had been distressed by an accident in the colliery in which her husband had almost been killed.'

'Tosh! Someone careless with dynamite, I expect! I'm glad Ferguson was there. I've commended him for his care in keeping watch over you, especially as young Jamie was with you. I'd never get over it if anything happened to my bonnie wee grandson.'

'The girl was no danger to me or to Jamie. And she assures me that he would make a good gardener.'

'Don't tell me you're taking on the steward's job, Anastasia,'

Conroy jeered. 'What do you know about gardening?'

She ignored that, and again addressed the old earl. 'I promised that her husband should be considered. I've sent a message to Mr Anderson, explaining that the man will call at his office.'

'That was rash of you,' the earl admonished. She smiled at her father-in-law. He had always admired her beauty and her sharp wit and now she had added that extra attribute of having produced an heir. 'I won't let it happen again,' she promised. 'If the man's not suitable, there's an end to it.'

'He'll have to be good to impress Anderson.'

Anastasia shrugged her shoulders, pretending indifference.

The men turned to discussing the troubles of Germany and Serbia. The Scottish regiment in which Conroy held a commission was about to undertake its annual manoeuvres and he would join them in a few days time. He wore a badge for 'Imperial Service' denoting that he had volunteered for service outside the United Kingdom.

'How long will you be away?' she asked.

'Two weeks – or maybe a few days more.'

'I don't believe there'll be a war,' declared the earl.

The discussion turned to politics. Anastasia pretended to listen with interest, but her mind drifted back to her meeting with the peasant woman – and Duncan.

That meeting on the eve of her baby's birth had been a catalyst. When she had seen Duncan again, spoken to him by the Bridie Burn, felt the touch of his hands as he assisted her, it had reawakened desire. As Jamie grew and her love for him deepened, the urge to see his father again had increased until it was almost obsessive. Sometimes she toyed with the idea of sending a message to Duncan, as she had done earlier, arrange to meet again. On one occasion she had actually set out – only to turn back before she had gone half a mile. It was too dangerous! She had to protect her child, and guard his heritage. The prospect of Duncan working in the garden excited her. She had no doubt that Anderson would engage him, following her subtly worded request, but had she been a fool to send it?

Where was her pride, her dignity? She recalled how she had laughed with friends when scandalous stories had been told of indelicate ladies who had affairs with servants. She had not believed it possible for anyone highborn to act in such a way. If he came to work in the gardens, she would weigh up her emotions. She would approach him coolly, look at him and see him as the simple peasant she knew him to be. Perhaps then she would be able to free herself of this obsession. She gave no thought to his feelings. Remembering how he had been enchanted by her, even on that last occasion, when she had been so incapacitated by her pregnancy, now, in the full glory of young motherhood she was as beautiful as she had ever been. It was a heady thought, and so pleasing that she smiled coquettishly at Conroy.

Recently he had come to her bed more often. His love-making was mechanical, he took her with little regard for her arousal, intent only on proving his own manhood. He was anxious to repeat what he believed to have been his achievement, and impregnate her again. Love was too strong a word for the relationship that had come into being between them. She found him too weak a character for that. They had drifted into a passionless relationship. It served both of them well enough.

Chapter 12

A NASTASIA knew the little house allocated to the under-gardener stood on its own. It was on Milton land but outside the high brick wall that circled the estate. It had previously been of no interest to her, and her impression was of a rather drab place. The next time she passed by, accompanying her father-in-law on a social visit, she noticed the cottage looked brighter. Lace curtains fluttered at an open window, the hedge was neatly trimmed, the path clean-swept and led to a gleaming white doorstep.

From the time of her first arrival at Achil House, Anastasia had always enjoyed wandering about the garden. The wide lawns in front of the house were divided by a paved pathway, leading to a circular walled pool where lilies bloomed and goldfish swam around a central fountain with a scantily clothed Greek goddess carrying an overflowing urn. The driveway swept around one side of the lawn, on the other was a pergola, leading to the walled gardens and a dove house, around which the snowy birds continuously made love.

Quite often, Anastasia saw Duncan at work, but never on his own. He was being trained in the ways of Mr MacEwan, who was a perfectionist, as was evidenced by the quality of the fruits and vegetables that came into the house.

One brilliant day in early July, Anastasia found Duncan cutting back mock orange and lilacs which had scented the garden so sweetly a few weeks previously. A lad was raking up and piling the clippings into a wooden barrow. She wandered around pausing now and again to drink in the scent of the roses. She leaned over to catch the perfume of one perfect bloom, but also to allow her eyes to rest on Duncan.

He was dressed in the thick, rough clothes of any working man, yet was magnificent. Bareheaded, his dark wavy hair, quite long, sprang thickly from his shapely head, the strong column of his neck thrust out of his collarless, striped shirt. He was tanned and healthy looking from working in the open air, the muscles and sinews in his arms rippled, as he stretched up to cut overhead boughs, then crouched down with easy suppleness to reach beneath the bushes, selecting with care the points for pruning.

He gave no sign that he was aware of her presence. She allowed herself the pleasure of turning into the path alongside the bed in which he was so busy. Would she have passed without speaking? She was never sure, for as she approached, he stepped back, to survey the overall shape of the shrub. He stood at the very edge of the path then abruptly, when she was less than two yards away, swung around, and those evocative brown eyes, flecked with gold, stared straight into hers.

The movement was so sudden she was startled. She stopped, aware of the beating of her heart. She almost stretched out her hand, for she was as close to him as that. Only will-power kept her from doing so. Neither of them smiled. His eyes held hers questioningly, in a long, perceptive stare, and it was she who wavered. Too late she realized that in reacting to the desire that emanated from him, she had betrayed her own deep emotion.

The boy shifted his feet, scrambled up from his position of kneeling on the ground, whipped off his cloth cap and twisted it in his grubby hands, shyly, with eyes downcast.

Duncan straightened up and faced her. 'I trust your ladyship is satisfied with the garden?'

She ignored that and asked, 'Do you like being here?'

'My wife and children are happy, that's enough for me.'

'Is it?' She smiled. 'Do you still go fishing?'

'Sometimes.'

'On Sunday afternoon?'

He nodded. The boy's voice cut between them.

'The laird's comin', Mister MacRaith.'

Anastasia turned and continued her walk. A moment later Conroy appeared in the arched entrance to the garden, back from military exercises, dark kilt swinging beneath regimental jacket, silver-knobbed stick tucked under his arm. He was followed at a respectful distance by Mr MacEwan. Anastasia hurried towards her husband and perfunctorily they kissed. 'Have you had an enjoyable time?'

'Fine. Great fellows in the mess. Then I stayed on with Cameron.'

'Yes. You said you would.'

'A letter's just arrived. Father suggested I should bring it out to you.' It bore a Russian stamp, and Anastasia recognized the writing as her brother's. She walked over to a garden seat. Conroy sat beside her, crossed his legs and leaned back contentedly.

Dear Sister – I am sorry to have to write with bad news, but I can no longer put off letting you know that Father is far from well. It happened so suddenly, we had no warning; the doctor says it is apoplexy, and that although it is possible that time may effect a partial cure, he cannot be sure of that, or if the end may come at any moment.

I do not know if it is possible, or even practical, for you and Conroy to make the long journey here to visit him, but he constantly asks for you. I have tried to explain to him that it will not be easy but he is not always lucid, and does not seem to understand the difficulties.

He has suffered some paralysis. He spent a normal day out on the estate and on his return, went to his room to dress for dinner, but whilst his valet was laying out his evening clothes, he experienced a violent seizure and collapsed on to the floor. He does not seem to be in great pain, but frets at being unable to move. I have delayed writing this letter for a few days, hoping that there might be some better news I could send.

You must consult with Conroy as to whether you should come to see Papa; as you know the shooting of the Archduke

Franz Ferdinand at Sarajevo on 28 June has roused enmity between Serbia and Germany, and our Tsar is in constant contact with his cousin Kaiser William. This may result in some minor skirmish, but I do not foresee any major difficulty. We have the best doctors and nurses and everything possible is being done to assist his recovery. With affection, as always – Stanislovas.

She read in stunned silence, then handed the letter to Conroy.

'Out of the question – quite impossible for me to go,' he said.

'I think I should go,' she said.

'Stanislovas says you can do nothing.'

'Papa is asking for me—'

'The ravings of a sick old man. I'm sorry, my dear, but I simply cannot leave the country.'

'I have a duty to go to him.'

'No. You cannot travel alone, so there is an end to it.'

'I shall not be alone. I shall take the servants, and Nanny of course, and a nursery-maid.'

'Nanny? Good heavens, Anastasia! You're not suggesting that you should take the boy?'

'Of course I shall take Jamie. My father has not yet seen him. Surely it is not too much to ask that he should see his newest grandson before it's too late?'

'That I absolutely forbid.'

'But why? The child will be as well looked after as if he was at home. You said yourself you did not expect trouble.'

'I don't, but there is always some risk. There was talk in the mess about what will happen between Austria and Serbia.'

'But you don't seriously think there'll be a war?'

'No.'

'Then I shall make arrangements for my journey as soon as possible.'

'You're asking me to go to Russia with you, Ma'am?' Nanny's grey eyes widened in her broad, pale face.

'That's right, Nanny.' Anastasia had requested the interview after church on Sunday morning. 'My papa is seriously ill and I must go to him. We'll take a nursemaid – two, if you wish – and of course men-servants to travel with us, as well as my maid, Effie. You'll have plenty of help, my father keeps a large staff in the house.'

'I dare say, ma'am.' Nanny snapped her lips tight shut. Seated on the edge of a low chair in Anastasia's boudoir, she pulled herself up. Her ample bosom was thrust forward, crackling beneath her starched apron, disapproval evident in every line of her face and body. Agitation shook the white cap on her grey hair and a pin fell out and landed in her comfortable lap.

'There is a large nursery suite, south-facing, overlooking the garden. It's a beautiful place, especially at this time of the year. You shall have extra free time—'

'Very good of you, I'm sure.' Nanny actually interrupted. 'And I'm sorry to hear about your Papa, ma'am – but I'm not one for going off to foreign parts. I never have been and I never will be.'

'Oh, Nanny – you must come with me,' Anastasia pleaded.

'There's no must about it, ma'am. I'm sorry, but I cannot go with you to Russia.'

'Jamie needs you.'

'I dare say he does, ma'am. I've grown really fond of the little fellow.'

'Think carefully, Nanny.' Desperation hardened Anastasia's voice. She resorted to a veiled threat. 'You won't easily find another place as good as this.'

'I won't deny as I'll be sorry to leave, but there it is. Wild horses wouldn't drag me over there, across the sea and everything.'

A fury of frustration was building up in Anastasia. 'Then you leave me no option but to give you notice.'

'Just as you wish, ma'am.'

Nanny stood up with the martyred air of one who knows she is in the right. She gave a perfunctory curtsy and left the boudoir with her lips tight compressed.

Anastasia boiled with barely controlled fury. She waited until the door closed, with almost insulting gentleness, then leapt to her feet and paced up and down the room. How dare that woman speak to her in such a manner! It had never occurred to her that Nanny would act so unreasonably. She was accustomed to giving orders to servants, not asking for their consent. Now she would have to find a new nanny. Another unwanted problem to be solved before she left! Not to mention that as the new woman would be a stranger both to Jamie and herself, it would hardly make for trouble-free travelling.

The door was thrown open without even a knock. Conroy strode in. 'What's this you've done? Nanny says you've given her notice.'

'The woman disobeyed my orders. I cannot accept such insubordination.'

'She says you asked her to go to Russia with you.'

'She was absolutely unreasonable.'

'But you are not going to Russia, Anastasia.' His voice was icy. 'I have told Nanny she is to stay on just as before.'

'I won't have her in the house, not after she defied me like that! Are you suggesting that I should never visit my family again, just because Nanny doesn't wish to travel? We've talked of spending Christmas with my father. What will we do then? She has to go.'

'I've rescinded the notice you gave her. I've asked her to stay, and she has agreed.'

'You'd no right to interfere, Conroy. The nursery staff is my department.'

'I've promised Nanny that this little altercation will never be mentioned again – you understand that, Anastasia?'

She stared at him truculently but made no reply.

'I forbid you to take him out of the country. He doesn't have a passport and you cannot get one without my consent. He is my son.'

She bit back the retort that would have sent his world crashing around him – but the repercussions from such an admission would have hurt her and Jamie more, much more.

'Very well,' she said. 'I shall leave him here.'

'You are determined to go, even though you know I cannot accompany you?'

'Yes.' She stood tall, defiant, coldly remote.

He shrugged. 'Do what you will.'

When he went away, he never consulted her. Sometimes she simply received a message after he had departed. Why should it be different for her? She adopted a businesslike attitude. 'I should be grateful if you would instruct your secretary to make the necessary reservations for me.'

'When do you wish to travel?'

'As soon as possible.'

'Very well. He shall see to it tomorrow morning.' Conroy moved away. 'Are you coming down to lunch?'

'No.'

'I'll have a tray sent up.' He left, banging the door behind him.

Anastasia stared after him. Her eyes filled with tears of anger and frustration. She could see no reason why she should not take Jamie with her. She would miss him terribly, and he would have enjoyed staying in her father's household. She had hoped to wheedle the earl into agreeing with her, then Conroy would have given his consent. Now her plan was thrown into disarray, because Nanny refused to go abroad, and Conroy had reinstated the woman. It was humiliating and infuriating.

A footman brought up a tray with hot soup in a silver tureen, cold meats, cheese, eggs, rolls and butter and fruit and cream. A maid followed carrying an ice bucket with wine. They set all out with care. 'Will there be anything else, your ladyship?'

'No, thank you.'

She took a glass of wine and walked to the window, sipped and began to feel calmer. She was desperately sad that she would not be able to take Jamie with her, it meant so much to her, to show her firstborn off to her family. Conroy had no imagination. If her father's illness proved fatal he would never see his youngest grandson. At Christmas, it might be too late.

She was heavy-hearted at the thought of being parted from her son, even for the month or two she planned to be away. Since his birth she had been happier than ever before, just by the fact of his existence. No matter what the day held, she had been able to look forward to her regular visits to the nursery. She would miss her baby every day, but she had to go to her father, there was no question about that – Papa was asking for her. They had drawn closer during that Christmas visit, she felt more kinship with him than ever before. They had sat up late talking with understanding and affection. She had changed, become more mature in her outlook, but her father also had mellowed.

She was furious with Conroy and deeply hurt that Jamie could not go with her, even for so short a time. She fully expected to be back at Achil House by the end of August.

Conroy had not resisted too strongly over allowing her to travel to Vilnius, probably because she was so determined. A small triumph, but it lightened her humour and brought her mind back to the day. It was Sunday. She had asked Duncan if he would be fishing this afternoon.

The words had been uttered without conscious thought and he had nodded in the same rather remote way. That encounter in the walled garden danced in her mind enticingly. Did she really intend to meet him again, secretly, in that beautiful magical spot? She pushed the answer to the back of her mind and, pretending she was totally indifferent, ate a little lunch. After only a few mouthfuls, she leapt to her feet.

It was a day to be outside. Fleecy clouds rolled slowly over the brilliant blue sky. Jamie was having his afternoon sleep. She would take him out later, spread a rug on the lawn for his toys and they would play together. The earl always napped at this time and Conroy had driven out in the gig. She was alone, free to go wherever she pleased. No one heeded as she walked out across the lawn to the little gate. With her hand on the latch she glanced back to make sure no one was within sight, then passed through and made her way along the woodland path. The lake shimmered in the sun. Presently she heard the familiar ripple of the Bridie Burn. She left the path, ducked and twisted beneath the trees, moving towards the sound of the water.

Duncan was leaning against a tree, so clean, fresh and handsome in an open-necked shirt with sleeves rolled high up his bronzed sinewy arms, black trousers, wide leather belt, brass buckled. He saw her and joy lit his face – intensely and so powerfully that she felt it, absorbed it, and was transported to a different world, a world in which only he and she existed.

He said, 'I was not sure if you would come.' He straightened from his leaning position, but did not move. He made no attempt to hide the strength of his feelings. Slowly, savouring each step, she moved across the grassy sward that separated him from her. She halted about two yards distant, absorbing the pleasure of his presence.

'Anastasia.' He breathed her name, as if it had a magical significance.

'Yes.' Her voice was a whisper in the still summer air. She had no time to say more.

He sprang across the short divide, clasped her in his arms, drew her body tight against his and took possession of her mouth. The sensuality she had experienced when he had climbed the creeper and intruded into her bedroom was re-awakened. She had neither will nor strength to fight it.

She gave herself up to the total delight of being female. The woman in her took over, drumming a message that it was for this, and only this, that she had been created. Every inch of her body pulsated with knowledge of the vital maleness of Duncan. Her excitement was increased by the greed of his lips. She curled her arms over his shoulders and ran her fingers through the springy curls at the nape of his strong neck.

Clinging to him, returning his extravagantly long kiss, she pulled his head deeper into contact. Excited by the softly moist pressure of his lips, she curved her body wantonly against his. The movement thrust forward her breasts, flattening them against his chest. She swayed her hips, delighting in the brushing of her loins against the swelling that was evident beneath the thick material of his trousers. He tightened one muscular arm around her pliant waist, the other one slipped lower, moving gradually until she felt its pressure around her thighs. With one easy sweeping movement he lifted her, carried her into the shelter of the bracken and gently laid her down on the ground.

She abandoned herself to him entirely, smiling invitingly and caressing him as he unbuttoned her gown. When they had made love before they had both been slightly drunk on vodka – this time there was no need for any stimulus. Suppressed passion had been there as each had separately approached the rendezvous – the moment their eyes met erotic sensations flared, overtaking all reason.

The earthiness of her bed increased her sexuality. Its dank mossy smell harmonized with some wild, primitive instinct that civilization had modified but never totally suppressed. Duncan was now more experienced as a lover, unhurried, sensitive to the effect upon her of his caresses. The intimacy between them was greater this time, and although he did not remove all her clothes, his hands, fingers, mouth and tongue discovered every secret part of her. And always he sought to please, to give as well as to take pleasure, until she felt she must drown in the wonder of it.

Afterwards they sat on the greensward beside the Bridie Burn, watching white-flecked water rush and tumble around the rocks, splashing them silver-bright. Duncan placed his hand over hers where it lay palm down on the grass, his fingers curled over it possessively, gentle and lover-like. He leaned over and kissed her lightly. Passion was spent but its residue bound them. Anastasia's eyes roved over him, loving the way he looked, hair ruffled, happily relaxed, like a little boy who has received a wonderful and unexpected gift.

'Thank you, my love,' he whispered.

She smiled at him. She did not easily say those words herself, but to hear them was a bonus.

'Will you come here again next week?' he asked.

A pang of regret prevented her from replying immediately. She was aware of his eagerness. Slowly she shook her head. 'Next

Sunday I shall be in Lithuania. My father is seriously ill and I have to go to him.'

Duncan turned and stared across the burn. 'How long will you be away?'

'It depends on how my father is – a month, maybe six weeks. Apparently he is asking for me.'

'You love him very much?'

'I suppose I do now.' She spoke dreamily, allowing her mind to wander back. 'I was afraid of him when I was a child. Then my mother died and I was so dreadfully unhappy. I didn't understand. I thought he was so powerful he should have been able to save her somehow.'

'Poor little Anastasia.' His tone encouraged her to continue.

'It was years before I got over it. Then, when I went back last Christmas, he seemed different.' She turned to face him. 'Or perhaps it was me, I was pregnant, soon to become a parent myself. That may have changed my attitude. He was delighted that I was to have a baby at last.'

'Were you also pleased, Anastasia?'

'I had longed for a child. It was like the answer to a prayer.'

'I have sometimes wondered – about your son.'

She understood exactly what he was asking, but she would not put that truth into words. There was too much at stake, and not just for herself. 'He is Conroy's heir,' she told him firmly. 'Jamie is beautiful, I love him very dearly.'

'He must look like you.'

It was an affectionate compliment, but she would not be drawn by it. Her smile was enigmatic. 'I can't say.' She leaned over and kissed him once more. 'I must go now. Jamie will have wakened and I like to play with him in the garden when it's sunny like this.'

He sprang to his feet, reached down one hand and pulled her up to stand facing him. 'Goodbye, sweet Anastasia, until we meet again, whenever that may be.'

'I cannot make any promise. I've no idea what the future holds.' She broke off, suddenly gripped by an sense of insecurity. 'I must go—'

Without another word, she ran. Duncan made no attempt to prevent her leaving. Nor did he follow her; he was soon hidden by the bushes. She reached the path and looked back for the last time, slowing her steps to a walk. Still in the wood, she heard a trundling sound, then the chuckling prattle of a young child's voice.

A woman strode towards her, pushing a wheel-barrow in which a young child was riding. Anastasia could see its straw-coloured hair. It was Duncan's wife, the peasant-woman, who had waylaid her and pleaded with her on his behalf. Anastasia watched with haughty suspicion as the woman pushed the barrow to one side, leaving the path clear. She had been collecting sticks for kindling. She curtsied, and remained in that respectful position until Anastasia was immediately in front of her. Then, with an earnest expression on her face, she spoke fast and urgently: 'Your Highness, I must thank you. You have no idea how happy you have made us.'

Anastasia had intended to hurry by with the merest nod of acknowledgement but, hearing that breathless little speech, she stopped. The woman had a pleasant voice and good manners. She was dowdy, of course, probably wearing the same dress as before, and there was something arresting in her clear-eyed honest face. But it was the glow of happiness which struck Anastasia and aroused a sharp stab of jealousy. This lowly woman slept beside Duncan every night!

Anastasia turned to survey the child in the wheelbarrow who was bouncing up and down, impatient to be on the move again. The little boy was probably about the same age as her own son, sitting in a nest of dry sticks, glowing with good health, just as Jamie did. But it was more than that which made her stare in disbelief. Her eyes roved over the little nose, fine blond hair, the shape of head, and most especially the huge dark eyes that regarded her. He was still now, solemnly returning her scrutiny. Before Anastasia recovered from her astonishment, the woman swooped upon her child, lifted him out of the wheelbarrow and clasped him against her, turning his face away. He objected and made his views known with a loud wail.

'I beg pardon, your ladyship. He doesn't usually cry.'

'It – it doesn't matter.' Anastasia had lost a little of her self-assurance.

'He's good baby really. Aren't you, Marty? And everyone says he's so like his dadda.'

Without another word, Anastasia walked on, thinking hard. She knew Jamie was not Conroy's son, but it had never occurred to her that Duncan had a legitimate child so close in age, and so alike in looks that the pair might have been the proverbial peas in a pod. That child presented a threat more serious than any she had ever dreamed of. The resemblance so striking she felt sure that anyone – everyone – must notice it.

Her imagination ran riot over the possibilities of a revelation. What questions would be asked! She would deny any accusations utterly, defend Jamie's inheritance with the fierceness of doting motherhood. No breath of suspicion must ever be attached to his parentage or to her moral character.

She must never see Duncan alone again, even though that would be one of the hardest resolutions in her whole life to keep. It would be safer to have him dismissed, turned out of that cottage. The situation was fraught with danger. She would never have agreed to his wife's request if she had known of the existence of that child. It was odd the way she had snatched him up like that, hidden his face, as if she did not want Anastasia to look at him. And then made a point of saying 'everyone says he's so like his Dadda.'

Surely that little woman could not know the truth? Could she be plotting anything, behind that mask of sweetness? Even Duncan was not certain whether he had fathered James, though he had obviously wondered. She was glad she had resisted the temptation to tell him. No one knew, other than herself. Heaven help anyone who attempted to raise doubts, or threaten her or her son.

She fretted that she had no time to deal with the situation before leaving for Russia. It would have to wait until she returned. They would have to be removed but to initiate anything hastily might awaken suspicion. She took comfort from the fact that she would not be away for long. It was unlikely that either Conroy or the earl would ever see the MacRaith child, but to make doubly sure the next morning she instructed the steward to send a message to Mrs MacRaith, forbidding her from entering the gardens.

That done, she completed her preparations for the journey to Vilnius.

Chapter 13

As Anastasia travelled through Germany lulled by the monotonous movement of the train, her mind drifted back frequently to that passionate encounter with Duncan. Yet even as she relived its sensual pleasure, her daydreams were splintered like spun glass by the mirror-image of the child's face. Marty, she'd called him. He was poorly dressed, grubby from playing in the woods, but so disturbingly like her own darling Jamie! If Anderson had carried out her instructions, there should be no danger the boy would be seen by either her husband or father-in-law. When she returned she would look into the possibility of housing the family off the estate. With that thought she was able to dismiss the problem from her mind.

Effie Cameron, her personal maid, was travelling with her, and three men servants, selected for their trustworthiness. Crossing the continent she was aware of a stronger military presence than usual. The movement of troop trains held up their progress so often the journey seemed endless, and she chafed at the delays. The carriage was hot, she felt sticky and tired and snapped irritably at Effie for the least little thing.

At last the express steamed into the station at Vilnius, where Juozas, her father's coachman, was waiting as before except that he was in his lighter summer uniform. 'How is my father?' Anastasia asked him anxiously.

'I am told that His Highness's condition remains the same, your ladyship.'

The count's carriage awaited her outside the station, with

others lined up behind for the servants and luggage. Effie saw her mistress comfortably settled, then took her seat in the same carriage, facing the back. The footman closed the door and jumped up behind as they set off along the busy street.

It was late July and the days were long. The city of Vilnius was clustered between two rivers, the old town a maze of streets, courtyards, close-packed two or three storeyed houses, built of creamy-pink stone and brown brick. Red-tiled houses mingled with palaces, and ecclesiastical and educational establishments, many topped by spires and cupolas, and everywhere there were trees, so that at times it hardly seemed to be a city at all. The background was of green, of pine-crowned hills. The road from St Petersburg came in from the north and to the south lay a vast marshy area. Moscow was over six hundred miles away.

The main street, so familiar to Anastasia, thronged with people, but Juozas drove with autocratic speed and skill. In no time at all they were out of the city, travelling across the flat dry plain, golden with ripening corn crops, dotted with peasant farmsteads.

They passed the old roadside shrine, a solid square trunk of wood, thatched and topped by a wrought-iron many-pointed cross. An old woman, black clad except for her white headscarf, knelt in prayer. They passed the lake where freshly harvested flax was tied in bundles to soak. Later it would be dried, combed, spun into lengths of brownish linen, then spread out in the sun to bleach.

Juozas reined in his team to negotiate the tall gates, already open. Anastasia's heartbeat quickened as the carriage rolled up the long drive to Count Suslenko's magnificent blue, white and gold palace. Anastasia alighted as soon as the carriage door was opened and the steps in place. Stanislovas stood where her father had always been on previous visits, his absence emphasized the sadness that underlay the welcome. He walked down the steps and kissed her on each cheek.

'How is papa?' she asked.

'Poorly. He makes no progress, he constantly asks for you.'

'I'll go up straight away.'

143

Stanislovas offered his arm to her to mount the steps and together they entered the house, crossed the parquet-floored entrance hall and climbed the marble stairs.

'Did you have a good journey?' he asked.

'Terrible! I've never known it to take so long. Troops everywhere. Do you think there will be war?'

'It looks as if some sort of skirmish is coming. But don't worry. It won't last long.'

He opened the door of Count Suslenko's room. An old serving woman sat by the window plying a crochet-hook. She stood up and curtsied as they entered. Anastasia smiled; Sabulaite must be over seventy and was devoted to the family.

Anastasia moved to the bed and gazed down at her father. He looked small, propped up in the great four-poster bed, piles of pillows behind him, his jaw dropping slightly to one side, his face thin, pale, eyes sunken and dark, beard greyer. He had always been so strong and energetic. Now he lay silent and unmoving. His hand was emaciated and ivory skinned; he picked continually at the woollen blanket.

She leaned over, not sure whether she might hurt him. Then aware of her presence his lips parted, drew back in a ghost of a smile. His eyes roved over her with an expression of tenderness and his mouth quavered in a way that brought a lump to her throat.

'An – as – tas – ia.' His voice was hoarse, slow and slurred.

'Yes, Papa. I'm here.' Her heart went out to this shadow of her strong, powerful father and she kissed him softly on each cheek, pleased that he recognized her.

'Glad – need – you – stay—'

'Of course I'll stay. I shan't leave until you're better.'

She made the promise impulsively, easily, with no idea of what it would involve.

It was 28 July 1914, the day Austria-Hungary declared war on Serbia. Three days later Russia mobilized its forces. Germany sent an ultimatum to both Russia and France. On 1 August Germany declared war on Russia and the day after that German troops marched through Luxembourg into France. Three days later Great Britain declared war on Germany. The First World War had begun.

The warm August days were lazily pleasurable in the usual way of a Russian summer, with young men and women, all accustomed to enjoying themselves. Anastasia was welcomed into their midst and bombarded with invitations to house parties and visits to dachas, in the tranquil Lithuanian countryside, among woods of silver birch, by river or lakeside. In the evenings there were sumptuous dinners and dancing to the wild violin music of a colourful gypsy band.

Anastasia easily formed a circle of admirers, teased them, flirted a little, enjoying herself. The young officers constantly sought her company, held her close as they whirled around the dance floor, flattered her with compliments, assured her of their undying devotion, but she only laughed at them, telling them they would forget her the moment they marched triumphantly into Berlin.

'Shall I pack my dress uniform for the victory parade along the *Unter den Linden* when we reach Berlin?' asked a very young officer.

'Send back for it when we get there,' was the equally confident reply.

Stanislovas and the other young officers rode off towards Prussia, filled with enthusiasm, convinced their mission was just and holy. They were going to protect their way of life, and the freedom of the world. There was little sense of fear as they dreamed of a quick victory.

The ladies waved them off, then looking for a new distraction began to attend classes in First Aid and imagined themselves laying cool hands on the flushed foreheads of handsome young men.

The first despatches from the front brought good news. General Rennenkampf captured Stalupönen and Intersburg. Jubilation increased as the army of General Samsonoff advanced.

Everything appeared to be proceeding just as had been predicted.

Then, in three terrible days, from 26 to 29 of August, the masses of peasant soldiers who made up the Russian army were outflanked, outmanoeuvred, surrounded and trapped. They had no chance against the highly trained military might of the enemy. The Germans called their victory the Battle of Tannenberg. The loss of life was enormous; thousands were taken prisoner and thousands more wounded.

An urgent order came from the government requisitioning part of the Suslenko Palace for use as a military hospital for Russian Officers. The count had made a partial recovery but was still too ill to understand properly. Stanislovas was somewhere on the front line. Anastasia signed the document giving authority on behalf of her family. She watched over the transformation of the palace into a hospital, and knew she would have to lengthen her stay. She negotiated with the military authorities to retain the west wing of the palace for family use, and sufficient servants to look after her father.

The first casualties arrived, their hideous wounds forcefully bringing home the horror of war. They came from field dressing stations at the front in Red Cross trains – those young men who had ridden off so gaily. She fed them and sluiced out their bed pans. Her beautiful, safe and comfortable home overflowed with the sights and sounds, smells and agonies of the mutilated and dying. The nurses who had been caring for the count were commandeered by the surgeon to work in the operating theatre.

Anastasia spent as much time as she could with her father and was thankful that Sabutaite, too old to work in the wards, was capable of attending to his needs, and so loyal that she sat by his side all day long. Effie and the two men-servants who had accompanied Anastasia from Scotland were also directed to work in the hospital.

News of the war seeped through to Ringbrae. It had little effect upon Irena's daily life.

Mr Anderson had called upon her one morning and instructed

her to keep away from the gardens and woods around Achil House. He made it sound like a threat. Afraid Duncan might lose his job, she agreed immediately, hiding her disappointment. She was delighted with her own garden, where there were raspberries, gooseberries and currants. The branches of old apple trees were drooping almost to the ground with the weight of their fruit. She helped Duncan to get the vegetable patch into a good productive state, working tirelessly. Often Ona walked out from Half Mile Row. Dougie and Gavin were both at school and little Bonnie, now three years old, played with Marty in the way little girls have with younger children. As the months passed their gardening efforts began to produce results, and they shared the vegetables and fruit. When it came to the apples, however, there were more than they could use. They gave some to neighbours and friends. Mrs MacEwan, whose washing she still did weekly, also had more apples than she could use.

'It's a shame to see them falling from the trees and going to waste, when people in the town could use them,' Irena said.

'Why don't you sell some?' Mrs MacEwan suggested.

'Would I be allowed to?' Irena asked.

'Of course. The produce of your garden is your own. When we first came to live here, before my husband was promoted to head gardener, I used to sell any surplus we grew. I don't bother now my man's getting better money.'

Irena seized on the suggestion. Ona helped her to gather the luscious fruit, then looked after Marty and Bonnie, whilst Irena walked from door to door. 'Would you like apples?' she enquired. 'Six for a penny, pick your own from my barrow.' By the end of the week she had earned more than a pound.

'Don't wear yourself out. Remember you've got a new baby on the way.'

'I know. But I've almost four months to go yet, and I feel as fit as a fiddle. I'm so happy Duncan doesn't have to go down the pit any more. We'd like more land if we could get it. Duncan wants to grow potatoes.'

'My husband might let you tak' a strip of ours,' Mrs MacEwan said. 'His arthritis is getting worse, Digging is too much for him now. It'd be a kindness if you took it. Guid for the both of us, I reckon.'

Irena regularly attended the Catholic Lithuanian church in Ringbrae and it was from the priest that she heard how the Russians had invaded Prussia and had been defeated in a terrible battle. Hundreds of Lithuanians had been among the Russian troops and the thoughts of all the immigrants turned with fear and sorrow to the plight of families and friends.

'It's terrible to think of. I don't know how they can bear it,' Irena said.

'Terrible.' Duncan held her in his arms and comforted her. He was glad he didn't have any family members to worry about.

'There's nothing I could do even if I was there.' Irena said. 'I'd just be an extra mouth to feed.'

'I know,' he said. 'But I feel I ought to do something. Several of the lads from Mick's Buildings have volunteered.'

Before the year was out she learned that that her homeland had become a battlefield, cut off from the outside world. Most of the news that came through was from the western front, where British soldiers were entrenched and bombarded. After Mons came the battle of the Marne, which saved Paris, then Ypres, to keep open the channel ports. Thousands of young men answered the call to defend freedom and marched off with patriotic enthusiasm and high spirits. Lord Eveson was one of the first to leave the area. Irena saw a photograph of him in a newspaper, marshalling his men on to a train, and was surprised to find her loathing for him tempered slightly despite her anger at what he had done to her.

The lists of the dead began to appear and the wounded returned home. Watching some young men swinging along on crutches in their blue hospital clothes she thanked God that Duncan was still at home.

'You've heard about Lady Anastasia, I suppose?' Mrs MacEwan, said one day.

148

Irena shook her head.

'Apparently her faither was taken sick an' her ladyship went off tae visit him in Russia. That was way back in the summer, an' she's no' returned.' She nodded her head emphatically. 'That's what I heard frae the cook. She took her maid, Effie wi' her, and men frae the hoose, an' they're all caught up in it and cannae get oot.'

'Count Suslenko lives in the same area as my family,' Irena said. 'I haven't heard from them for weeks.'

'It's dreadful – dreadful. Ye shouldnae have all this worry, hen, wi' only a few weeks to go afore yer new bairn's born. They said it'd all be o'er before Christmas, an that's only four, five weeks away.'

That evening after she had put Marty to bed, Irena sat down heavily, beside the fire. Duncan sat opposite her, a saw held between his knees, sharpening its teeth with a file. His head was bent over his task, his handsome face concentrating, a perfectionist in everything he did.

Irena watched with tender love, the curve of his strong neck, the softness of his slightly open lips, totally absorbed in his work. He remained as attractive to her as on that day when she had first seen him, when she was a newly arrived immigrant in a strange country. How fortunate she was that he had married her! She picked up her crochet work and set the hook dancing and twisting through the soft white wool.

'Mrs MacEwan says Lady Anastasia went to visit her father and can't get back because of the war,' she remarked.

'Christ!'

She looked up in alarm. Blood was spurting from Duncan's finger. She threw aside the crochet work, pulled herself up out of the chair.

'Oh, my darling – what've you done?'

He was sucking at the side of one finger. 'Saw slipped.' His voice was curt.

'Come to the bowl and wash it. I'll get a piece of clean linen—' Relieved to see the cut was not deep, she covered it tenderly, put pressure on to staunch the bleeding. 'Hold your hand up,' she advised.

149

'No need for all this fuss.' He pulled his hand away quite sharply and got back to work on the saw, 'I promised to have this done before tomorrow. Go to bed, Irena. I've almost finished.'

It seemed a long time before he joined her in bed. He crept in quietly and she felt strangely lonely, close though she was to him.

Irena's baby daughter was born on 20 January 1915. Ona was called in to help as before and there were no complications. Irena scanned the little face, soft as a crumpled rose, trying to find features that linked her with Marty, hoping to dispel the ghost of his paternity. But this baby bore no visible resemblance to her brother. She was smaller, crowned with a mass of dark hair, and according to Ona, looked so much like her mother it was laughable.

'What shall we call her?' she asked Duncan.

This time he had no hesitation. 'I thought Catherine would be nice – Catherine Irena.'

'Why Catherine?' She was surprised that he was so positive, remembering how he had shrugged off the decision over naming Marty. It gave her the impression that he felt differently about this child.

'It was my grandmother's name,' he said. 'The only relative I've ever had.'

But for the war, Irena's happiness would have been complete.

Chapter 14

SOON Irena's homeland was totally occupied by Germany.
There were reports of farms ransacked, buildings burned,
crops ruined, refugees fleeing from their homes. It was agony to
think of it. Duncan shared Irena's sorrow. She lived in dread that
one day he would be swept up in this tide of madness that was
taking away all the fit and able-bodied young men.

She had begun to build up a small business, expanding from
selling their own produce, to buying from other gardeners as well.
Duncan spent long hours working in the gardens at Achil House
but Irena involved him in her enterprise as much as possible.

She bought a flat-bottomed cart and a little pony and Duncan
built a wooden stable for Toddy. Four days a week Irena drove
around the streets of Ringbrae, selling produce. Sometimes she
took the children along, but more often they stayed with Ona,
who had become indispensable, helping in so many way different
ways. She employed a lad on Saturdays. The business prospered.
Soon there was spare money and Duncan agreed immediately
when she said they should invest in land. He always agreed, whatever she suggested.

On the Western front, trench warfare had become firmly estab-
lished and news of terrible losses in battle continually came
through. In May 1916 conscription was extended to include
married men.

By the beginning of 1917 Irena had bought a paddock for the
pony and another small field which they cropped with potatoes.
The children were healthy and happy. Life would have been

perfect, but for the war. And Duncan had grown quieter, that great laugh of his rang out less and less often. She knew his enforced inaction haunted him. Yet she was utterly unprepared when he walked into the house one afternoon in March and announced that he had called in at the Recruiting Office.

'Oh, no!' she breathed. Her life was about to be shattered.

'I volunteered for the Merchant Navy, on the Antarctic run.'

He took hold of her hands the strength and warmth of their familiar pressure steadied her a little. His eyes told her his determination was unshakeable.

She burst into tears.

He held her close. 'Don't cry, Irena. You never cry – you're so strong—'

'Strong!' she repeated bitterly. 'That's what my father said when I left home to come to Scotland. And it's not true! I'm not strong at all – I don't want you to go—'

'I must.'

He kissed her. Her mouth clung to his, she pressed her body against him, clasping him fiercely, tightly as if she could hold him by force. He stroked his fingers through her hair, then cupped her face with his hands and gently drew back.

'I'll never manage without you,' she said.

'Yes, you will. The other women have to and you're more resourceful than most. You've already set up a good little business.'

'Only because you've been here to help and support me.'

He extricated himself from her arms and grasped her by the shoulders. 'You must and you can. Don't make it harder for me than it has to be.'

She dashed the tears from her eyes with the back of her hand.

'That's better. And don't worry – I'll come back.'

How many men had said that in the last few years?

Never did time fly by at such frightening speed. On the afternoon before he had to leave they walked in the grounds of Achil House.

'Marty – don't get too far ahead of us,' Irena called.

'He can't come to any harm there,' Duncan assured her.

Irena had obeyed the warning delivered by Mr Anderson three years previously. She would never have dared to go there, but Duncan was leaving the next day and she could not bear him out of her sight for an instant. Cathie, pretty as a picture in her frill-yoked summer print, was riding high and proud on her daddy's shoulders.

Marty, sturdy, adventurous, only two days off his fourth birthday, took no heed of his mother's call. A gap in the high hedge lay ahead and he planned to slip through and hide, then jump out and give his parents a fright. Just before he reached that spot a large ball bounced out and a boy scampered after it. Marty pounced on it immediately.

'Put that down,' the boy ordered.

Irena recognized the child immediately. Little Lord Eveson. The likeness between the two boys had if anything become more pronounced. It was evident in their physique, light brown hair, bright dark eyes and wide smiling mouths. Only their clothing made them look different. She hurried forward intending to grasp Marty's hand and draw him back, but before she could reach him, the Earl of Milton emerged from the cover of the hedge, following his grandson.

'Ready?' Marty shouted. Completely ignoring the elderly gentleman he dropped the ball, stood back and kicked it with all his might. It bounced past James, who turned and ran after it.

'Marty,' Irena called again.

'Let them play,' said the earl. 'It'll give me a rest, he's had me running around all afternoon.' Irena bobbed a curtsy, and he nodded his head in acknowledgement. He made no objection to her being there, and obviously recognized Duncan. 'Ah, MacRaith. I hear you're off soon.'

'I leave tomorrow, sir. Just wanted a last look around the garden before I go.'

'Good. Good. Got to keep up the war effort. Need all the men we can get to beat the Hun.'

'Yes, sir.'

153

'Don't know if you remember my daughter-in-law, Lady Anastasia? Reason I ask is she went to visit her father just before war started, and she's been caught up there ever since. Can't get any news of her. I thought if you're over there you might have the chance to get a message to her.'

'If it's at all possible, I will contact her ladyship – on your behalf.'

'Come up to the house this evening. There's something I'd like you to take to her.'

The ball came bouncing between them, both boys chased after it, knocked each other over and rolled on the ground laughing merrily.

'Marty!' Irena scolded.

'No, no,' the earl interrupted. 'It's just what Jamie needs, a lad of his own age to have a rough and tumble with. Your boy must come and play with him again. I'll send for him.'

Irena was scarcely aware of what he was saying. Her whole being was dreading tomorrow, when she would go with Duncan to the station and wave him goodbye. They were bound for some port in Russia. Recently they'd heard that revolution had broken out and the Tsar had abdicated. She could not bear to think of the horror Duncan would be going into – and yet she found it impossible to clear such thoughts from her mind.

Later that evening Duncan stood at the imposing front door of Achil House. The brass bell jangled with exactly the same note that he recalled so clearly from that evening, now almost five years past. How very different had his mood been then! Again he heard the measured footsteps approaching.

The butler, whom he now knew as Mr Ferguson, obviously recognized him as the gardener, but that did not alter, by even the slightest twitch, the disdainful expression he maintained for all underlings.

'Go to the servant's entrance.'

'I come at the earl's invitation,' Duncan stood his ground. 'Tell his lordship I am here.' He looked the butler straight in the eye and it flashed into his mind to wonder if he remembered that previous occasion. The look on the butler's face suggested it would please him to slam the door in Duncan's face but he stepped back and held it open. Duncan strode into the huge marble-floored hall, and looked around with interest. Opposite the main entrance door rose the most imposing stairway that he had ever seen. Almost as wide as the hall itself, it led up towards a group of classical nudes, then branched right and left, to an upper landing. The doors were all shut, the house very quiet.

'Whom shall I say is here?' Ferguson enquired, the curl of his lip intended to show his disapproval.

'Duncan MacRaith.'

'The under-gardener, are you not?'

Duncan nodded.

'Wait here.' Ferguson moved sedately across the hall and disappeared through a doorway.

Distantly Duncan heard him say, 'My lord, your under-gardener is here. He says you asked him to call upon you.'

The earl's response was mumbled. But almost immediately Ferguson was back. Duncan was ushered into a luxurious drawing room. His first impression was of a great deal of gilt furniture, and huge gilt-framed oil paintings. Of these the one to the left of the splendid marble fireplace caught and held his attention. It was Anastasia, almost full length, languidly leaning against a pillar. The artist had caught the luxuriant abundance of her hair, her eyes held a dreamy expression, and her beautiful mouth wore a mocking smile.

'MacRaith,' said the butler, he bowed and withdrew.

The earl was seated in a comfortable armchair, on a small table at his elbow was a decanter of whisky. He held a book in his hand and carefully marked it with a strip of tooled leather before turning towards Duncan.

'I've written a letter.' He heaved himself out of his chair, ambled across the room to a large leather-topped desk and fumbled with some papers.

Duncan stared at the portrait. Was it possible that he might see her again?

The earl's voice interrupted his thoughts. 'You remember my daughter-in-law?'

'I do, my lord.'

The two men regarded the picture, each with his own memories.

'A fine piece of work,' said the earl. 'Excellent likeness of a very beautiful woman. When I look at it I wonder if she will ever return. I'd give my right arm if she'd never left.' He paused and turned to face Duncan. 'Lady Anastasia went to visit her sick father and got caught up in this ghastly war.'

'Where is her ladyship now?'

'As far as I know, still at her father's house. We received letters and telegraphs at first, but it's almost a year since we had any news. Place was requisitioned as a military hospital, but the count continued to live in one wing and Lady Anatasia stayed on to look after him. She said something about nursing in the hospital too. Heaven knows how the poor girl is managing. Now this accursed revolution has broken out! Of course the rebels will be crushed. Britain is sending forces to see to that. Mustn't be despondent.' He held out an envelope.

'I've written a letter for you to give to your commanding officer, explaining the circumstances. I've asked him to give you all possible facilities on our behalf. That may help.'

The rich and powerful always helped each other, thought Duncan.

'One other thing. I'd like you to take this photograph of Lord James.'

The little boy, riding a horse on wheels, was dressed in a navy and white sailor suit. His face was enlivened by a wide smile, intelligent eyes stared boldly at the camera, the image of Marty.

'His mother will be happy to see this,' Duncan said. 'I hope I may find her.'

'It may not be easy, but do your best. Do your best.' The earl's voice was gruff. He pushed the photograph and the letters into the envelope then handed it to Duncan.

'While I am away, sir, I hope my wife will be permitted to live where she is?'

'Yes, of course. Don't worry about that. I'll see to it myself. And I'll send a footman to fetch your boy up here to play with my grandson. Now I expect you want to get back to your family.' He rang for the butler.

'Show Mr – what did you say your name was?'

'MacRaith.'

The earl grasped Duncan's hand and shook it firmly. 'Good luck, Mr MacRaith. Bloody good luck.'

'Thank you, sir.'

Disapproval registered plainly on the butler's face as he ushered Duncan out and shut the door firmly behind him.

Walking through the gardens, Duncan found himself imprinting the place in his memory; he wanted to be able to picture it all when he was far away. Those roses he had pruned had responded well, the lawn showed signs of improvement from the spiking in the autumn. He must tell the boy – he pulled himself up sharply. Tomorrow he was leaving. The Lord alone knew when – if – no, he mustn't think like that – of course he would come back. Recollections coloured his mood as he continued on along the path through the woods.

He could not resist deviating to that precious spot beside the Bridie Burn where he had lain with Anastasia. He lingered for perhaps five minutes, then involuntarily shivered – someone had walked over his grave. Suddenly, unreasonably, he felt haunted. He could not stay there a moment longer – he had to get away quickly, he ran – crashing through the undergrowth, heedless of tearing thorns until he emerged, breathing heavily, on the path again. He ran, and did not slow his pace until he came within sight of the cottage. Home, clean, cosy, nicely decorated, with furniture they had bought second-hand and repaired.

Irena and the children had been looking out for him, standing outside the little wicket gate. Marty, with a whoop of excitement, ran to meet him. Duncan caught his son up into his arms and swung him around and around.

'Me, too,' demanded Cathie.

He caught her up and she chuckled as he whirled faster and faster.

'And you Irena?'

He set the children aside, hushing their clamour of 'More, more,' and crushed her close in his arms, and swung her around too. He saw tears in her eyes, but they all tried to smother fears in laughter.

Irena had set the table with as many of his favourite foods as were available. She must have spent several days' ration coupons to put on such a fine spread. Ona came over, and Connie, who brought a half bottle of whisky and some little pancakes. Mr and Mrs MacEwan sat with them for a little while, smiling but sad. It comforted Duncan to know that Irena would be left with such kind friends.

They sat up late into the night eating and drinking, reminiscing, singing. Good wishes rang to the rafters of the little cottage.

He was a little drunk and very emotional when at last they went to bed. Unsteadily he stripped in the flickering candlelight, looked across to where Irena was undressing and caught hold of her before she had time to pull that long linen nightgown over her head. He knelt at her feet and pressed his face against the naked flesh of her soft belly. She stroked his head, stood with her feet a little apart and he pressed his tongue through the pubic hair to lick at the moistness within, until she moaned with pleasure.

She allowed him to push her gently back on to the bed and she held on to him, drawing him down with her. With exquisite tenderness he made love to her, every sensation heightened by the near-terror of the unknown future.

Sleep did not come immediately. He could not dismiss the thought that this might be the last time ever that he would lie with her. He had no need to ask what she was thinking, for he felt her cheeks wet, kissed the tears away, and whispered her name over and over, as if it was some sort of talisman for the future, as if it could assuage the agony of parting.

Chapter 15

IRENA'S spirits were as leaden as the sky above, when she and the children walked with Duncan to the railway station at Ringbrae. Duncan carried a bundle with his spare clothes, some food for the journey, and as much money as they could spare. Marty ran ahead, jumping about, leaping up on to the bank and off again.

'Behave yourself,' Irena snapped.

'Let him be,' Duncan said.

How could she help it! Tears pricked behind her eyes.

'Carry me, Daddy,' pleaded Cathie.

He swung her up on to his shoulders. On the Main Street of Ringbrae Marty walked beside Irena and held her hand. Trams rattled along the centre, miners trudged by, steel-tipped boots sparked on the pavements. Duncan recognized some and exchanged greetings. At the station a group of men were gathering, wives, sweethearts and mothers close to them. Some kissed or hugged but few were talking.

Irena wished the train would never come, but all too soon it was there in a cloud of smoke and huff of steam. Duncan kissed each of the children in turn, lifted them and hugged them. Then he drew Irena into his arms and held her close. She raised her face for his kiss, his lips clung to hers, and she could no longer hold back the tears that spilled from brimming eyes. He lifted one finger and wiped them away. 'My dearest. You promised not to cry.'

'I'm not crying. It's just that my face is wet. Oh, Duncan, my darling, look after yourself.'

The guard was closing the carriage doors. A last quick kiss, then he was on the train, leaning out of the open window. The whistle blew. The train moved and he was torn from her. She began to run alongside, but Cathie tugged at her skirts, holding her back.

The carriage was a mass of waving arms and caps. Then it chuffed away round a bend and disappeared. Irena stared bleakly after it, then with a child holding on to each of her hands, walked out of the station.

'I've been sent to fetch your boy. Lord James wishes to play with him.' The footman delivered the message peremptorily. It was the afternoon following Duncan's departure and Irena was in the garden, preparing an onion bed, raking over the ground she had dug earlier in the day. She had slept badly, missing the comfort of his body beside her, agonizing, not knowing when, or if ever, he would lie there again. She had risen at dawn determined to put in a long, hard day, to tire herself out by nightfall.

Marty, grubby and happy, had been collecting snails to race across an old tin tray. Aware that this unfriendly stranger was speaking about him, he sidled towards his mother and clutched at her thick woollen skirt.

'As soon as you can get him ready,' the footman added.

Irena stooped down so that her face was on a level with the child's and spoke to him quietly. 'You remember that nice boy you played with when we walked up to the big house with Daddy? You are to go and play with him again.'

'Will you come too?' Tears began to gather in Marty's big brown eyes.

'Not this time. This gentleman will take you, and bring you back later.'

'I'd rather stay here and play with my snails—'

'I'll look after your snails. Come – let me clean you up.'

'Don't want to go,' he protested, as Irena led him into the house.

Reluctantly he allowed himself to be washed and changed into clean knee length shorts and a hand-knitted red jersey. She thrust one of his favourite sugar coated cakes into his hand for comfort and smiled encouragingly, but her heart sank as she watched him being led away, with an expression that suggested he might be going to the gallows. He turned back mournfully more than once, then had to trot to keep up with the smart pace of the footman. She felt quite miserable herself but an order from the big house had to be obeyed.

A little later Ona arrived with her three children and the house filled with sound again.

'I've brought the seeds you wanted, and some of those flowers you mentioned, though I don't see how you're going to sell those.'

'It's worth a try, Ona.' She was determined to be positive. 'No one around here sells flowers, I got a book from the library called *The Art of Floristry*. Mr MacEwan has said I can start some things off in his greenhouse, so we'll get them early.'

Since she had bought the pony and cart, she had been able to expand her business, building up a regular round. At first she had sold only the fruit and vegetables they had grown themselves but now she also bought from other growers and more recently from wholesale markets. In addition to Ona, and the Saturday boy, she employed Connie's daughter, Agnes, who had left school. Isabella Buchan also helped out occasionally. Irena had maintained a warm friendship with her and Joe, remembering it had been on their wedding day that her marriage to Duncan had been arranged. Isabella now had two little girls.

'What I'd really like,' Irena said, 'Is a flower shop.'

'People haven't got money to spend on flowers.' Ona said.

'Well, perhaps not now. When Duncan comes back.'

'Have you heard? Lord Eveson's been killed.'

Mrs MacEwan was sitting with the thin sheets of the local newspaper spread out on the table in front of her. Irena had called in, as she did every day. The newspaper was dated 30 October 1917, and the big black headline read, *'Heir to the Earl of Milton, killed. Conroy, Lord Eveson, loses his life in Allied battle at Ypres.'*

She could feel no sorrow for him. The hatred driven into her soul by his brutal violation of her body had faded but lost little of its bitterness.

'When will this dreadful war end?' moaned Mrs MacEwan.

Every loss of life emphasized the horror and added to her fear for Duncan. It was over six months since he had left and there had been no word from or about him. Where was he? Was he alive? Had he been caught up in the Revolution? It had begun in St Petersburg in early 1917 tearing the country apart. She'd been shocked by the brutal murder of the Tsar with his wife and family, though she had no cause to love them. They'd been cocooned in unimaginable riches, whilst families like her own lived in poverty. Perhaps the Tsar deserved to die, but that the rebels had killed his four young daughters and the poor, sickly little Tsarevitch appalled her.

Mrs MacEwan was fascinated by anything to do with the Milton family.

'Ye ken what that means, Irena? Little Lord James is heir to the title – and him no' but a bairn five years old! And I wadnae be surprised if it's no' long before he inherits. I thought the earl looked quite poorly when I opened the gates for his carriage last week.'

'What would happen then?' Irena asked.

'Och, likely there'll be trustees appointed tae manage the estate and look after the wee laddie, till he reaches manhood. Aye – it'll mak' great changes. There are those that dinnae like the earl, but I've always found him fair and considerate and your Marty loves to get up there an' play wi' the little laird.'

'That really surprised me, Mrs MacEwan. He took to little Lord Jamie from the very first time the footman came and fetched him.'

She paused, thoughtfully, her unease regarding the two boys as strong as it had ever been. It seemed unnatural, the way they always wanted to be together, and when he was at home Marty did nothing but talk about Jamie. Mrs MacEwan was regarding her with a strange expression, kindly but thoughtful. Of course she could not possibly have any idea of those doubts – but Irena felt obliged to speak again, quickly.

'They do so many things together. You know I taught Marty to ride on Toddy?'

'Aye. I do that. I thought the child would split his wee legs when he first tried to stretch them over that creature's belly.'

'Well, now when he visits Lord James they saddle a pony for him and the two boys go out together with the groom. Marty likes that very much. And sometimes he goes with Lord James to the school-room and joins in lessons.'

'They'll be wantin' him to live up there before lang.'

Mrs MacEwan said the words lightly, but they brought a chill to Irena's heart. It was as if Lord Jamie had adopted Marty as a brother. Often she woke up in the middle of the night, missing Duncan, yearning for his presence, his kisses, for his arms around her to comfort and make her feel she belonged. In that distraught state she became convinced that Lord Eveson was the father of both boys. Occasionally Marty brought home with him a parcel of good, but outgrown clothes. They saved her buying new and Marty was happy to wear them.

She seldom saw Lord James, except fleetingly when he passed by in the big silver limousine, for he was never allowed to visit Marty's home. When she chanced to see him the likeness between the boys always disturbed her afresh, and she marvelled that no one else remarked upon it. What would Duncan's reaction be when he came home and saw them together? Her active mind dreamed up horrific visions of some distant meeting in which Duncan turned from Marty with rejection seamed in every line of his face.

The picture was so real that Irena groaned aloud, and searched for some escape from the situation. Somehow she must find some-where else to live.

Her business was flourishing and vegetables made good prices. She took the initial moves into the flower trade. She grew as many as she could, even some that were exotic, and had a greenhouse constructed on her own land. She negotiated a contract with a florist in Glasgow, taking flowers and plants to them by train.

Life would have been hard, had it not been for her enterprise, not only for her, but also for Ona and Isabella. They worked for her and had no income other than what she could pay them. There was no government allowance for the Lithuanian women whose men had been sent back to Russia and no widow's pension for Ona. The earl had honoured his promise to Duncan and allowed Irena to live rent free in the cottage. Only by her own hard work and initiative was she able to survive and care for her children.

Sometimes the blaring of a klaxon horn announced that the Earl of Milton, comfortable in his chauffeur-driven Rolls Royce, was at the gates.

'You sit still, Mrs MacEwan – I'll open them,' Irena said.

She had just walked back from church, with the children, and was having a cup of tea with her neighbour, and talking about the armistice which had been signed the previous week. The war was over at last.

Marty raced ahead, out of the cottage and was at the tall wrought-iron gates before she could stop him. He clambered up on to the lower bar, clinging on so that he could ride when Irena, after bobbing a brief curtsy, swung the gate open.

'Get down, Marty, go inside,' she called anxiously.

Marty jumped off, but only to run across the drive to hang on the other gate. The earl leaned back in the plush-covered seat, as with stately smoothness the big car swept through. Suddenly the earl drew himself sharply upright, and rapped on the glass partition that separated him from his chauffeur. The car stopped and the Earl lowered the window.

'Jamie, what the devil are you doing here?'

'I'm not Jamie, sir. I'm Marty.' The boy chuckled as he looked up into the earl's astonished face. Irena had dressed him in a clean white sailor-suit with navy trimmings, only recently discarded by Jamie's Nanny. He was a handsome, fair-haired, bright-eyed child. With horror she realized that the clothes emphasized the likeness. The earl turned from the child to her and there was doubt and dismay in his eyes, his face suddenly haggard and grey.

'This is my son, your lordship,' she said quickly. 'Nanny gave him these clothes, they belonged to Lord James.'

'I'm not really like him,' Marty said. 'Lord James is taller than I am – and his hair has some goldy-red in it.'

His words were spoken with assurance, in the pleasantly cultured accent he had learned whilst taking lessons with his playmate. Irena's fears gathered again. Colour began to return to the earl's face. 'Drive on, Angus,' he said sharply.

Irena stared after the car. The incident increased her determination to move away, to break the link that had been forged between the two boys.

Two days passed. Marty watched and waited but the footman did not come to fetch him to play with Lord James. Never before had there been such a long lapse and her child's disappointment hurt Irena.

'I could walk up to the big house on my own,' Marty suggested. 'I know the way.'

'No, my darling. You may only go if you're fetched. I expect Lord James has other things to do.'

'He hasn't, Mummy.' He said positively. 'He'll be waiting for me. Mr Davison said he'd put some bars up in the paddock and teach us to jump next time we go riding.'

'Perhaps he's got another friend over.'

Marty gave her a withering look. 'I'm Lord Jamie's friend. He said he likes me better than anybody else.'

'Well, you can come out with me. I'm just going to harness Toddy.'

'Don't want to.'

'I'll buy you a glass of iron brew and a bannock,' Irena bribed him unashamedly. 'It's either that or you'll have to stay with Cathie and Mrs MacEwan.'

'All right.' Marty made it clear that the drive in the flat-bottomed cart, loaded with boxes of apples, was second best. They were wrapped up in thick clothes against the cold.

'I wish we had a limousine, like Jamie has,' he grumbled.

'I dare say you do,' Irena snapped. Then she softened her tone, she understood the child's frustration, and could do nothing to alleviate it. 'I've explained to you before, Lord James's parents have a lot more money than we do.'

That was another reason why it was sensible that this friendship between the boys should be broken. She had often worried about their obvious devotion to each other, wished it had never come about, but it was tough on Marty that it should end so abruptly.

The station smelled of coal smoke, was noisy with the clanging of buffers and the hiss of steam. A porter helped Irena to unload boxes of apples from the cart on to a flat four-wheeled trolley. The paperwork was done and the freight charge paid to Glasgow. The boxes would be picked up by the retailer, with whom she had negotiated a good price for regular supplies. Marty forgot his ill-humour and ran the length of the platform to say hello to the engine-driver. When they moved on again she allowed Toddy to amble at his own pace towards the allotments in Ringbrae. Half way along Main Street she noticed an empty shop, with a poster in the window announcing, 'FOR SALE OR TO LET'.

'Whoa. Whoa, boy.'

She sat on the cart assessing the possibilities of the place. It was well situated, plenty of pedestrians were passing to and fro. A tram rattled along and stopped in the middle of the street almost opposite. Three blank windows above the shop suggested there was accommodation. The whole place had the dusty and uncared-for look of emptiness, but she could soon alter that.

Marty held the reins whilst she peered through the dirty glass of the shop window. There was a counter and some shelving on the walls behind; a door stood ajar, obviously leading into the living room at the back. Her interest grew. She further read the notice – 'FOR SALE OR TO LET. APPLY ROBERTSON AND CRAIG, SOLICITORS, DALKER ROAD, RINGBRAE.'

She couldn't buy the place, but she might be able to rent it. It would be a big undertaking, but why not? The war was over. Surely Duncan must return soon! She closed her eyes momentarily and imagined how wonderful that would be. She conjured up his face so strongly that she almost expected when she opened them again, to see him walking down the street towards her. It was only wishful thinking. But it would happen one day, it must! It must! She could not bear to think otherwise, even though she'd had no word from or about him since the day he left. When he came back they would work at the business together. She would serve in the shop and he could do the collecting and delivering, and oversee the cropping of the land. She had purchased another small field alongside the one they had bought before he went away, a total of three and a half acres. She was already earning quite a good living, and when the two of them were working they should easily double it.

At the solicitor's office she met Mr Craig, and liked him because he treated her with respect. He informed her of the rent and the rates. If she took care, it should be within her means. He offered to show her over the premises immediately, but she pleaded another engagement and made an appointment to view the following day. That would give her time to think the project over.

At the back of one of the rows were allotments. Two ex-servicemen worked there, one hanging from his crutch, another with only one arm. Both were managing, with difficulty, and Irena gave them the best price she could for their surplus produce. One had beetroot dug up and ready bunched. The Lithuanian women liked to have the tops as well as the roots when making the rich red soup. Three women had turnips, potatoes and cabbages ready to sell.

Irena checked everything for freshness and quality. Her deals were soon completed. Marty had run over to a row of rabbit hutches and hurried back to her.

She drove Toddy at a brisk pace to Main Square. Connie was leaning against her door post, talking to another woman. Agnes sat on the step, crochet-hook flying in her nimble fingers. Connie pulled a sheet of paper from her apron pocket, grubby, dog-eared, torn out of an exercise book. She waved it excitedly.

'It's a letter from Vincie. We've heard at last. He's all right. He's in some sort of camp.'

Irena wanted to be happy for them, but her only thought was, why had she not heard? If Vincie could send letter, why couldn't Duncan?

'When did you get it?' she asked, and knew her voice sounded strained.

'This afternoon. It's only just arrived.' Connie looked sympathetic. They all knew she'd had had no word from her husband. 'Maybe you'll find one from Duncan when you get home.'

'Yes,' Irena said 'I'll go straight back.'

Frank, the boy who acted as her general handyman, was waiting to unharness the pony. 'Postman brought a letter for you, Mrs MacRaith,' he said. Marty followed as Irena hurried in. The brown fibre doormat was tidy and straight on the square patterned linoleum of the floor. An envelope was lying face down and her heart leapt. She snatched it up, closed her eyes and pressed it against her heart, breathing a prayer. It was a moment before she could bring herself to hold it out and take a clear unemotional look. The envelope was long and narrow, moreover it was clean, its whiteness almost shone. Commonsense told her this thing in her hand had not travelled all those miles from Russia to Ringbrae. The letter Connie had shown her had been dirty and dog-eared. The precise copperplate handwriting was not Duncan's.

'Is it from Dada?' Marty asked.

'No,' she said, wiping away the moisture that welled into her eyes. Her voice was dull.

'Why are you crying, Ma?'

'No reason, it's just that I hoped it would be from Dada.'

'I did too.'

'Never mind. We're sure to hear soon. You go and help Frank to rub Toddy down.'

Disappointment lowered her spirits as she tore open the envelope.

The sheet of paper inside bore the crest of the Earl of Milton. Her hands shook as she opened it. Her mind went blank as she read it.

I, the undersigned, Bailiff to the Earl of Milton, hereby give you notice to quit and deliver up to me possession of the premises, No 2 Lodge Cottage, which you hold as tenant on behalf of your husband Duncan MacRaith. As you know the tenancy goes with the position of under-gardener, and since your husband has failed to return to Scotland despite the ending of hostilities, his employment here is also terminated from this date.

In order to cause you the minimum of inconvenience I am prepared to allow you four weeks in which to make other arrangements. You must therefore vacate the said premises on or before the 31st day of January 1919. Please note that you should leave the said premises in a good and clean condition.'

It was signed with a flourish by the Bailiff.

Cold fury gave Irena courage as she stormed up the steps that led to the white-painted double doors of Blair House. How dared he do that to her! Had she not suffered enough from the Milton family without this! She had no doubt that she would have to leave the cottage, and she would be glad to go, but not before she had spoken to the earl.

After reading the notice to quit she had screwed it into a ball and thrown it into a corner behind the cupboard. She had forced herself into a cold, calm attitude. She had fetched Cathie from Mrs MacEwan's, and chatted quite normally as she did so. She made sure the little girl thanked the old lady nicely for having her, and left some vegetables, cleaned ready for cooking, on Mrs MacEvan's kitchen table.

As was customary Frank had his evening meal with them, and Irena asked him to stay on and look after the children, as she had some business to attend to.

Marty and Catherine both hero-worshipped Frank, who would play games and tell them stories.

She dressed with care. She had bought a fashionable outfit to wear when she travelled to Glasgow or Edinburgh for business appointments with shopkeepers and hoteliers to whom she sold her produce. It was a two-piece – with a skirt shorter than she had ever worn, even as a child! It seemed so daring, reaching only to just below her calf. The shop assistant insisted that 'Madam's neat ankles' were perfect for the new line, and would be seen to best advantage if 'Madam' would discard her button boots in favour of strap shoes with two inch high heels. Unable to afford pearls she selected a rope of prettily coloured beads. She put the outfit on with confidence that evening aware that previously it had attracted several admiring looks.

Frank's jaw dropped open when she emerged into the living room, where he was helping the children to build a stable with wooden blocks. Despite her tense mood she could not help smiling at the amazement written on his thin, spotty face.

'Where are you going, Ma?' Marty asked.

'Not far, my darling. I shan't be long, but I expect you both to be in bed when I come back.'

She kissed and cuddled each of them in turn and the sight of her children's upturned faces, so innocent and trusting, strengthened her resolve. She hurried away along the lane then glanced back and was touched to see them still in the doorway in their long flannelette night clothes, waving to her. It was their future she had to think of. How cruel was that notice to quit! Only she was there to fight for them and she had planned exactly what she would say when she saw the earl.

The butler opened the door in answer to her ring.

'I wish to see his lordship,' she said.

'Whom shall I say is calling?' He gave her an enquiring but by no means dismissive look.

'Mrs Irena McRaith'

Mr Ferguson's eyebrows twitched. It was a name he remembered. His eyes roved approvingly over her. Some of these 'Pole' women were not bad-looking when they discarded those little white headscarves and voluminous homespun skirts.

'Step inside, I'll enquire whether his lordship is at home.'

Irena entered the marble-floored hall. 'If his lordship is not at home, I shall wait,' she announced.

To make her resolve crystal clear she crossed to a chair and sat down. Ferguson's eyebrows twitched up another notch. He made no comment and walked away with his usual slow dignity, tapping on a door and opening it. Irena sat very still, keeping her body upright, moving only her head as she took in the wide stairway, classical Grecian nudes, domed ceiling with stucco plasterwork, oil paintings in moulded gilt frames, beautiful Chinese carpets, so indicative of wealth. Far from intimidating her, the sight hardened her resolve. She heard the door reopen, but did not look round until Mr Ferguson spoke.

'His lordship will see you, but you must be brief for he has another engagement.'

Her heart beat fast as she entered the elegant drawing-room. The earl stood with his back to the fireplace.

'Mrs McRaith' the butler announced.

'You may go, Ferguson.'

Irena walked forward until she was only about six feet away from the Earl and met the hostility in his shrewd old eyes straightforwardly. His face was deeply lined, dour, his thinning hair white. He had always had power. This was epitomized in his stance and expression. 'What is it you wish to say?' he barked.

Deliberately she kept her voice gentle. 'When you saw my son helping me to open the gates, you noticed how much he looks like Lord James.'

'Rubbish—'

'No, your lordship. It is not rubbish, and it is the reason why you have forbidden the boys to play together.'

'Lord James has no further need of your son's company.'

Keeping her eyes fixed on his face she continued speaking despite his interruption. 'Also you have given me notice to quit—'

'The cottage is needed.'

171

'You have other empty houses on the estate—'

The earl made a spluttering noise. He was not accustomed to have his decisions challenged. Irena continued, quietly, 'It is because you have seen the likeness the two boys bear one another. And therefore – ' She paused.

The earl's eyes blazed with anger, his mouth was working, but he did not interrupt. She held her head high. Quietly, but firmly, she added, 'Perhaps you thought they might be – half-brothers?'

'How dare you make such an assertion!'

'I dare because it is true—'

His lip curled. 'You're a shameless harlot to stand there and speak to me like this. I'll have you thrown out.' He reached towards the bell cord, threatening – but he did not pull it.

'Not before I tell you what happened to me.' Her voice rose in pitch but remained ice cold in emphasis. 'I became pregnant after your son raped me.'

He froze, there was fear in his eyes and his hand dropped from the bell pull.

'You're lying.' He lowered his voice, his tone became a fraction less authoritative.

'I was virgin, a Catholic, I was about to be married when Lord Eveson found me on the steps of the church in Main Street. A 'Pole' woman meant nothing but a few moments' pleasure to him.'

The bitterness in her voice, and the honesty in her eyes vouched for the truth of her words. The earl staggered towards an armchair, then regained control of himself. Holding on to the winged back of it for support, he pulled himself upright again and glared at Irena.

'You have no right to accuse my son of fathering your bastard when he is no longer here to defend himself. That is what you want me to believe, don't you?'

The ugly name hurt, but she had to accept it. 'You have seen the likeness for yourself,' she told him simply.

'A slight resemblance, nothing more.'

'A strong likeness. That is what I have seen over the years, and it is what you saw that Sunday.'

'You're a wicked woman, and a liar. You've concocted this story now my son cannot defend himself.

'You must have known the reputation of Lord Eveson. Ask your coachman, he will remember. Or the priest who found me the following morning and took me to the convent.'

A startled look crossed the earl's haggard face. 'You haven't discussed it—?'

She threw back her head scornfully. 'I wanted only to forget the horror of that night.' She shuddered at the memory, then pulled back her shoulders and continued with relentless determination. 'I would never have spoken of it, if you had not sent me that notice to quit my house. Now it is different. I have my children to think of. My husband is not yet back from the war. I cannot.' Again she paused, then emphasised each word. 'I cannot and I will not leave my home when I have nowhere to go.'

'This is blackmail!'

She shrugged. 'You force me to fight back.'

The earl lowered his head. There was silence in the room, apart from his rather laboured breathing. She watched him anxiously. He was old and he looked gaunt. In other circumstances she would have felt sympathy. His mouth moved. He seemed to have difficulty with his speech, licked his lips, then said sharply, 'I will never acknowledge your bastard as my grandson.'

'We have no need to say it.'

'What do you want?' His voice was hoarse.

Irena did not hesitate. 'You buy for me a small shop with living accommodation.'

His eyes narrowed. 'Do you know of such a place?'

'There is one in Main Street. Robertson and Craig are advertising it.'

'*If* I do this for you, and I say only *if* – you will have to move further away than that.'

'How far?' she asked suspiciously.

'Far enough so that neither I nor any of my family ever have to set eyes on you or your accursed offspring again,' he growled.

She lifted her head proudly. 'I have no more desire than you have for any contact between our families. I was never in favour of Marty being brought here to play with Lord James, but no one consulted me. You sent for him and I had to allow it. Do you think I want people to wonder about the legitimacy of my son?'

'Then you agree to moving away, to Lanark perhaps.'

It sounded like a foreign land. She knew only this area and the difficulties of moving leapt into her mind. 'The shop in Main Street is well placed for trade and I already have regular orders in and around the town. I cannot afford to lose my customers. Also I have land here and the people who work for me live in Ringbrae.'

'A resourceful woman like you could soon find others to work for you.'

'You may dismiss employees without a thought, I cannot and will not do that. Determination held her rigid. 'The shop in Main Street is what I want, and I do not see that we need ever meet again, after I move there.'

She waited. The earl appeared to be deep in thought. His fingers tapped restlessly on the back of the chair.

'If I do this, can I trust you never to come here again, never to ask for anything more?'

'You have my word for it.'

'Never to speak to anyone else about – about this matter?'

'That I promise also.'

'I ought to have you sign something – but that might be too damned awkward to get drawn up. I suppose I'll just have to trust you.' He regarded her thoughtfully.

'As long as you arrange for the transfer of the shop to me. I have kept silent all these years, and would have done so, to my grave.'

She held out her hand. 'We shake on it,' she said.

'I'll see my solicitors tomorrow and have the conveyance drawn up. No need to give reasons.'

Chapter 16

November 1919

'IRENA, do take a day off. You'll wear yourself out,' Ona said. They'd been to church and were walking back to Irena's shop in Main Street.

'We're going to the Glenny Woods, Auntie Irena,' Ona's daughter Bonnie announced. Thin, long-legged and seven years old, she jumped and hopped on the irregular slabs of the pavement. 'Mammy says we can take a picnic.'

'Can we go?' pleaded Marty and Cathie together.

They were within sight of the shop with a name painted in green, outlined in gold, on a white board – D & I MacRaith.' Almost a year had passed since they had left Lodge Cottage and moved into the rooms behind and above the shop. Had it been wishful thinking to put Duncan's initial on the headboard with hers? It had not been easy without him. Life was always so busy.

'I really don't think I can spare the time.'

'You never do anything with us nowadays,' complained Marty.

'You work too hard,' Ona said again. 'You've expanded the business no end, but you owe it to the children to spend more time with them.'

'It's not that I don't want to, my darlings—'

'Come with us, Mammy,' Catherine wheedled and Irena found her plea irresistible.

'All right.'

The Glenny Woods lay behind a trickling burn where she loved to go when she first arrived in Ringbrae. It was a joy to turn away from the dirty, spit-gobbed pavements and follow the track between bare hedges, over the old stone hump-backed bridge and up a slope into the woods of beech, silver birch and pines. The dead leaves crackled underfoot as the children shuffled through them.

Irena swung around in delight. 'It's lovely. I'm so glad I came.'

'Like home, in a way,' Ona agreed.

The wistful note in Ona's voice awoke an echo in Irena. 'I know. Oh, Ona – I wonder what's happening back there? Are Mamma and Dadda still alive? They're elderly now and they've had such a hard life. All those years when the country was occupied by Russia and then the revolution.'

There were no answers to those questions, never any replies to letters. They had given up writing.

Irena voiced the fear that haunted her every day. 'Why doesn't Duncan come home? The war's over. It's a year since they signed the armistice.'

'He's not the only one,' Ona reminded her, grimly. 'Very few of those who were sent away to the Russian Front have come back.'

'So many killed and wounded, it's so sad. Some of the wives whose husbands have been reported missing or killed have been told they must go back to Russia.' Ona said bitterly. 'But what is there to go back to? Terrible things are still happening. It's civil war there now, worse than it was under the Tsars.'

'And my Duncan is there somewhere. That thought is always with me.'

'At least you have hope,' Ona pointed out sharply.

Irena felt contrite. 'I know how hard it's been for you, since Petras died.'

They reached a clearing from which there was a panoramic view. The children were running, calling to each other hiding among the trees. Ringbrae lay below them, scabbed and brown on the green plain, erupting with dark, dirty bings, the cage wheels of a pit head turned, smoke hung over the houses. The distant countryside was softly coloured in russet and heather and in the distance blue-grey hills rose high and dominating. To call that part of Lanarkshire beautiful would have been an exaggeration, but from that viewpoint it was impressive. She could see the narrow ribbon that was Main Street, and looked for her shop, but was too far away to make it out.

'Let's look for mushrooms,' Ona said. 'I found masses a week or two ago.'

She led on up the slope to a part of the beech wood where sunlight sprayed through the bare branches, paling the damp dead leaves beneath. Suddenly they were in a paradise of fungi, brown and rounded as if a batch of penny buns had spilled from a baker's tray. Laughing excitedly, Irena began to pick them.

'We'd better call the children for their picnic, then we can put the mushrooms into the basket to take home.'

She wandered happily on and found some lilac coloured wood blewits and more boletus. Country folk in Lithuania learned in childhood to recognize the edible varieties. Despite the lateness of the year there was a profusion of fungi pushing up through the ragged grass or hiding coyly beneath fallen leaves.

The children enjoyed their sandwiches and 'little ears', cakes of twisted dough, which Ona had baked. An apple each finished the feast. Afterwards Irena and Ona carried on picking fungi until the basket was full.

'Perhaps we could sell some in the shop?' Ona suggested.

'I tried that once, but the Scottish people called them toadstools and were afraid to try them. A policeman said I'd make the whole town ill. He made me throw them out. It was such a shame.'

'They don't understand.'

'I'll fry some tonight, the children love them. The rest we can give away, or dry for the winter.'

Ona called the children. 'Time to go home.'

'I'll beat you to the bottom,' shouted Dougie.

The other children chased after him.

'Wait,' Irena called.

They didn't want to hear, they rushed down the narrow twisting path and were soon out of sight. Ona snatched up the basket and hurried after them. Little Catherine tripped over, scratched her hands on some sharp stones and wailed in protest. Irena calmed her, then taking her hand, followed the rest of the party at a more leisurely pace. Halfway down, nearing the old stone bridge, the path was crossed by a bridleway winding around the hillside. Irena heard the sound of horses' hooves.

A chestnut pony was approaching, led by a groom and ridden by a young boy, Irena immediately recognized the child as little Lord James. She was relieved that Marty had rushed away down the hill, as he might have been upset by seeing the friend with whom he used to play. Holding the leading rein was a groom in the Milton livery and a smartly dressed young woman. Irena knew her slightly. It was Effie Cameron, who had gone with her mistress, Lady Anastasia, to Russia. Following the death of his grandfather, the child was now the Earl of Milton.

Irena was surprised to see them for she had not heard that Lady Anastasia had returned. She waited at the side of the track, and as they drew nearer her attention was caught by the alert expression on the child's face, by the light brown wavy hair that sprang thickly up and the whole shape of his bright eyed intelligent head was so familiar to her that she could not take her eyes from him. Duncan! He was the living image of – Duncan! But that was impossible. Duncan was her husband, a coal miner with not a drop of aristocratic blood in him! She must be going off her head, seeing a likeness both to Marty and to Duncan reflected in the eager face of that small boy.

The group was almost up to her now and memories and impressions flooded into her mind. The old earl had ordered Duncan to call on him at Achil House the evening before he left for Russia. She and the children had waited by the gate for Dadda to come back – and her heart had ached at the memory of him swinging blithely along through the wood towards them. He had caught them up in his strong, comforting arms and swung them around, each one in turn. She had scarcely been able to keep from crying and she knew now that her fear for the future had been prophetic.

Her longing for him was an agonizing scream inside. As the pony came level with her it all flashed like rich tapestry on to the wide canvas of her mind.

The earl had asked him to take a letter to Lady Anastasia. They had been surprised that two such powerful families had been unable to keep in touch. The earl had given him official letters to take to ease his passage across Russia.

Effie Cameron was one of the little group, walking beside the boy on the pony, with one of the Milton grooms holding the leading rein.

Irena knew Effie slightly and knew that she was maid to the countess.

'Effie.' she called softly 'Please can I have a word with you?

Effie stood still, an inquisitive expression on her face. 'It's Mrs MacRaith, isn't it?

'Yes, Effie. You went to Lithuania with Lady Anastasia, didn't you?'

'I did, indeed. We stayed at the Suslenko Palace, Lady Anastasia's old home.'

'I ask because I wondered if my husband, Duncan called there. The earl gave him some papers to take to her ladyship.'

'Yes. I remember that,' said Effie. 'It was just before her old father died.'

Irena's heartbeat quickened. 'You see, Effie, I've heard nothing from him since he left on a ship bound for Russia.'

The groom was growing impatient. 'We're not supposed to talk to strangers, not when we have the little Laird with us,' he said.

'I won't be a minute, Hamish. You carry on.'

·'We'll wait at the top of the lane,' the groom said. 'But don't take long.'

Cathie, growing restless, tugged at her mother's hand until she let the child go. 'You know the Suslenko Palace, just outside Vilnius?' Effie asked.

'I have heard of it, though I have never been there. It was one of the finest palaces in the whole of Lithuania.'

'When I was there it had been taken over as a hospital, first by the Russians and then by the Germans. I was nursing there when your husband arrived.'

'Oh, dear God! Was he ill – wounded—?'

'No. He was very tired from making such a long journey, but perfectly fit otherwise. He brought a letter and a photograph of Lord James.'

'You've seen Duncan?' Irena cried in joyous disbelief. 'Oh, Effie! And you say he was quite well?'

'He was then. It's over a year ago.'

'A year ago! I haven't seen him for two and a half years!'

'Everything's chaotic there. That bloody revolution! Lady Anastasia's father was ill for a long time, then after he died there was a big funeral at the cathedral. The palace was full of Germans. We should have gone back to the palace, but my lady said we should try and get away. She persuaded Duncan to take us to the house of some friends, out in the country.' Irena's hands flew to her mouth to stifle the gasp. She stood rigid, afraid of interrupting.

'When soldiers came looking for us, we hid in the cellars. Then we were snowed in, there was no alternative but to stay there until the spring. We would have starved, but your Duncan used to go out into the forest and shoot wild boars and other animals and birds. When the snow melted at last, he insisted we must stay and work on the farm until the land was ready for the sowing. Lady Anastasia was anxious to go earlier, but I think he was right, because the family had sheltered us through the winter. Then at last we managed to get on a train to St Petersburg.'

Irena's thoughts were in turmoil, picturing Duncan and Anastasia living so close together, travelling across Lithuania and Russia.

'Lady Anastasia hoped to find relatives in St Petersburg,' Effie continued. 'But the rebels were in charge – her uncle's house was occupied by ruffians and thieves. It was terrible in the city. Terrible! We got out as soon as we could, and managed to get on to a train bound for Archangel,' Effie continued. 'It was filthy, and infested with fleas. I felt quite ill.'

She looked a picture of health now – and she was home! Where was Duncan? Why had he not come back? Every word increased Irena's aching longing for him. What had happened to him? Was Lady Anastasia home?

'But we hadn't gone far when the train was derailed – crashed into a tree that had been felled to fall across the track. It was days before any help arrived, then we moved on again. I don't know how long it took. We couldn't count the days. When we reached Archangel we thought our troubles would be over, the British were in charge, they arranged a passage for Lady Anastasia and me.'

'And for Duncan—?'

Effie shook her head. 'We were separated. They said he was a deserter, because he had not joined the White Russian Army. They refused to allow anyone to see him – not even Lady Anastasia.'

'Who were they?' Irena questioned fiercely.

'The British Expeditionary Forces were in charge. There was nothing we could do. Lady Anastasia begged and pleaded with the leader to send Duncan back with us, but the next day they said he had already gone to a prison camp, in Siberia. Everything was in chaos – so horrible.' Effie shook her head with an expression of hopelessness. 'I'm sorry Mrs MacRaith. That is all I know.'

'What can I do?' asked Irena.

'Nothing. Absolutely nothing. The whole country is in turmoil, and will be until these Bolsheviks are crushed.'

'No doubt you've heard, when Lady Anastasia and I were on our way to Finland, our train was derailed again. I don't know who by. It was awful. Lady Anastasia was thrown across the carriage. Killed outright! It was terrible. So sad, especially when

181

we thought we were on our way home. I felt so helpless.'

How was it that Effie had come home, and he was still out there? It was unfair, as all life was unfair.

Cathie tugged at her skirt. 'These are for you, Mummy.' She held up a grubby fist, clutching sprigs of heather and feathery grasses. Irena's eyes filled with tears, and she caught the little girl up into her arms.

'They're beautiful, my darling,' she murmured, hiding her face against the peach softness of the child's cheek.

'You haven't looked at them,' objected Cathie. 'I don't like that lady. She's made you cry.'

'No, she hasn't. She's given me good news. She's seen Dadda.'

Irena grasped that piece of news and concentrated her whole being upon it.

'Will Dadda be home for Christmas?'

'I hope so. Oh, my darling. I do hope so.'

Ona invited Irena and her children to spend Christmas at her house. She had set the scene in her kitchen in Half Mile Row as close as possible to the traditions that had been handed down over the generations. Straw was spread over the table and covered with a white linen cloth. On this were set thirteen different vegetarian dishes. In Lithuania they would have processed around the farm buildings, carrying lanterns, voices raised to the night sky. In Ona's crowded little room they walked slowly round the table. Ona's lodgers, both miners, sang lustily. The children's faces glowed with excitement.

Irena thought only of Duncan – where was he? Was he able to celebrate Christmas? She tried to believe that somewhere in Russia he was joining in this same ritual. It was too awful to think that he might be incarcerated within some prison, alone and miserable. Effie believed he was alive – the words they had exchanged kept floating into her mind. Hope had sprung into her heart after that meeting. So why, oh why, did he not come home?

She recalled how she had she had proposed to him and they

had flaunted tradition by not having a match-maker. The old folk had muttered that no good would come of it, and she had wanted so desperately to prove them wrong – but fate had given their lives a bitter twist.

The carol finished. They all took their places at the table. Ona took a piece of unleavened bread, tore it apart, then the plate was passed around the table, and everyone took a small piece, in preparation, so it was said, for Christ's coming. As the meal ended a loud knock was heard. The children jumped and giggled with excitement.

'Stay in your seats,' Ona commanded. 'Auntie Irena, will you go and see who's at the door?'

The children watched, wide-eyed. Irena opened the door and said the ritual words. 'God be with you, Old Man. We have five children here this evening.'

She pretended to speak to Old Man and teased as if considering whether they had been good. Then the magic words: 'You've left presents for them? Under the bed – in the cupboard, outside—'

They hunted and scrambled, wrenched curtains aside, determined, by fair means or foul, to be the first to haul out one of the parcels. There was nothing grand. A home-made wooden boat, jointed dolls, which Ona had dressed in scraps of silk, satin and lace. Also colouring books and crayons, a board game, oranges, sweets and pennies.

One of the lodgers had a mouth organ and they sang the ballads, carols and hymns, haunting evocative folk music as they remembered and dreamed of the land of their birth. The little ones fell asleep in their arms and much later all five children were all put into one wall bed; the lodgers went to their adjoining room. Ona and Irena climbed into the other wall bed. The little house was overcrowded, but that evening more than most, they needed each other's company.

Even then sleep did not come.

'I keep thinking about Duncan.' Irena said.

'Aye. It's only natural. '

183

'I must know what has happened to him! If I went to Russia—'

Ona sat up in bed sharply. 'You're not thinking of anything so harebrained as that? You've no idea where to look? He might be anywhere in that huge country.'

'I'd start in Mossenos and find out what's happened to our family. Effie said Duncan helped her and Lady Anastasia to get to St Petersburg, then to Archangel.'

'Now I know you're mad! Your children need you here.'

'I know. I'd have set off months ago, but for them. I keep thinking he needs me. If I go, Ona – would you look after the children for me?'

There was a long silence. Irena knew she was asking too much. She sighed and turned over.

'Leave it until the Spring,' Ona said. 'You can't do anything in Russia at this time of the year.'

'I know – but then? Please Ona – help me—'

'If he's not home by then, we'll talk about it again.'

'Thank you.' She leaned over and kissed her sister.

From then onwards Irena began to make preparations. She wanted to know where her husband was, and if no one would tell her, she would go herself and look for him. It was all very well for the authorities to say they could get no firm information from Russia but she did not believe they really tried. What did they care about ordinary people?

As the year advanced, so did her plans. She persuaded Ona to leave Half Mile Row and move in with her. There were six spacious rooms behind and above the shop and Irena and Ona had no difficulty in sharing the kitchen. She had installed a modern gas cooker, and a pump over a sink, so they no longer fetched water from the yard. With gas lighting, the shop and house were as up to date as any in Ringbrae. She had a telephone connected, to keep in touch with retailers and suppliers in Glasgow and Edinburgh. The children got on well together, and they were among the healthiest and best turned out in the school.

When her dear old friend Mrs MacEwan died quite suddenly in March. Irena was devastated, but nothing was allowed to interrupt her preparations. By the beginning of June she would be ready to set out for Lithuania. She schooled Ona to take more responsibility for running the business. They had worked together on the horticultural side from the start when she sold her surplus crop of apples. Both had an inborn love of the land, and now with practical experience acquired over years, Ona knew as well as Irena did the pattern of cropping that best suited the soils of each field.

She had paid for Agnes, Connie's daughter, to take a training course in wreath and bouquet making. Now eighteen she had developed from a clever, pretty child with bouncing golden ringlets, to a poised and lovely young woman, artistic as well as intelligent. Her charm and skills brought in many orders. In the aftermath of war people wanted to enjoy themselves; they threw parties and gave presents. Her cut blooms and arrangements, bouquets and buttonholes were in increasing demand. Agnes was in her element working with flowers, and managed that side of the business so competently that Irena had no qualms about leaving her in charge. She was also able to do book-keeping, a side of the organization that defeated Ona.

Parting from the children would be by far the hardest part to bear. Marty and Cathie would miss her almost as much as she would miss them, but this undertaking was for their sakes as well as hers. They needed their father – he had been absent for so long. They might have forgotten him, if she had not constantly reminded them and talked about him. She'd had a photograph taken of Marty and Cathie hand in hand. Ona loved them as if they were her own, and the two families had grown up together. Irena hired a girl to live in and help.

Quietly, patiently, she made preparations for the long, lonely, possibly dangerous, journey back to her homeland. She had no idea what to expect when she got there, knowing only that the war, the German occupation and the revolution had wrought havoc, but how much she had yet to discover! With difficulty she acquired the necessary papers. She packed serviceable clothes, reverting to peasant style having heard revolutionaries despised westerners. She had put money aside in packets and little bags, in which she could hide coins in the pockets and folds of her voluminous skirts. She had taken care of everything and was ready to go.

Chapter 17

IRENA stood on top of the gentle slope that rolled down through the scrubby fields to the plain. Mossenos lay about a mile ahead. The single-storey log houses were scattered on either side of the dirt track that constituted the main street. At the far end of the unmade road the wooden church rose higher than the houses, stubby spire topped by a cross. She could see the house where she was born, familiar, yet now somehow changed. The forest seemed further way. The day was clear, there was a blue sky with friendly white clouds, a perfect summer day. Why was it so quiet?

Irena strode on. Would her family be there? Papa and Mamma, and Magde, who had been expecting her third child.

And her younger sisters, Selina and Anita, had they married, or were they still single and at home? She ran the last few yards, called out, and just before she reached the door, it opened.

A woman stood there. A thin, haggard, middle-aged woman. Irena's step faltered, then came recognition: 'Magde!' She dropped the suitcase, opened her arms and sped forward.

'Irena!'

Amazement and joy restored Magde's face so that it resembled again the girl she had once been. Irena hugged her tight, tears began to flow.

'Where is everyone?' Irena asked.

'Oh, dear, dear, dear!' Magde shook her head in deep sadness. 'Death and destruction. Death and destruction; that's all it's been. There's only me and Anita left here, with the three children.'

They sat, side by side on the old bench, beneath the broken

veranda. Irena listened as Magde talked and talked.

Her husband, Vladas, had been forced into the army, sent to the Caucasian front, after the Germans had taken Vilnius. They'd billetted soldiers at the farm, and they'd taken her store of food and killed the animals. Anita had been raped and had given birth to a little boy. 'Mamma died. She seemed to fade before our eyes. I believe she wanted to die – and when she'd gone Dadda gave up too. They're both buried in the churchyard,' Magde said.

A group of children ran into the farmyard. When they saw Irena they hid behind the cowshed, suspicious of a stranger. 'Come and meet your Auntie Irena,' Magde called.

'You were only about four when I went away,' Irena said to the eldest girl.

'I'm twelve now. Stasys is eight. And this is Pranas, he's four.'

'He's Anita's child,' Magde said.

'We've been helping with the haymaking. We've come back to fetch tea.'

Irena followed Magde into the house and helped to pack cold tea and chunks of bread into a linen-lined basket. The bread was coarse, and hot from the wall-oven. The older children carried the basket between them to the field; memories flooded Irena's mind. Magde continued talking. 'My Simonas died last year,' she said. The hurt showed in the stark simplicity of her statement. He was the middle one of her three children.

'He was a lovely child.' Irena remembered.

'Diphtheria. A lot of children in the village had it.'

Irena held her hand. They sat in the silence of grief for a few minutes, then Magde said, 'Tell me about your family.'

Irena opened her suitcase and showed the photograph. She told Magda why she had come back to Lithuania.

'The war has taken so many men.' Selina had worked in the hospital. 'It used to be the Suslenko Palace,' said Magde. 'The count's daughter married an Englishman.'

'I went with Grandpapa to the wedding,' Irena said.

'Of course! I'd forgotten that. She came back when the count was taken ill, and then she couldn't get out of the country. Selina married one of her servants.'

'Are they still at the palace?'

'No. The hospital was evacuated when the Germans came. Everyone was sent to Russia.'

Every day for the following week Irena walked from village to village, to Vilnius, and to the now ruined Suslenko Palace asking if anyone had seen or heard mention of a tall foreigner. She was tiring herself out, all to no avail. She would have to move on, but where to? Then it seemed as if a miracle happened. Magde's husband came home. He was dirty, smelly, dishevelled, exhausted from days of rough travelling. He staggered into the house late in the afternoon. Too tired even to eat, he drank half a glass of vodka and flopped out on the bench. Magde covered him with a quilt and left him to sleep.

The routine of the whole household was changed to revolve around him. Magde hovered and fluttered about, holding up a finger, whispering. The children were subdued, fearful of this big bearded man who had burst back into their lives after being away for years. The quiet which Magde insisted upon scarcely seemed necessary, for Vladas showed no signs of stirring. He awakened briefly at around midday, went out to the privy, and consumed three bowls of bone and vegetable soup. The pot had been simmering for hours, ready for just this moment and Magde watched whilst he ate, with a smile playing uncertainly around her lips. He finished the soup, grunted a few syllables, held her hand for a moment then went back to sleep.

Irena took over the work that Magde would normally have done, dropping easily into the old familiar tasks, outside in the fields, helping Anita, and looking after the children. She stayed for longer than she had intended, as Magde fussed over her husband, spending hours at his side, talking to him whilst he rested. It was not until the evening of the third day, that Vladas recovered sufficiently to join the family for the evening meal.

Then it became a celebration, and after a few vodkas he began to tell them what had happened to him. How he'd been sent to

Omsk, had fought with the Siberian Army under Admiral Kolchak, how they had been expected to break through the rebel lines and reach Archangel, but had been beaten back. They'd not had enough guns or ammunition, no warm clothes and little food. Many had died.

Magde glowed with contentment. The return of Vladas brought a semblance of normality to life in the homestead. Irena began to think of moving on.

'I saw Selina,' he said unexpectedly. 'In Omsk. With her husband. They both work in a hospital, there. They share a room in one of the big houses. They've got a little girl. I visited them. Selina said to tell you not to worry about them.'

'That is good news,' Magde said.

Vladas stretched. 'It's good to be home! I can hardly believe I'm here.' His gaze roved around the table, then rested on Irena. He frowned. 'I thought you'd married and started a family in Scotland.'

'That's right. I'm Mrs McRaith now.' She showed him the photograph of Marty and Catherine.'

'Then why aren't you at home looking after them?'

He listened in silence as she told him. How forlorn and hopeless her words sounded, even to her own ears! Russia was so vast. 'I thought if I came here myself, I might find him,' she finished lamely.

'There are a lot of Lithuanians in Omsk,' Vladas said. 'I heard that some of them came from Scotland.'

Irena's heart lurched. 'You didn't come across Duncan MacRaith?'

'I never met any of them. They were in a different unit. It was Alastair, Selina's husband, who told me. He liked to meet up with them so that he could speak in English. He finds it very difficult to learn either Lithuanian or Russian.'

'Are they still there?' Irena asked eagerly.

'I reckon so, poor sods. I don't suppose much has changed since I left, and that was over a month ago. What a journey! I hope I never have to do that again.'

'Why don't they leave, like you did. Vladas?'

'It's not as easy as that. You have to have papers, permits, passes, ration documents or money.'

'I've got money. I'll go there. I don't care how far it is. If there are men there from Lanarkshire, Duncan may be among them. If not, at least someone there may know him.'

She lay awake late into the night. The wooden walls were thin, the logs ill-fitting, and sounds of love-making came from next door where Magde was with Vladas. An agony of longing for Duncan overwhelmed her. Duncan, dear, darling Duncan – how could she go on living without him!

She stayed one more day. She made wreaths of wild flowers, flax and ruta and took them to the graveyard. She knelt by the graves, her father's and her mother's, and remembered them as they had been, with gratitude and love. With adult eyes, as a mother herself, she saw now the troubles they had surmounted, and remembered with understanding and tolerance their occasional shortcomings. She wept, not entirely for them, for they were at peace, but for all the suffering that was in the world. She placed a wreath on the grave of Simonas, the smallness of the grassy mound was a poignant reminder of how little he'd had of life. Longing for her own children surged through her. Momentarily she wondered if she had the strength to go on. She felt torn apart. Doubts crept in. If Duncan had wanted to return to Scotland, surely he would have found a way? Vladas had managed it. Some men were glad to be free of wives and families, clear of responsibilities – she had read that speculation in her brother-in-law's eyes. Effie had remarked that Duncan was a resourceful man, and that was true. Irena did not want to think of Anastasia, but she could not help thinking about what might have happened during that winter when they had been hiding in the country together, and the weeks and months of the journey to Petrograd and Archangel. Her imagination could all too easily conjure up pictures that were deeply disturbing, even the inexplicable likeness between Marty and Lord James, but she refused to allow her mind to dwell upon that. Resolutely she set her sights forward again. Nothing would deter her from her purpose. She had to find Duncan.

Vladas gave her all the information he could to help her on the journey. The railways were in a broken down state. The system had been inadequate and badly organized before the war and since 1914 virtually no maintenance had been carried out. The armies of both sides frequently blew up lines, sabotaged engines, derailed carriages. Much of the rolling stock was useless and rusting in sidings. Her journey would take her from Vilnius to Minsk, to Moscow, then on the Trans-Siberian railway.

Vladas went with her to change the last of her sovereigns and helped her to get a better deal than she might have done on her own. She insisted on giving a few roubles to Magde, despite her resistance. Irena decided to leave her suitcase and carry the minimum of necessities, tied in a linen cloth. It would be almost impossible to buy food; that was why Vladas had been so weak when he got home. Magde packed a smoked sausage which would keep for months, some bread, cheese and a bottle of water.

Sadness overshadowed her departure from the farmstead. Who knew what the future held for any of them? It was unlikely they would meet again in this world though that was never said. Somehow Irena found the strength to stand back from the parting, hiding her emotions, forcing a smile.

CHAPTER 18

THERE were times when Irena thought she would never survive the journey. The need to scramble, push, and to fight to get on to the train, left her battered and bruised. Inside the carriage all the seats were taken and she had to grab and hold on to a small corner on the floor where she could sit with her bundle resting on her knees. The smell of unwashed humanity was overpowering. Sometimes felt she would suffocate if she could not take a breath of fresh air. Yet she had no option but to stay where she was.

The train was at a standstill more often than moving. Once they sat in a siding for twenty-four hours, waiting for some bigwig, some general, or for a troop train, to pass by on the single track. No one on the train ever knew why they were held up. Carbolic was splashed around every morning, the thick white liquid masking the human smells briefly, then allowing putrid odours to build up again as the heat of the day increased.

Twenty-seven days after she had left Mossenos the train drew to a halt in the station at Omsk. Irena had become so accustomed to the stench that she scarcely noticed it. Her clothes, her hair, her whole body was impregnated.

She fought her way off the train, against the tide of would-be travellers, then leaned against a brick wall, feeling sick. She would have vomited, but she had eaten so little she had nothing to bring up. Then she squared her shoulders and reminded herself that the journey was over.

She was there – she was in Omsk! Outside the station she found a decrepit carriage with a bony horse standing dejectedly between the shafts. She read out her sister's address to the driver, he held out his hand for money, and unable to understand Russian, she held up half a rouble. The driver jerked his head and she climbed into the rickety carriage.

The horse walked slowly along the cobbled streets, trams clanked, their wires sparked, pedestrians shuffled along dirty pavements. Twenty minutes later he stopped outside what must once have been a very grand town house. With her grubby bundle in her hand, Irena walked up the steps and through the open door. Several people were sitting about in the spacious entrance hall. They stared at her.

'Selina and Alistair MacDonald?' she asked.

'*Anglichan?*'

She nodded. A man pointed to a door on the first floor. It was reached by climbing a wide sweeping stairway, once a thing of grandeur, from which half the bannister rail was missing. At the top of the stair was a balcony. The front overlooked the hall and on the other side were several doors. Irena was uncomfortably aware of the eyes that followed her. She rapped sharply with her knuckles.

The door was opened just sufficiently to allow a thin, anxious face to peer out. A white linen square was tied over the young woman's head, her blue eyes were wary. In her arms she held a litle girl, aged about two years, with mop of ginger hair. The woman and the child both stared, and Irena smiled. Disbelief and bewilderment opened Selina's eyes so wide, they seemed enormous in her peaky, pale face.

'Selina,' Irena laughed with relief. 'It's me! Oh, how wonderful to see you!'

A moment later she was inside the room, Selina banged the door shut behind her and they clasped each other, kissed and hugged, then stood back and gazed in joyous incredulity, until little Justina, confused by all this carrying-on began to whine, demanding attention for herself. When she had been settled Selina fussed around Irena, fetched bread and a cup of water. She apologized for having so little to offer, and pushed extra wood into

194

the stove to heat a large kettle. Irena ate and said she had never tasted better bread, and told her story and why she had come to Omsk, and passed on news of the family back in Mossenos.

Half an hour later Selina's husband, Alistair, came in. Alistair was quite tall, and it was obvious why his little daughter had that rich auburn hair. Irena liked him immediately. He had been working in the hospital and looked tired and distressed.

'Did you get paid?' Selina asked him.

He raised his arms and dropped them in a gesture of helplessness. 'They haven't got any money.'

'How do they expect us to live, if they don't pay you! And you work so hard too.'

'It's not their fault. The money hasn't come through.'

'I've got money,' Irena said.

She pressed coins into his hand. He went out immediately to buy food. Whilst he was out, Irena took the opportunity to strip and wash and Selina loaned her a skirt and blouse. What a pleasure it was to feel clean, to have fresh clothes, unsoiled and sweet-smelling, against her skin! Selina put her dirty garments into a bucket to soak, and covered it with a piece of sacking to be dealt with later.

Alistair returned triumphantly from the black-market with bread, sausage, cheese, apples, gherkins, eggs, bread, milk, sugar and a bottle of wine. A feast such as none of them had eaten for a very long time.

'Vladas heard there were Lithuanians from Scotland in Omsk,' Irena said, as soon as there was a suitable opportunity.

'That's right. In the barracks on the hill. They've been in General Kolchek's army, fighting the Reds. What a mess it all is. They were sent to fight the Germans, and now they've been caught up in this terrible Civil War, and nobody knows what's really happening.'

'I'll go to the camp with you tomorrow and ask for your husband,' Alistair volunteered.

The camp was little more than a cluster of long wooden shacks, within a perimeter fence of barbed wire. The gate was open, and beside it were two Siberian policemen, both armed with rifles. They wore summer uniforms, brown tunics, belted over baggy trousers, feet and legs thrust into knee-high leather boots, flat topped caps with shining peaks covered their close-shorn heads.

They nodded in recognition as they saw Alistair. He introduced Irena and explained, in English, that they were looking for Duncan MacRaith A guarded expression hardened the face of the older of the two men.

'Why you vant him?' he asked.

Their accents confirmed what Irena had already suspected – they were Lithuanians from Scotland. She spoke to them in their own language.

'I'm his wife. I came to ask if he can be discharged and return to Scotland, to his family.'

'A great many of the men here would like to go back to Scotland.'

'Then why are they not permitted to leave? They came to fight against the Germans. Now that the war is over, it's unfair to keep them here against their will.'

'Psst! If the Commissars hear, you'll get thrown into prison alongside your husband.'

'In prison? Duncan is in prison? Why? What has he done?'

The sentry shrugged. 'They say he's a counter-revolutionary. He'll get a trial, one of these days, if he's lucky.'

'It's not true. He's a working man, a coal miner. Where is this prison?

'In the fortress, there.' He jerked his head in the direction of a tall solid windowless tower. It had been built many years previously and probably dated from the days of Peter the Great. 'It used to house those who opposed the Tsar – now the Bolsheviks have taken it over to hold counter-revolutionaries. His words were interrupted by a rattle of rifle-fire from the direction of the tower. It was followed by an ominous silence. He crossed himself. 'They shoot counter-revolutionaries,' he said.

A chill gripped Irena. It was a moment before she recovered, and then it was with tremendous anger – icy, bitter and beyond control. She ran forward and rushed through the gate.

'Hey – stop – you can't go in there—'

She ignored the shouts, turned towards the tower, running now.

'Stop – or I'll shoot—'

She glimpsed the barrel of the rifle raised in her direction, but in the grip of mindless fear and anger, ignored that too. A shot was fired, over her head. Her step faltered but only momentarily. The heavy wooden door of the fortress swung open and more soldiers appeared there, holding rifles, pointing them straight at her. Reason returned. She stopped. She raised her hands above her head. The sentry from the gate lumbered up alongside her. He put a rough hand on her shoulder.

'She's the wife of Duncan MacRaith,' he shouted to the guards. 'She wants to see him.'

The guards lowered their rifles and the sentry pushed her forward.

'Search her.'

The man's hands were insultingly intimate. Irena glared at him, but stood still.

'Take her to the commissar.'

His office was a haven of calm, with comfortable, old, scuffed furniture, which had once been opulent. Dust danced in the sunshine that poured through the open windows. The officer wore a gold-encrusted uniform, coloured scarlet and gold; perhaps he had once been a Cossack and had changed sides. He sat behind a broad desk topped with green leather. Irena was taken in by two guards. She halted, facing him, and, without waiting to be asked, poured out her story.

'My husband is no counter-revolutionary,' she said. 'He came from Scotland to Russia when we were fighting Germany. It was his country he wanted to fight for, not for the Tsar. He is a peasant, a coal miner.'

'He kept company with a known subversive, the daughter of Count Suslenko.' He turned aside and spat his contempt of the name.

Irena spat also. 'I am no lover of the Suslenkos and nor is my husband. He never joined the army of the Tsar.'

'We have evidence that he assisted Suslenko's daughter to escape.'

'I don't believe you. He couldn't have known who she was. He's a man like any other.' Her lip curled a little. 'He's always been easily led by a pretty face. It won't be the first time – just let me see him. I'll find out the truth about that.'

A sarcastic smile spread over the commissar's face. Irena pressed on.

'You're a man of the world, I can see that. What good will it do to keep him here? I've come from Scotland to find him, all I want is to take him back there. His family need him. See—' She took the photograph out from a pocket in the folds of her skirt – 'These are our children. It's three years since he went away – I implore you, as you must once have loved your mother, please let me see him.'

The commissar snapped at the guards. 'Take this woman to visit Prisoner MacRaith. Then bring her back here to me.'

'Thank you – thank you.'

Joy flooded her heart, overflowed in a surge of happiness, brought a smile to her face. She would see Duncan again! She recalled his handsome face, his swashbuckling manner, thought of him swinging her off her feet on that memorable day just before he went away, and crushing her in his arms. She imagined smothering him with kisses.

One on either side of her the guards marched her to another part of the building, and sent other guards to fetch the prisoner. They led down a flight of cold stone steps, through long grey corridors. A shiver ran over her, caused not only by the physical change of atmosphere, icy though it had become. The very walls of the place seemed to hold misery and despair.

The guards opened a door into a small, cold room. It held a long table with a chair at each end. She was told to sit down. The waiting seemed endless, her eyes fixed on a door at the far end of the room. It opened, and another armed guard came in and stood beside it. Then two more, with a wild looking unkempt man between them. He blinked, as if unused to daylight. Duncan! Her hands flew to her face in horror. She leapt to her feet, and would have rushed down the room to him – but the guards caught hold of her and roughly pushed her down again on to the chair.

His hair straggled uncombed almost to his shoulders, lustreless and matted. His face – his wonderful handsome face – was lost behind a dark matted beard, cheeks shrunken, pasty-white, an unhealed cut ploughed a furrow of dried blood just above his left eye. A filthy crumpled tunic, torn and unbelted, hung on his sagging shoulders. Stooped, like an old man, so thin he scarcely had the strength to stand as he shuffled into the room, with his eyes on the ground.

'Duncan. My dearest, my darling Duncan.'

Endearments flowed straight from her heart to her lips. She spoke softly, afraid of startling him, seeing him as an invalid. Slowly he lifted his face, as if he had difficulty in focusing, bewildered, slowly turning his head from side to side. The guards pushed him into the chair. He slumped over the table and peered towards her.

'Duncan. It's me – Irena.'

What a terrible length that table was! Love made her reach towards him; it was a useless gesture, he was eight feet away.

'Irena?'

CHAPTER 19

His voice was a croak, through cracked lips, muffled in his beard. It was a question, weighted with disbelief.

'Yes. It's me, Duncan.'

'Irena! What – what are you doing here?'

The words came slowly, simple and ordinary, but proved he was aware of her presence.

'I came to find you.'

He raised his right hand, rested it on the table and reached forward with his fingers outstretched towards hers. Her reaction was immediate. She lifted her body from the chair, and threw herself along the table towards him. For the briefest of moments the tips of her fingers touched his, then the guards grabbed hold of her, hauled her back and thrust her hard down into the chair again.

'Leave my wife alone.' Duncan's voice held something of the old timbre.

'I'm all right,' she said quickly, reassuring him, smiling through her tears. She turned to the guards. 'Forgive me.I shouldn't have done that. I won't do it again.'

The guard's face was forbidding. 'Five minutes left,' he warned.

She gripped her hands into tight fists and concentrated her mind. She had to work out a way to get him released.

'Do you know why they're holding you here, Duncan?'

'They say I'm a counter-revolutionary.' His voice was dull as if he was repeating words he had said many times before.

'Why?' she asked.

200

'I don't know.' The note of impatience showed his spirit was not entirely broken. 'The war was over when I got to Archangel. They should have sent me back, but they put me on a train to Moscow and said I had to join the White Army. I didn't want any part in the Civil War. I came to fight the Germans.'

'You were never with the White Russians?'

'Never. I don't understand politics. All I want is to go back to Scotland, to work and provide for you and the children.'

Her heart bled for him, but she had to keep on questioning. 'Tell me about Lady Anastasia.'

He looked down, away from her. 'Not now,' he pleaded. 'It's too long a story.'

'They want to know.'

'She had a terrible time.' His voice was gruff. He was defending her. He didn't say she meant nothing to him. 'The palace was used as a hospital and she was a nurse there.' The gossamer thread of love between Duncan and herself was stretched, about to snap. 'Please, Irena,' his voice came louder. 'Tell me about you, and the children. How are they?'

She pulled herself together. 'They're fine. They're good children.' She took out the photograph and held it up for the guard to see. 'May I show my husband?' she asked meekly.

He looked it over and the innocence of those young faces must have softened his heart a little, for he walked down the room and allowed Duncan to see the photograph briefly.

'One minute left. Finish your talk.' He returned and handed the photograph back to Irena.

One minute and neither could think of anything to say. The tears that Irena had kept in check streamed down her cheeks. Sobs choked her. Duncan was crying too. The guards lifted her from the chair, for she was incapable of obeying their command. Like an automaton her limbs moved as she was led away. She glanced back as she reached the doorway. Duncan had been hauled to his feet. Her imagination showed her clearly the cold damp cell he would be taken back to. Fury and despair etched deeply into every line of his face, and was echoed like knife cuts in her own.

The guards pushed her forward. She stumbled as they hurried her away and a great cry burst from him – a long, furious moan. Savage and primitive, the sound of a wild animal at bay – she struggled to get free, to turn back, to run to him – but the grip of the guards tightened on her arms. They forced her out, through the heavy iron-studded door and banged it shut behind her.

That great cry was an agony of despair, a reverberating anguish around her head, caught in the web of her consciousness as she was bundled along, half carried, half pushed back through the gloomy corridors.

She was thrust into the commissar's office, tears streaming down her face. She had held them back until that last minute of parting, when the whole horrible injustice of his imprisonment overwhelmed her. Too miserable even to think of wiping them away, she cared nothing for how she looked. Through bleary eyes she tried to focus on the commissar.

'Let her sit down,' he instructed the guards.

They placed a chair beside her, but she remained standing, facing this man who had condemned Duncan to so much suffering. She wanted to shout, to rant and rage and give vent to her feelings, but even at that moment natural common sense warned her to be calm. A wrong word could put Duncan in even greater peril. She placed one hand on the wooden back of the chair and gripped it hard.

'Thank you, Comrade Commissar, for allowing me to visit my husband,' she said.

With a determined effort she managed to make her voice sound gentle and clear, even though her heart snarled at the hypocritical words she had chosen. Her success in making that small speech helped to restore confidence. Her head was rapidly gaining control over her emotions.

The commissar inclined his bullet head in acknowledgement of her appreciation. 'I'm sure he was pleased to see you.'

How could he make such a fatuous remark? He must be as stupid as he looked. She nodded, not trusting herself to answer immediately. She must use her all her intelligence, concentrate her mind on this man in front of her, and if necessary flaunt her charm. She was fighting for Duncan's life. Her eyes were clear, she would not allow any more tears to dim them.

'Sit down,' he ordered.

This time she obeyed. 'Thank you, Comrade Commissar.' Her deference appeared to please him.

'Now, what do you wish to say?'

'I think that perhaps you do not know the true story of why my husband came to Russia,' she began.

'He is a spy, a counter-revolutionary—'

'Forgive me, Comrade Commissar, but that is not true. That is what you have been told, but I fear you've been sadly misinformed. My husband is no enemy of the people. He would never do anything to harm your cause. He came to Russia voluntarily only because he wanted to help the fatherland, to defend Britain against the Germans.' She embroidered her story a little, put in all the facts she knew, everything that might help Duncan. 'I am Lithuanian, and you know that the great leader Lenin has acknowledged how badly we have been treated by the Tsars, and has graciously granted independence to my country.'

'He helped the Suslenko woman to escape. She's not one of the people, she's a counter-revolutionary—'

'She is not a peasant, but she did her best during the war. Her home was turned into a hospital. She nursed the wounded—'

'She did not leave when the Germans advanced. Those who were loyal moved eastwards to continue their good work.'

'I understand that her father was too sick to move. There was no one else to stay with him.'

'He should have been left to die. He was an oppressor of the poor.'

'But that has nothing to do with my husband, Comrade Commisair. My husband landed in Archangel in 1917. He came to fight the Germans – but the war was already over. He wanted to return to Britain; he had no wish to help the White Russian Army, but they put him on a train bound for Moscow. Rather than fight

203

against the Red Army he escaped and made his way back to Vilnius.'

'He should have joined the Red Army.'

'He intended to do so, Comrade Commissar.'

'And where did he meet up with the Suslenko woman? Did he tell you about her?'

Irena looked down, twisted her hands in her lap, appearing embarrassed. She cleared her throat. It was not entirely an act as she answered.

'That woman took advantage of his good nature. He did not realize he was being made a fool of. I know my husband. He is weak where women are concerned.' She paused then raised her eyes and gazed at him emploringly. 'I – I know you are too good a man to ever behave so – but would you have told your wife if you had found yourself in such circumstances?'

'You may be forgiving. There is no reason why the state should be so,' he said sternly. 'Perhaps his silence is for other reasons. If the Suslenko woman is a subversive, then your husband must be one also.'

'No. I assure you, he is not. He is a good man, a worker, a man of the people. I implore you to believe me, Comrade Commissar.' She leaned forward regarding him earnestly, willing him to help her. 'He would do no harm to you or to your noble cause.'

'Then why has he not said so before?'

'I think it is because everybody is so busy, he has never had the chance to explain. You are the first to hear the true story, Comrade Commissar, and it is only because you are a just man and a good man that you have been willing to listen to me.'

He leaned back in his chair, pleased with the compliment.

'I can accept that he never joined the army of the White Russians. But why did he not join the Bolsheviks?'

'He was taken prisoner before he reached the barracks. He would join tomorrow if you would free him.'

'You think I'm soft, eh?'

'Not at all, Comrade Commissar. I'm not pleading for mercy, only for justice.' She turned to the Guards. 'You heard all that my husband said. Was there one word of subversion?'

The guard glanced at the Commissar, who granted permission for him to speak.

'The prisoner did not say anything subversive.'

'Did he refuse to join the Red Army?' Irena asked.

'I don't think that was mentioned.'

'Precisely. How can you condemn a man for not joining the Red Army when he has never had the opportunity to do so? He refused to fight with the Tsarists against you.' She turned again to the guards. 'He was never with the White Russians – you heard him say that, didn't you?'

'Yes.'

'He risked his life, threw himself from a moving train—' Her voice rose, she embroidered the story shamelessly, seeking to impress, aware that the commissar was wavering. 'Duncan is a proud man. He would not let them force him into fighting against his own people. He is a hero – and this is the way you treat him!'

The commissar's eyes narrowed. 'You say he would fight with the Red Army if he is released?'

'Yes. As soon as he is fit. His health has suffered from being in jail.' She sighed, shook her head sadly, allowed one tear to tremble on her eyelash. 'Oh, Comrade Commissar, what good does it do to keep him in jail? He will be no use to anyone if he is stays there much longer.'

'He cleared his throat. 'I shall have to contact the District Commissar—'

She felt a glimmer of hope. 'Thank you, Comrade Commissar.'

'I shall put the case of prisoner MacRaith to the Local Commissariat. Call in two days' time and I will tell you their verdict.'

'Thank you, Comrade Commissar. May I ask one more favour? I should like to leave money with the guards so they may buy extra food for my husband?'

'If you wish.'

She deliberately made the request in the presence of the commissar, as she then felt it less likely that they would put it all into their own pockets.

Two days later Irena called again at the camp, only to be given the terse message that she must report the following afternoon for further interrogation. Her request to visit Duncan was refused.

Promptly at 2 p.m. she presented herself, and was told to wait. Two hours later she was still there. The guard shrugged. Waiting was just part of the way of life. The officials would probably see her, since they had made an appointment, but who could say when? At six o'clock she was told to return the following day.

Another twenty-four hours of frustration, fear and mental torture had to be endured before she was actually ushered into a bare bleak room. Six hard-faced officials sat stolidly behind a long polished table. She stood facing them. On the end of the line sat the commissar. She related exactly the same story as before. They threw questions at her, trying to trick her, to make her say something different. She answered freely, fully, her mind sharply focused, sifting the questions and taking care with her answers. The fight for Duncan's life was not yet over.

At the end of almost three hours during which she seemed to have repeated her own words over and over, she was dismissed.

'Why do you not ask Duncan MacRaith himself?' she asked.

'He was questioned yesterday.'

'We will let you know our verdict in due course.'

Every day for a week she returned to the camp. The guard would turn over a few papers, run a finger down a list pinned on the wooden wall, then shake his head. The reply was always the same – until the eighth day.

'Tomorrow the commissar will give you the verdict on Duncan MacRaith,' she was told.

Her mind was in turmoil as she walked back to the overcrowded house.

Selina looked grave. 'Do you think he'll be released?' she asked.

'I just don't know. They gave me no indication.'

Selina moved away then suddenly swung round. 'We don't have room for him here.'

They already shared the one room with another family. It was ineffectually partitioned by a line of blankets pinned from wall to wall, roughly down the centre.

'I hoped we might stay here, just for a night, before we start the journey back home.'

'Selina's afraid of the other people in the house,' Alistair said, apologetically. 'Some of them are unfriendly. They're suspicious, because I'm not Russian.'

Irena understood. They had talked earlier about the jealousy and greed of some of those with whom they shared the house. She had been surprised that Alistair did not wish to return to Scotland, but he said he liked his work at the hospital. He felt he was doing more good as a nurse than if he resumed his former occupation as a footman. The life of a servant was not one he wished to return to.

'I mustn't be too hopeful, the news may be bad, and I don't know what I'll do then.' She swallowed. 'But I'm not going to think on those lines. I have to make arrangements about what to do if Duncan is released. He was very weak when I saw him, but I hope he has been better fed these past few days.'

'I'll come with you to the jail tomorrow,' Alistair offered. 'We'll hire a drosky, then we can drive him straight to the railway station.'

'You are very kind.'

Selina burst into tears. 'I feel awful – not allowing you to bring Duncan back here – but those people really frighten me – and I've got Justina to think about.'

'It's all right, Selina. I understand. We'll manage.'

The drosky was pulled by a pair of horses in surprisingly good condition, and the coachman wove his way skilfully through the rattling trams and thronging pedestrians. Outside the town, on the road to the camp, he whipped the horses into a gallop. Irena was grateful to have Alistair's company. If the decision went against Duncan, she feared her own strength would fail her.

Alistair waited in the drosky, watching over the precious bundle which contained food, and a change of clothing for Duncan. It was still early when she presented herself at the reception desk.

'Wait there.'

An hour passed. Time hung leadenly. Her heart alternately lifted with hope, then plunged deep into depression. At last she was ushered into the untidy, neglected office of the commissar.

'Good morning, Comrade Commissar,' she greeted him.

'Ah, yes,' he mumbled. 'Duncan MacRaith.'

'That's right.' Her voice creaked with tension.

He fumbled among the papers on his desk. He didn't look at her. She was sure it was bad news and tried to steel herself. She wished she'd brought a knife with her, she imagined plunging it into the fat belly that hung over the desk.

'Ah. This is it. The warrant for his release.'

She reached out a shaking hand. He held the document up. In her joy she leaned over the desk and kissed his fat fingers, before grasping the precious piece of paper.

'Thank you. Thank you, Comrade Commissar. May all the blessings of this life be showered upon you.'

He smiled. He was a kinder and more friendy man than he had seemed. 'The guards will fetch your husband. Show them that warrant and he is a free man.'

She walked backwards in deference, as she would have done in Tsarist times to the nobility.

'God be with you, good Comrade Commissar.'

They brought Duncan to her in the outer office, a guard on either side of him, supporting him. He was weaker than she had supposed. His face wore a bewildered exression, his eyes rested on her but there was no light in them.

'You're free, Duncan.' she called out. 'Free.'

She handed over the warrant, and picked up discharge papers, ration card, travel permit and the host of duplicate documentation devised by the bureaucratic Tsarist system and already expanded by the Bolsheviks.

'Free,' she repeated.

He seemed unable to grasp the meaning of those wonderful words. He stood with shoulders drooping, staring about as if unaccustomed to the daylight. She sped across the room towards him. Brushing the guards aside she clasped him in her arms, and was shocked to feel the emaciated state of his body, revolted by the stale prison smell that hung about him. She took his head between her hands with a caressing movement, trying to bring some life back into his eyes. She pressed her lips to his and could have cried at his lack of response.

'Don't you understand, Duncan? Oh, my love – I'm going to take you home.'

'Home?' he mumbled unbelieving.

'Yes.'

'Irena?'

A spark of recognition at last. 'Yes. It's me, you old silly.' She hugged him tight, scarcely able to believe that after all the lonely months of longing, Duncan was there. Somewhere inside those smelly old clothes, was the man she loved, too bemused and battered and depressed to understand. She lifted her head and looked up at him.

A flicker of light came into his face, his arms closed around her, and there was strength in them. He tried to speak, but whatever it was, the words simply choked in his throat.

'Come, my dearest,' she urged. 'Let's get out of this place. This way.'

'It's really true? I can go with you?'

'Absolutely true.'

'Then what are we waiting for?'

He moved forward, half-stumbled, but clung to her with urgency, as if he feared someone would yet prevent him getting out.

Outside the prison, he blinked in the daylight. Then lifted his head and drew in a deep breath of clean fresh air.

'It's wonderful,' he said. 'I can't quite believe it.'

'Wonderful for me too,' she said. 'This way. I've a drosky waiting by the gates. My brother-in-law is there too. We're going to the railway station.'

He stared at her, shaking his head, then reached out a hand and stroked her face. She smiled at the tenderness of the gesture, caught his hand and kissed the palm. A smile creased his sunken, rugged features. It was another flash of the real Duncan, and her spirits danced.

'How on earth did you get here, Irena?'

'I came to find you, Duncan. And thank God I did.'

Chapter 20

R ED flags flew over the bleak dirty station, and on the front of the train. Irena, Alistair and Duncan threaded their way through the mass of loitering soldiers, along the platform, seeking a space on the already crowded train. A company of Red Guards pushed everybody else out of the way. Two carriages were allocated to them, the rest of the hundreds of passengers had to fight their way through wherever they could. Alistair shouldered his way on and by some miracle found one seat. He made Duncan sit on it immediately; there were others ready to rush if it was vacated even for a minute. A loud whistle from the engine deceived them into thinking it was getting up steam ready for departure.

'I must go,' Alistair said. 'I'm sorry you couldn't stay with us until Duncan had his strength back—'

'It's probably for the best. He'll soon get fit now he's free. Give my love to Selina – thank you for all your help.'

She kissed him warmly. He pushed his way out of the carriage and was immediately lost to view. Almost an hour later the train actually moved.

Duncan tried to persuade Irena to take the seat, but she would have none of that, and he was too weak to protest forcefully. Beneath him she pushed the precious bundle with the carefully packaged food, which would have to last until they reached Moscow, almost two thousand miles away. She settled on the

211

floor at his feet, leaning back between his legs. He rested a hand on her shoulder and she reached up and grasped his thin, cold fingers, trying to instil some of her warmth and strength into him. In the drosky he had changed into the clean clothes Alistair had sorted out for him. The old prison garments would probably end up as a rag rug. Three days after leaving Omsk they crossed the Urals. Although still in Russia, they were out of Asia and into Europe.

There were no lights in the carriages, often they slept, talked a little, but never on intimate matters. Irena ate little, always giving Duncan the tastiest and most nourishing pieces from the packed food. Sometimes they bought tea from vendors who pushed a samovar on a trolley along the platform when they stopped at a station.

As the days passed she noticed that Duncan's hands were regaining strength. He squeezed her fingers, and she responded by caressing his. Under cover of darkness in one of the tunnels she felt his fingers creep beneath her outer garments and seek the soft warmth of her breast, fondling it. She caught hold of his hand, turned it over and kissed the palm. Rejoicing at the vitality that was stirring, she crept up and sat on his knee, seeking his lips with hers – then slid down to the floor again quickly, shyly, as the train burst out of the dark tunnel into the brilliance of daylight. He cupped her chin in his hand, forced her to look up at him and thin though his face was, the old mischief was dancing in his eyes.

They crossed Moscow by tram. They waited on another crowded platform until they were able to board the train for Berlin. There she trimmed his beard and his hair, using only a small pair of nail scissors. He watched her with trusting eyes.

'Now I can see it's you, Duncan!

'It's me all right,' he growled.

Nowhere and at no time were they alone together. Yet whenever their eyes met it was as if they were the only two people in the world. Gradually they told each other of happenings, of incidents, of friends, picking up the pieces that had been shattered by their separation.

'You've left the Lodge Cottage?' he asked in disbelief.

'Yes. I've opened a fruit, flowers and greengrocery shop in Main Street. It's doing quite well.'

'You own it? However did you manage that?'

That was not a question she was ready to answer. She shrugged it off. 'It was going cheap, and I'd put by a bit. Ona's running it while I'm away. She lives with us and is looking after the children.'

'Show me the photograph again. I couldn't see right when you came to the jail.'

He looked at the photograph for a long, long time.

'Cathie is even prettier than that,' she told him. 'And Marty's a fine strong laddie, you'll be proud of them both.'

'I'd lost hope that I'd ever see them again.' He fell silent.

After a time, she asked, 'What are you thinking, Duncan?'

'I was wondering if I'll get my old job back in the garden at Achil House.'

'You won't need it, Duncan. You can work in the shop, or if you don't want to do that, see to the horticultural side, we can build the business up together.'

'I don't know if I'd like that. Maybe I should go back to the pit.'

'Oh, no!' She was definite on that.

'You said Lady Anastasia was in a rail accident?'

Irena hid her feelings and answered matter-of-factly. 'So Effie said,' she continued.

Duncan said, 'I delivered the letter to her – the one the earl gave me before I left Scotland. She was delighted to see how strong and handsome her son is.'

'He's certainly a fine looking laddie – and so is our Marty.' Was this the moment to ask him about Lady Anastasia – to voice her doubts about Lord James and Marty? Tentatively she said, 'The old earl is dead, and Lord Eveson too. He was killed in the war.' She watched Duncan closely as she added, 'The little boy, Lord James, is the Earl of Milton, now.'

'Well, fancy that!'

It was an exclamation of surprise, but it told her nothing. He made no further comment, and her lips would not form any questions. She let it pass. What ever had been between Anastasia and Duncan it was over. It could never happen again. She hesitated to say anything that might open up a rift – she loved him too deeply.

It was not until the train crossed the frontier, and they were in Germany that they really relaxed. Only then did they feel safe from the influence of Russia and the revolutionaries, safe from re-arrest, from recruiting officers, from bureaucratic commissars and all the horror of Russia in turmoil. The train picked up speed as it travelled on to Berlin, arriving in the mid-morning. Their connection to Hamburg would not depart until the evening.

'Let's get out of this place,' Duncan said. 'I want to get out into the fresh air, to find a bit of countryside.'

'We're in the middle of the city—'

'We'll take a tram.'

They sat on the top deck, and he put his arm around her and drew her head down on to his shoulder. The tram run ended in a huge area of parkland the nearest thing to countryside, with grassy paths and trees, shrubs and flowerbeds.

Wansee Irena read on a notice board. Beside the huge lake was a restaurant.

'Time for lunch,' she suggested.

The first hot food they had eaten for days was delicious and they celebrated with a carafe of sparkling wine. They picked a table in dappled sunshine, beneath a trellis of climbing plants. It was a heady mixture – good food, warmth, freedom and safety. With war and revolution behind them, they relaxed.

Hand in hand they sauntered away from the restaurant, along gravelled paths. It was a weekday and not many Berliners were free to enjoy the peace of the *Wansee*, rowing boats were mostly tied up, a few small children playing on the swings. Whenever there was a choice Duncan took the path that led deeper into the woods.

'I dreamed of woods like these, when I was in jail,' he said.

He slipped an arm around her waist, drawing her close. The path led up a slope, away from the lake, the trees closed in thickly on either side of them. Duncan led her beneath their leafy mantle, holding low branches aside for her to duck under, deep into an almost impenetrable wood, until they came to a small clearing, a sunlit fold of the hill that was a bowl of warmth. Far below she glimpsed the silvery water of the lake.

Duncan sat on the soft grass, close nibbled by rabbits; she dropped down beside him.

'It's wonderful to breath fresh air!' He was thinking of prison again. She nodded, ready to listen if he wanted to talk about it. He lay back, stretched out, and the sun brushed red glints on the waves of his dark hair. His eyes were half-closed, his mouth softly relaxed. She was beginning to grow accustomed to the beard, its shape improved by her careful trimming. He opened his tunic almost to the broad brass-buckled belt at his waist, enjoying the warmth of sun, his pale flesh darkened by soft hair. The cage of his ribs stood up with skeletal precision.

She delighted in looking at him, then lay back on the grass beside him, not touching him, gazing into the leafy branches against the blue sky. After a few moments she felt him turn on his side. He leaned over her and his sweet breath was a caress on her face, she smiled and he kissed her. He began to unbutton her blouse. Instinctively she put her hands up to restrain him.

'I want to make love to you,' he said.

'It's a public place—'

'There's nobody for miles around.'

It was true. They had left the trodden paths a long way back and all was quiet in the woods. She relaxed in loving sensuous pleasure, displaying herself as he opened her blouse, thrilling to the hardening of her nipples as he kissed her breasts. The touch of his lips excited a tender depth of carnality, of wantonness that was primitive within her and which had been subdued for far too long. She ran caressing fingers over the back of his head, stroked his cheeks and his shoulders, aware of the masculine strength that yet remained in them.

Slowly he undressed her, and kissed each part of her body as he exposed it. The pleasure and desire that gleamed in his eyes as he looked at her awoke matching sensations in her. Only when she was lying completely naked did he throw off his own clothes, standing up as he did so. She could have wept at the emaciation of his arms and legs, and the pallor of prison that clung to his skin, but still in her eyes he was beautiful. She held up her arms to him, parted her legs and he dropped upon her. Unashamed sensuality wove a magic that reached to the very core of her being. She drowned in a cloud of sweet eroticism, in total communion with him. The turf softly bedded her body. Far above leafy branches swayed against an azure sky, a lark soared, bursting with his song of glory. The rhythm of life was complete.

When reason returned Irena hurried Duncan back to the tram, worrying lest they should be late and unable to get on the train, refusing to listen when he said they had plenty of time. They were an hour early. He smiled at her foolishness.

For the first time there were sufficient seats for all travellers. What luxury to settle into a window seat! Duncan chose to sit beside her, rather than in the corner opposite. Contented and relaxed they slept as the train puffed its way across Germany.

On the boat they stood side by side to watch the lights of the port grow gradually fainter until their pinpricks of light faded completely.

'Soon we'll be back in Scotland,' Irena said. It was a wondrous thought.

'I hardly dare to believe it – even yet!' He whispered, with his mouth nuzzled close to her ear.

The air grew chilly, and she shivered. Duncan put an arm around her. The boat was only half filled. There was room to stretch out on the plush covered seats in the saloon. She had only a few English coins. She counted it and decided there was enough to buy them each a half pint of beer.

'I haven't tasted anything as good as that for a long time,' he said.

Soon he was asleep again. She watched him tenderly, dreamily looking forward to the moment when they would arrive at the shop. She could telephone before they got on the train and tell Ona where they were and what time they would arrive in Ringbrae. Perhaps she would bring the children to meet the train at the station. They would take a taxi home, she could pay for it when they got there. This was not a day for counting costs. Her return to Ringbrae with Duncan was an event to be celebrated!

She smiled at herself as she remembered how timid she had been when she had made this trip that first time, nearly nine years ago now. What a lot had happened since then! Thank goodness the man she was supposed to marry had not waited – she had to cudgel her brain to remember his name – Tamosinskas. How awful it would have been if she had been married to him. Or to Lazaraitis.

Duncan stirred in his sleep. His head slipped down to rest on her shoulder, he made murmuring sounds. She took his hand and caressed it, murmured his name, telling him he was safe. He had nightmares about the prison. It would take time for the misery to be erased. She must help him to put it behind him. He'd be better when they were at home with the children. It wasn't the same house, but it was furnished with many of the same things and old friends would rally around.

She looked forward to picking up the reins of her business. Surely Duncan couldn't have meant it when he spoke about going back to the pit? Or returning to his job at Achil House? Those thoughts made her uneasy. How could there ever have been a relationship between Duncan and Lady Anastasia? Was it possible that the likeness between her own darling Marty and the young Earl of Milton, with all his wealth, power and freedom, was no more than a coincidence? She turned her thoughts to more practical matters. She hoped Duncan would take over the horticultural side of her business, cropping her fields; that was something he would really like, it was man's work. If her early

217

success continued, before long they would be able to buy another field, perhaps put up greenhouses, open another shop. She had ambitions to expand and diversify. There was no limit to her dreams and plans now her husband was back.

Duncan was awakened by the touch of Irena's lips on his. He reached up to pull her face down and she responded easily and immediately, then drew back, giving a bright little laugh. 'Wake up, Duncan. The boat's almost into dock.'

He leapt to his feet caught hold of her hand, pulled her after him as he rushed out on to the deck. Together they leaned on the rail and watched as the boat steamed towards its berth.

'Scotland!' he cried.

He raised his hands in the air and gave a mighty whoop of joy – a wild sound that rose loudly into the cool fresh air. He was oblivious to the strange looks other passengers cast at him.

Scotland. Home. His own country. Hope had deserted him, until Irena came. He had explored every possible avenue of escape, grasped every opportunity to gain his freedom, fought every inch of the way until, almost a broken man, he had resigned himself to his fate. In bitter despair he had come to accept that death would be his only release – until that day when he had been led from his cell and Irena had been there. Even after that he'd had no hope that he would ever be released.

The boat bumped on the dockside.

Ona was at Ringbrae station to meet them. Marty and Cathie rushed to Irena the moment she stepped off the train. She bent and kissed Marty. Cathie held up her arms for Irena to lift her, but she hid her face shyly from the big, bearded stranger that she scarcely remembered.

'She'll get used to me in her own time,' Duncan smiled. He contented himself with running the back of one finger down her soft pink cheek.

'It's wonderful to see you both back,' Ona commented. 'I've been run off my feet with the business and everything.'

'No great problems?'

'Nothing of importance – you'll take it all in your stride, as you always do. I'll go into details with you tomorrow.'

Outside the station Irena a hailed a taxi. They drove from the station and along the streets of Ringbrae, blackened with coal dust. The familiar sulphurous smell of the burning bing made her wrinkle her nose. People were huddled against the chill of the weather, rain poured from a leaden sky – there was no beauty in the scene, yet their hearts were high.

'Thank God to be back,' Duncan said, fervently.

'Amen to that, but that's over now, we must put it all behind us. We have the future to look forward to.'

The taxi pulled up outside the shop. She stepped out, put a hand on Duncan's elbow, and pointed up to the board, painted with clear letters – *D & I MacRaith*. Duncan read it aloud, then turned to her and raised one interrogative eyebrow.

'You will come into the business with me, won't you?' she asked.

'Looks as if I've no option – you've included me already,' he said.

'But will you want to?'

He nodded. 'Of course.' He squeezed her hand. His eyes roved over the shopfront. 'I never expected it to be so big, or so fine. You really own this place?'

'I've got the deeds to prove it,' she boasted.

'I just can't understand how you did it.'

She didn't answer that. She might tell him the truth one day – but then again she might keep her secret. Marty tugged at her hand.

'Let's go in, *Mamyte*. Auntie Ona's set the table with all sorts of good things.'

'Come on, Dadda. I'm starving.' Marty held out a hand to Duncan.

'You don't know what starving is,' said Duncan, 'but, yes. Let's go in.'

Irena looked from the child to his father and smiled. The likeness had never seemed more evident.

Word quickly spread around the Lithuanian community in Ringbrae and district that Duncan MacRaith was back from Russia, that somehow his wife Irena had managed to persuade the authorities to allow him to return. Others were less fortunate. Hundreds of men never came back and many women and children left Scotland, some under compulsion, others voluntarily.

Joe Buchan was one of those who elected to stay in Lithuania for he lived in that part of the country which was then free. The death of his two older brothers meant that he could inherit his family farm, and Isabella and her children were on their way to join him there.

'They left only a couple of days ago,' Ona told Irena.

The two sisters had gone into the kitchen to put the kettle on.

'I wish I could have seen Isabella before she left,' Irena said. 'I do so hope all will be well with them.'

'They're hard-working people. I'm sure they'll make out. I'll miss Isabella, though. She and I grew very close when you were away.'

Irena nodded. 'I'm so grateful to you for keeping everything going so perfectly, Ona. You must have worked like a slave, with the shop and the children – I don't know how to thank you.'

'We all pulled together,' Ona shrugged away the gratitude that was making Irena feel quite emotional. 'We've been like one big family, in a way.'

'And we must stay that way—'

'No. It can't be the same.' Ona shook her head, positively. 'Not now Duncan is back. Please don't misunderstand me, Irena – I'm delighted to see him, really happy for you both—' She fumbled in the pocket of her skirt for a handkerchief. 'I'm sure I'll easily find a wee house for myself and the children, but I'll miss living over the shop, running the business and all that—'

'Ona, I've been wondering – I wasn't going to mention it yet, but since you've raised the subject – I'd like to buy another shop, and if I did – would you run it for me? Be my manageress?'

There was a momentary pause whilst Irena's words sank in, then Ona's plump face beamed. 'Why, yes. I'd really like that. Where would it be?'

'I don't know yet. Probably in Motherwell, or Hamilton, somewhere like that. We'll look around, and see what's going, it'd have to be somewhere you'd like, and right for the children.'

Then Ona threw her plump motherly arms around Irena and hugged her yet again.

Duncan's voice called out from the living-room. 'What are you two scheming up now?'

'Nothing. Just making a wee cup of tea,' Irena answered. She beamed at her sister. 'Oh, it's wonderful to be home again. And I've so much to tell you.'

That evening family and friends gathered around Irena and Duncan, to celebrate with them. It was open house to everyone. Sprigs of pungent blue-green ruta decorated the centre of the spotless white tablecloth on which was spread a plentiful variety of cooked meats and fish, pickles and salads; rye bread and cheeses, cakes and fruit. Stanislovas and Vincie brought along a barrel of beer on a wheelbarrow.

Irena noticed with amusement that Frank made a devious detour of the table to enable him to sit beside Agnes. Then he leaned close to whisper in her ear, bringing a glow to her lovely young face as she responded with a sweet, shy smile. The floral arrangements that decorated the table were a tribute to Agnes's artistic skill and Irena could not help thinking what a nice young couple they made together.

The fiddler struck up a tune and immediately everyone joined in. Lithuania's reputation as the land of song was upheld that night. The old country folk have traditional airs for every special occasion, for birth and death, betrothal and marriage, to celebrate the ploughing of the first furrow in spring, the cutting of the first sheaf at harvest. Songs that centuries of tyrannical rule have tried to suppress, but the proud, defiant voices of the people have never been stilled.

221

They were raised in melodious harmony, as late into the night the old songs rang out from the comfortable rooms behind the flower, fruit and vegetable shop of *D & I MacRaith*. Duncan and Irena were home.